The
Monster
Squad

The Monster Squad

John Angus

St. Martin's Press
New York

Design by Junie Lee

Library of Congress Cataloging-in-Publication Data

Angus, John.
    The monster squad / John Angus.
      p.   cm.
    "A Thomas Dunne book."
    ISBN 0-312-11319-6
    1. Policewomen—Oregon—Fiction.   I. Title.
PS3551.N49M66   1994
813'.54—dc20   94-31312
                                              CIP

First Edition: December 1994

10 9 8 7 6 5 4 3 2 1

The Monster Squad

Cats have green eyes.

Or so they say. I've never really looked closely at the things, not being particularly fond of unpredictable animals with razor-sharp claws.

During most of my life my name had been shortened to Kate or Katie, shortened from Caitlin, that is. That hadn't been nearly good enough for the wiseasses in Vice. Everyone needed a nickname, and it had to be something like Greaser, or Fish Eyes, or Jock. Kate wasn't acceptable at all, so Cat replaced it, because of my green eyes . . . and sharp claws.

Being nervous and new and wanting to fit in, I hadn't protested when they'd started addressing me like that. It probably wouldn't have done much good, though. The guys liked nicknames, but they were in love with ones that pissed people off.

That was one of the reasons I tried not to show my annoyance when I was hissed at or meowed at or had some jerk claw his fingers at me. After six years, it was all as familiar as breathing. At least they didn't use the obvious, if crude, parallel around me, though Fish Eyes had insisted on telling pussy jokes for the first couple of years.

Anyway, "pussy" was more a term for a weakling than a description for a woman, at least to these guys, and I'd proved myself far from that in the last six years. I'd had to. I hadn't belonged here when I'd arrived. They knew it. Lieutenant Brooks knew it. Even I knew it.

Unlike the other denizens of Temper Street's vice squad, I'd been chosen strictly for my looks and sex. No experience necessary. They'd each had five or more years under their belts before being accepted, after rigorous competition. I'd been almost fresh out of the Los Angeles Police Academy, with only five months in a patrol car.

Circumstances like that had been known to cause more than a little resentment, never mind the necessity.

The squad at Temper Street then consisted of twelve guys. Stress the guys part. They were tightly knit and mutually supporting. Accepting a broad into their ranks, let alone a rookie broad, was the last thing they'd wanted to do.

Brooks had been adamant, though. They needed to get themselves a broad. Borrowing broads from different divisions or from uniform when the need arose wasn't nearly good enough. It was too uncertain, took too long and required too much paperwork.

They needed a broad of their own, a young looker so they could use her as john bait, and to hang on their arm to impress the druggies and pimps when they went undercover.

So I was added and they became a baker's dozen, and had to stop using the word "broad," at least when I was around.

Some women might not have liked being offered a plum assignment purely for their looks and sex. I wasn't too sure myself at first, but hell, how often did an opportunity like that come along? Working radio cars was no picnic and offered little opportunity for promotion besides the boards. So I'd accepted.

It had been a long six years. Several times I'd wondered if staying in radio cars wouldn't have been better. There was a lot of status with being a detective, and working plainclothes for Vice had gotten me the title long before I would have otherwise. But Vice was dirty, gritty, dark and dangerous, especially for a woman. Working Vice had often been compared to swimming in a sewer, with good reason. The people we dealt with were the scum of the city—pimps, drug dealers, addicts and hookers.

It got you dirty. It couldn't do anything else. You got compassion fatigue, your vocabulary became obscene enough to shock a sailor, and you took violence as a matter of course. Being a cop, seeing all society's misery and violence and death changed you, and not for the better. In Vice you saw the worst of the worst, becoming harder and meaner.

There were some cops who wanted nothing to do with Vice, promotions or not, and I had recently become one of them. It wasn't just the slutty outfits I had to wear, or the junkie and whore personas I had to put on so often, or even the danger that was a constant. It was the bleakness, the grayness of life in the sewer.

I was sick of it.

I'd asked for Robbery, so nice and clean compared to Vice, but knew there was an even chance they'd stick me in Juvenile or Auto Theft, or some other undesirable unit. I'd applied anyway. Even Juvie was better than Vice. God knew I'd be able to relate to the teenagers. Here I was thirty-two and still trying to play a teenager on the street.

That was starting to get a little hard, too. Looking younger than my age had been a major advantage six years ago and, I suppose, still was. But even with expert makeup, thick blond bangs, and ponytail I was starting to look like a pretty old teenager now.

"You got a client, Cat," I heard in my ear. I wore a Walkman on my hip, or what looked like a Walkman. It was actually a police radio.

"I see him," I said under my breath. The john was in a Cadillac. He was slowly, slowly, slowly driving along up next to the curb where I was standing. His eyes were carefully studying me as I slumped back against the lamppost, acting clichéd but arching my back casually to push my breasts out against the thin tank top I was wearing. Shyness didn't work here.

He stopped and I strolled over beside the Caddy, a smile on my lips. The tight jeans I wore cut into my thighs as I bent downward.

"Hi, honey."

"Are you a whore?"

What a sweet-talker, I thought.

"What you got in mind, honey?" I asked. The guy was about fifty, his thick hair just starting to gray. He wore an expensive suit and silk tie. He looked like a banker, and I hoped getting busted would screw him good.

"Are you a whore or not?" he growled impatiently.

"You a cop?"

"No. I am not."

"You kinda look like a cop to me, honey."

The best defense is a good offense and if I didn't ask, they would.

He pulled a bill out of his jacket and held it up. It was a hundred-dollar bill.

"If I give you this, will you have sex with me?"

"Sure, honey." I felt like laughing. What a classy guy.

"You are a whore then," he sniffed.

"That's me, honey. Where you wanna go? I got a motel room just back here." I pointed over my shoulder.

"I bet you're just crawling with diseases," he said, his face sullen and angry.

Uh-oh, I thought. I was starting to get a bad feeling about the guy. My right hand moved to the little purse that hung beside me and the .38 inside.

"Naw. I'm clean, honey. You don't gotta worry."

"You're like the rats that spread the plague in the Middle Ages!" he breathed. "Your filth kills the innocent and guilty alike!"

His face was getting red, and his eyes bulged.

Jock's car started up across the street and began to move forward into traffic. I got my hand around the automatic and clicked off the safety as I started to back away slowly.

"Hey. Forget it then, honey. I'll just go home and take a bath," I said, the hair rising on the back of my neck.

I'd seen hate before and this guy HATED me. His face was beet-red as he glared at my retreating form. Then his hand darted between his legs and pulled up a long-barreled revolver. He whipped it up toward me as I jerked my own gun out of the purse. Then he fired.

I felt the impact against the side of my head, a hammer blow that dazed me and flung me back against a mailbox. He fired again, the bullet hitting me high on the left shoulder as I dropped down the side of the box and landed on my ass.

I fired into the side of the door, my vision blurring as I heard the squeal of Jock's tires. The Caddy engine revved and the black monster rushed away. I held my hand up, though it wobbled from side to side, and kept pulling the trigger, firing almost without knowing what I was doing. Glass crashed and tinkled and then there was a tremendous thunderclap of metal against metal as Jock's Chevy hit the side of the Caddy and smashed it into a parked Toyota.

I kept firing the ten-shot automatic at the general outline of the Caddy until I ran out of bullets. I held it there for a minute, seeing a confused scuffling around the driver's side of the car. I blinked and closed my left eye tightly as blood colored my vision even more. I shivered and dropped the gun, feeling cold as I sank back against the box.

Someone shook me and I blinked out of my right eye at Greaser's face as he knelt beside me. He was doing something around the side of my head and I pushed at him feebly.

"It's okay," he said. "It's okay." He repeated that several times, his voice tight and anguished. I was surprised at that. Greaser was one of the guys who'd been the most hostile to me.

Sirens wailed in the distance, the sound rising and falling as my head swayed drunkenly. Jock and Joker were beside me, I noted absently. Jock was pressing something against my shoulder, which burned fiercely.

"Fuckin' johns," I breathed weakly. Then I blanked out.

I woke briefly to pain. I was lying down on something hard, the sidewalk, I realized. There were people all around me, cops, I thought, confused. The uniforms were wrong. EMTs, then. I must be hurt or something. A needle stuck me in the arm and a light flashed in my face, a little round one from a flashlight one of the EMTs held. I blacked out again, though I could still hear a siren somewhere.

I woke again, the light much bigger, much brighter this time. More people around me as I was lifted from place to place. I heard voices talking but couldn't make out what they were saying, the words were too slow, with a kind of echo. I was in a hospital, I judged, looking down casually. Someone held my head back as a sheet covering my chest was pulled away.

I wasn't wearing my tank top anymore, that meant I was naked, at least from the waist up. I wondered why that didn't embarrass me. Another pinprick in my arm and I blanked out again.

I woke up to peace and no more bright lights. No more voices calling back and forth above my bed. I felt a high buzz that kept me from thinking much at first. My mind cleared slowly. My head felt tight, hot. I started to reach up, but found I couldn't, as sudden pain shot through me. It cleared the haze a little more. I looked down and saw the bandages on my shoulder, then reached up with my right hand and found a thick bandage on the side of my head.

So. I was alive, at least. There were several moments of deep, all-encompassing relief, then the throbbing in my head began to grow louder and harsher, almost making me wish I were dead. My shoulder didn't seem so bad; at least, there was little pain there.

I couldn't see much around me. There was a pair of those hospital sheets hanging from the ceiling on either side of my bed. Machines whirred and beeped behind me somewhere. I couldn't see anything past the foot of my bed but a wall.

A nurse showed up then. A modern nurse, not one of those maidens with starchy white dresses and a funny hat. This one wore a blue sweater and a tired smile.

"Awake at last," she said, sounding genuinely pleased.

She pointed a little light at my left eye, then my right, then clicked it off and slipped it back into her pocket.

"How do you feel?"

"Head hurts." I said. Speaking was an effort. My voice was gravelly and low.

"You've only got a local for the shoulder right now," she said. "We've kept you off general anesthetics the last few days. You've been unconscious for a little bit."

7

"How am I?"

"Well, speaking is a good sign. Do you remember your name?"

"Yeah."

"What is it?"

"Caitlin."

"Good."

Another woman appeared then, wearing clean surgical greens. She was younger than the first, a frizzy-haired red-head. She yawned, but also smiled as she moved to the other side of my bed.

"Hi, Caitlin. I'm Dr. Reed. How do you feel?"

"Weak. Throat's dry," I managed to get out.

"You've been asleep for a while." Another flashlight in my eyes, one at a time.

"Can you move your left foot, Caitlin?"

I moved my foot.

"Does it hurt?"

"No."

"What about your right?"

I moved that one too.

"Good. What about your right arm? Can you move it up and hold it steady for me?"

She held my hand then.

"Squeeze my hand," she said.

I squeezed.

"Good."

"My head hurts."

"I bet it does." Reed moved around to the same side as the nurse and played with something up behind me. I was too tired to bother looking.

"Can you remember your age, Caitlin?"

"Thirty-two."

"What about your mother's name?"

"Susan."

"Do you remember what happened to you?"

I had to think about that one. The images were blurred, confused, rushed.

"Caitlin?"

"Someone shot me."

"Twice," the nurse said.

"Am I all right?"

"Well, you'll live, I guess," Reed said.

"That's good," I sighed. Nothing else seemed important then.

Reed appeared again, yawning.

"Do you remember how you got shot, Caitlin?"

"A banker in a Caddy shot me. I think he hated whores. My head hurts like shit."

"We don't want to zonk you out, Caitlin. You've had a head injury and we're trying to determine if you've fully recovered from the surgery."

"What surgery?"

"Don't worry about it. It looks like everything went well. We'll call your father and let him know. He's been bugging us every other hour for the last week."

Week?

"Week?"

"Week," Reed confirmed.

"There goes my sick leave."

"Try to sleep. Dr. Simpson will be in in a few hours. He'll check on you then."

I was too tired to wonder who Dr. Simpson was. Besides, the nurse brought me a plastic container of water.

"Don't raise your head," she warned.

There was a drinking tube attached to the container. She slid it between my lips and I drank slowly.

I drifted in and out of consciousness for a while, nurses

9

checking on me every few minutes, taking my blood pressure and looking at my eyes. Then a man appeared, wearing the traditional white jacket. He was in his late fifties, probably, and mostly bald.

"How do we feel this morning?" he asked, seeming pleased to see me.

"My head hurts," I complained.

"That's good," he said, poking a flashlight at my eyes.

I restrained a very obscene reply.

"Do you remember your name?"

"I already did that." I was starting to feel bitchy. Headaches do that to me.

"Humor me."

"Caitlin Elizabeth O'Neil."

"Good. Good."

I lifted my legs, wiggled my toes, then raised my arm and squeezed his hand. He squiggled on a clipboard and said "Good"—a lot.

"So how am I?"

"Doing very well, all things considered."

"What does that mean? How long will I be here?"

"Oh, you'll be with us a little while yet."

"You the guy who operated on me?"

"No. That would be Dr. Caldwell. He's the neurosurgeon who worked on your head wound. Dr. Millen and Dr. Pashner worked on your shoulder. I am in overall charge of your case. I'm Dr. Simpson, by the way." He sat down on the edge of the bed.

"You were struck by two bullets. The first hit the side of your head, fortunately at an angle, and didn't penetrate much beyond the skull.

"Although the bullet didn't penetrate the skull cavity, the blow was sufficient to cause swelling of your brain. We kept you under all this time until it subsided. The second bullet struck you in the . . . well, in the shoulder, let's say. No organ damage, but a lot of bone splintering took place. Dr. Millen spent a lot of time putting your shoulder back together again. I'll show you the X rays of what it looked like before when you're in a little better shape."

"How long until I'm better?"

Simpson hesitated.

"It's difficult to say. Your shoulder will need a lot of time to heal, then, well, there'll have to be some therapy to get it working again. If all goes well, you can be out of here in a few days, but your shoulder won't be back to normal for weeks. It might not ever be completely restored, though you should recover the majority of flexibility and movement in time."

I couldn't find it in myself to care that much. It was enough to know I'd live and wouldn't be a cripple or a vegetable or something. A nurse pumped on the lever beside my bed, raising my head, then presented me with a cup of orange juice. Brooks showed up while I was sipping carefully.

"Cat?"

"Hi, boss."

"Well, thank Christ." He came forward slowly, as if afraid to startle me. He wore one of his cheap brown suits, his brown hair brushing the collar.

"How do you feel?"

"Shitty."

He grinned and nodded. Brooks had a round face, all baggy like a chipmunk. He looked about fifty, ten years more than he really was. We'd gotten to know each other a lot better than either of us would have expected six years ago. He'd once told me that he knew every sexual position ever invented, and offered to prove it. He'd been joking, and I'd taken it for that, but as we'd gotten closer, well, on a couple of occasions I'd given serious consideration to taking him up on his offer. If he hadn't been my boss I would have.

"The doc says you're gonna be all right."

"Yeah. So I hear. What happened to the fucker that shot me?"

"He's downstairs somewhere. You put a bullet in his side, shot out a kidney."

"Good."

"Strong bastard, though. Took three guys to put him on the road, even with a bullet in his gut."

"Who was he?"

"Some asshole. His kid died of AIDS last week. Far as we can tell, the kid was a closet queer. The old man doesn't buy that, though. He read where a lot of hookers got AIDS, so figures the kid got it from a hooker."

"So he decides to off a hooker."

"Something like that. He's pretty embarrassed at getting a cop by mistake. Says he's sorry."

"Swell."

"You and Jock wrecked his car too. The insurance company doesn't want to cover it. He's mad at that. Wants us to pay for it."

"Fuck him," I sighed.

"Yeah. You should be out of here in a few days. Then you get to spend a few weeks at home on full pay. Nice time of year for a vacation too."

"I don't think I can get my bikini on over this." I smiled tiredly, looking down at the sling around my arm and the thick bandage around my shoulder.

"So you can watch soap operas. I know how all you broads love soap operas." He grinned.

"Up yours."

"Your mom and dad are on their way over. I called them when the doc called me, but he'd already called them anyway."

"When did they get here?"

"They flew in the next day. They've been staying at the Sheraton. Your mom threw a tantrum because they wouldn't let her stay here beside you."

"Glad I missed it."

A nurse appeared around the curtain.

"You'll have to leave now, sir. She has to rest."

"Yeah. Sure. Okay," Brooks said to her.

"Listen, kid. I'll be back. The guys all wanna see you too. The doc says you'll get out of ICU later."

"That where I am?"

"That's the place. I'll see you later." He gave my hand a soft squeeze, then slowly turned away.

After Brooks left, I lay there for a while, happy again at just being alive. But boredom started to get to me. I've always been kind of hyper. Lying on my back in a hospital nearly drove me nuts. Hour after hour of doing nothing. I examined everything around me, not that there was much to look at, just a couple of curtains on either side, my bed, and the camera.

There was a camera on the far wall, up near the roof, trained directly at me. It made me feel like someone was staring at me all the time.

"Darling!"

"Hi, Mom," I said with a weak smile.

My mother bent over and hugged me lightly, as if afraid she'd break something. She was crying, but trying to hide it. My mother looked as crummy as I felt. Her blond hair was flat, and she had no makeup on. She usually didn't need much. At fifty-eight, she could still pass for forty-something on a good day.

"The doctor says you're going to be all right."

"So I hear. How are you and Dad?"

"Oh God! How do you think?" She sat down beside my bed, holding my right hand tightly.

13

"We got a call at three in the morning saying you'd been shot! Your father almost had a heart attack."

I sighed and shook my head. Dad was as healthy as a horse, but Mom always had him on the verge of a stroke or a heart attack.

"We called the airport and managed to get a plane leaving a few hours later. Then, when we got here, they said you'd been shot in the head and you were unconscious! You can imagine how I felt. I haven't managed a wink of sleep in the last week."

My father appeared then, smiling broadly. I couldn't help smiling in return.

"Forgot to duck, huh?" he said with a grin. He came over on the other side of the bed, leaned over and kissed me on the cheek.

"Hi, Dad."

"Hello, Katie. How do you feel?"

"I got a headache you wouldn't believe."

"Can't they give you something for that?" my mother demanded.

"They want to see if my head is all right first."

"I thought they said it was fine."

"So they say. Maybe you can go and yell at them for me."

"Well, you just bet I will!" She sprang out of her chair and disappeared around the curtain, on attack mode.

"She's been out of her mind with worry the last week. We all have."

"Sorry."

"Don't be a little fool. Not exactly your fault, is it?"

"I was the one that forgot to duck."

He smiled.

"Well, you'll know better next time. Don't say that around your mother, though."

"I'm waiting for an I-told-you-so from her."

"You'll wait awhile. I told her not to talk about you quitting."

"How long do you think she'll be able to keep that in?"

"Not long, but hopefully until you're out of the hospital."

My mother returned then, Dr. Simpson in tow.

"Still have that headache, Caitlin?" he asked.

"Yeah."

"Well, we want to take you downstairs for a test, then we can give you something to dull the pain."

It dulled everything else too, giving my mother no chance to criticize my choice of career. I dropped off asleep. When I woke up I was alone again and wondering how long I'd been under.

After lunch, which consisted mostly of juice and milk, with a little bread, I was moved, bed and all, down the hall, out the door of ICU and down another hall to an elevator. They took the elevator up several floors, then rolled me down another hall to a room with sunlight streaming through the window.

I didn't get to keep my bed, though. I had to act like a sack of potatoes while several nurses and an orderly lifted me over into another bed. My shoulder started hurting then and kept on hurting for the next week.

There was another bed in the room, a few feet to the left of mine. It was empty, so I had the place to myself. Well, not really to myself. My mom and dad had shown up for the move.

"This is a nice room," my mother said, looking around from corner to corner, then checking the view.

"Now that you're in a room, we'll have to get you some flowers to brighten things up."

"I won't be here long, Mom."

"Then we can bring them home with us after you go."

I got the distinct feeling she meant home to Chicago, not home to my apartment.

"I've got nowhere to put them at my place, Mom."

"Who cares about your place? I'm talking about our place."

"Mom—"

"Oh now, don't be foolish. What do you think, we'd leave you on your own, and you barely able to move?"

"I can look after myself."

"Course you can, Katie," my father said. "That isn't the point. You can't go back to work for weeks, if ever. You can sure use some help for the next little while. Makes sense for you to come home with us for a little. Lord knows we've got the room."

"What do you mean, if ever?" I said impatiently. "I thought you guys weren't going to bug me about being a cop."

Dad looked guilty and turned to look at Mom. She shrugged.

"You might as well tell her," she said.

"Tell her what?" I demanded.

"We were going to wait until you left the hospital," Dad said.

"Tell me what?" I repeated.

"About your shoulder."

"What about it?"

"The doctors say it might not recover enough for you to go back to your job."

"What?!"

"Dr. Simpson said that shoulder injuries are very tricky things. The bullet did a lot of damage to your shoulder and it might not recover enough for you to stay with the police."

"He said it probably wouldn't," Mom corrected, not seeming at all sorry.

"He didn't say you'd be unable to use the arm or anything," Dad hastened to add. "Just that it probably wouldn't return to one hundred percent. It'll be fine for normal things but probably wouldn't pass the police physical."

I just stared at them, wanting to say they were crazy, but

knowing better. In the movies you could get shot in the arm or the hand or especially the shoulder, and almost ignore the wound. A little bandage and you could go on fighting bad guys for hours.

Real life was something else again. Bullets caused a lot of damage wherever they hit. A .45 in the arm could blow your arm clean off. I'd known plenty of cops retired on disability because of wounds that would have caused barely a shrug or a limp on Arnold or Clint or Chuck. You could be a secretary or paper shuffler with a damaged arm or leg, but not a cop.

"They said you'd likely get seventy percent of your former movement back," Dad said.

"Seventy percent," I said softly. Seventy percent wasn't enough, not to be a cop.

2

I got Simpson in and confronted him. He called Millen, and the two showed me an X ray of my shoulder that looked like a spiderweb littered with tacks and paper clips. Their professional judgment was I'd get seventy percent back, but no more. Seventy percent wasn't enough to be a real cop. I might spend the next twenty years in a uniform, being a clerk or answering the phone, but going out on the street would be out of the question.

"As far as bone and muscle damage is concerned, there's no worse place, other than the spine, for a gunshot wound," Millen said gloomily. "As you can see, the force of the impact does an incredible amount of damage there, both to the bone and the soft tissue."

"But I thought you fixed it."

"Fixed it? Well, you'll be able to use the arm again, but we can't completely mend damage as bad as this. With a lot of work and effort you might get more than seventy percent, but you shouldn't count on it."

It turned out to be a week before I was released, the most miserable week of my life. I was poked, pushed, prodded, stuck, and had to go through every type of indignity you could imagine. My head felt better each day but my shoulder continued to ache, a constant reminder of the dead end my life had suddenly hit.

By the time I was released a week later, I'd given up fighting my parents and allowed as how a trip home might not be such a bad idea. By then it had become damned obvious, even to me, that I was going to have a lot of trouble moving around for a while. As for work, well, no matter what, even light duty was out for months.

So I let myself be pulled along with my family to the airport and made the flight east to Chicago, where I proceeded to sit around the house and be bored for long weeks. The boredom was made worse by my now uncertain future. What could I do if I wasn't a cop? And what would I do if they let me remain a cop in some administrative support position?

I just didn't see myself sitting at a desk for the next thirty years. I'd never wanted a paper-pusher job, couldn't imagine doing one. I loved being outside, moving around, going from place to place every day. I loved the unexpected. True, I'd grown less than fond of life as a make-believe whore, but there were an awful lot of other jobs as a cop I would relish.

I was nearly six feet tall. I'd been that way since twelve, when I'd practically rocketed upward. I'd been terribly insecure about it, but the size had brought an intimidation factor which I seized upon to make myself sort of a schoolyard cop. With five brothers showing me how to fight, I'd done a pretty damned good job, too.

I guess becoming a cop had just been a continuation of that. Growing up blue-collar Irish, respect for the police was bred into me, so becoming one had seemed natural, even if my family hadn't been terribly thrilled.

But now I was facing a blank. I had no idea where I'd be or what I'd be doing in six months.

In the meantime there was the boredom, relieved by bouts of pain and frustration when someone, usually my dad, drove me downtown to the rehab center.

There I got to work on my shoulder, which was no fun task. It didn't want to do anything right, and still felt as if it were in pieces. It took a month of rehab before I could even move my left arm without pain. They were used to patients' cursing there, but I think I might have set a record, having a larger than normal vocabulary in that area of the language.

Once I could move the arm, I started in on moving it faster, and with more dexterity. It was another few weeks before I could raise my arm above my head easily. By then, my mother and I were driving each other crazy, and I was losing what little temper I had left. I could function reasonably well, so I said good-bye and went back to L.A.

They held a tearful farewell party, but I think we were all sort of relieved. My relationship with my mother had never been the best. She'd always wanted me to be the giggly, girlish type, like my sister Liz, and had never made any secret of how strange and unaccountable she thought my life was to date.

I've always exercised regularly. When your job involves wrestling mostly male suspects, you'd damn well better be stronger than your average woman, and, if possible, your average man. I wasn't any professional body builder or anything, but my arms and legs had muscles below the skin, and I'd regularly beaten men in arm wrestling. In L.A. I bought one of those exercise machines you see on late-night television, a Solo Flex, and began to do some serious workouts, spending several hours a day in various exercises. I spent more time at the rehab center, and for two months, exercising was a big chunk of my life.

I grew more and more confident as the time passed. My

arms, and the rest of me, for that matter, were stronger than they'd ever been, and though the movement of my left arm was a little uneven, I thought I could do the job again. The problem then became: would the doctors agree?

I talked to the guy in personnel, who called me back and gave me an appointment for two days later. That gave me two more days of moping around. I exercised as much as I could stand, hoping every little bit would improve my shoulder. I figured they'd probably keep me on desk duty for a week or two but hoped the doctor would tell me the recovery was doing well enough that I could expect more, eventually. At least he'd be able to tell me how much work I still had to do.

The weather was great, so I got my bikini and slipped up to the roof for two days of tanning, trying to put a little more color on my skin before I had to see the department's quack.

I got there bright and early, after a sleepless night worrying about what I was going to do with myself if I couldn't work as a cop anymore. The department had a lot of places it could stick people like me, of course. I'd wear the uniform, complete with gun, but basically I'd be in some kind of administrative job—filing papers, maybe working as a clerk or chauffeur or something like that.

I knew now that I would never be able to go on working in some kind of office position, not for the department. If I couldn't be a street cop, then I didn't want to be a pretend cop. I'd quit and find something else entirely.

My night of tossing and turning was a waste. The doc didn't even see me. Instead his secretary, or nurse, or whatever she was, said I had to get a psychological clearance first, from another departmental quack.

So I waited another couple of days, kicking around the house and getting a better tan, exercising, doing a little shopping, and going down to the target range to practice my shooting. I tried a lot of quick-draw firing, thinking that if I'd been faster I might not have gotten shot in the first place. Course, it's hard to do a fast draw from a purse.

The shrink wanted me to talk about my anger, which I didn't have any problem with. I was uncomfortable with shrinks. It was as if they were analyzing everything I said for its meaning. I never knew when I was saying something that might make them think I was a wacko or something.

Did I hate the man who shot me? Damned right I did! How could I pretend otherwise after all the trouble and pain the bastard had put me through? Was I afraid of getting shot again? No more than I ever had been. Did I think my judgment was affected by being shot by the jerk? No. Did I think I would be faster to shoot someone I found threatening? No. Not unless they pointed a gun at me.

Every question was a judgment call. I tried to figure what he wanted to hear. I couldn't be too nonchalant. Shrinks liked emotion. If I didn't show some, I was liable to be accused of repressing anger or something. At the same time, too much emotion would worry them about me maybe being unstable, a ticking bomb just waiting to go off and kill a bunch of innocent civilians.

I don't know exactly what he thought of me, since he wouldn't tell me anything, but he approved me for duty, so I suppose I gave mostly the right answers. I got another appointment, this time with the first quack, and sat around the house some more, getting incredibly bored.

Then I got a phone call from some guy in Internal Affairs. Actually, it was a message on my machine, telling me to get down to the Internal Affairs building first thing in the morning and talk to some detective there named Stewart.

It was already first thing in the morning when I checked the machine, so I drove downtown to see Internal Affairs. I was a little confused about what they wanted, thinking I might have been assigned there somehow, for some kind of light duty. I would have preferred to work for someone else, almost anyone else, but you didn't get your choice about things like that, and I had asked for a transfer. Anyway, it would only be temporary.

Internal Affairs got good press. In all the TV shows and movies they were always finding rotten murdering, thieving cops and solemnly bringing them to justice. The only thing TV got right was how everyone else in the department hated them, including me.

The truth was that they were all a bunch of climbers. They went in there because it was a fast-track route to promotion, without the dirt or stress or ridiculous hours of Vice. They all had more of a bureaucrat mentality than was good for anyone.

As for the crimes they investigated, well, in my experience, most of the cops taken down by those brave folks were drinking on the job, getting free coffee or lunches, or moonlighting at a second job without permission. They also bravely assisted vicious pimps and drug dealers who complained about a cop's using excessive force, or cursing at them, or making racial remarks. Get cut off in traffic by a patrol car and it's Internal Affairs to the rescue.

Cops who got so far out of line that they murdered someone or dealt drugs, or something, were almost always caught by Homicide, Narcotics, or Robbery, not by Internal Affairs.

Stewart proved to be an emaciated man about my height and age. He was prematurely bald, except along the sides of his head, and had narrow eyes and a hooked nose, like an eagle. He met me in the lobby and led me upstairs and down a quiet hall to a small square interview room.

The only contents were four chairs and a cheap wooden table, at which we sat down. He spread a file open on the table as he took a seat across from me. He glanced up at me, then back at the file, then slid a silver pen out of his breast pocket, looking all set.

I wasn't impressed.

"Detective, do you know why you're here?" he asked.

"No."

"This office was tasked to investigate the shooting which took place on May 14 on Jefferson Avenue. Although the circumstances were pursuant to guidelines, re, the shooting itself, there have been questions raised about the ammunition in your weapon at that time. You're aware of what I'm talking about?"

He gave me a fatherly look, stern yet understanding, linking his fingers in front of him as he waited for my confession.

As he'd talked it had dawned on me that rather than some kind of job interview, this scrawny little prick was complaining about the bullets I'd used to shoot the nut who'd shot me.

"Are you talking about the hollow-points I used?"

"Unapproved, as you well know," he said, nodding.

"You've gotta be kidding."

"You know that hollow-point ammunition is against regulations, Detective, for very good reason."

"Bullshit! A nine-millimeter packs just as much punch."

"Then why didn't you use one?"

"Because I prefer the thirty-eight! It doesn't kick your wrists as much."

"It is, however, banned by the department."

"I don't believe this shit!" I glared.

I hadn't exactly anticipated a brass-band welcome-back from the department, but I guess I'd figured on some kind of, I don't know, acknowledgment, a "Well done," that sort of thing. Instead I had this skinny jerk-off whining about my using the wrong ammo. I'd completely forgotten about it, considering it trivial compared to getting shot.

Besides, that rule was an old one that no one had gotten around to changing. When the .38s were the only approved handgun, cops had used hollow-points to give them more punch. The department, in its wisdom, had decided cops didn't need more punch and had outlawed the bullets, which mushroomed on impact and caused a hell of a lot more damage than normal .38-caliber bullets.

Now that every crackhead in the city was toting a machine gun, the department had approved much more powerful 9-millimeter handguns, but hadn't bothered rescinding the ban on hollow-points. The thing was, though, that 9-millimeters, with their much higher muzzle velocity, had a lot more kickback than .38s. They were hard to handle if you weren't very big. The guys loved them, but most of the guys on the department had sixty to seventy pounds on me. Women, and smaller men, needed both hands to control the guns when firing, meaning you had to stand and plant yourself to get an accurate shot. Firing one-handed with any accuracy was unlikely, especially if you were rushed, which was when it counted.

"If you disagree as to your guilt in this matter, you can choose to plead this before a departmental disciplinary hearing, Detective. During this hearing you may, if you wish, be represented or accompanied by a union representative. If you choose to forgo the right to a hearing, the matter will be moved directly to your division captain, who will decide the proper degree of punishment. That will be based on your record and an interview during which you will be permitted to make explanations as to the cause of the violation. However, in this case you will not, as you would in a departmental hearing, have the right to representation, and/or accompaniment, by your union representative."

He said all that without pausing to breathe, and he didn't look at me while he spoke, instead shuffling forms in the folder before him. He pulled several out of the pile and slid them across the desk to me.

"If you do not choose to contest the charge, sign here, here, here and here. A finding of use of unauthorized ammunition will be entered in your permanent record, along with whatever disciplinary action your captain takes. This action may include, depending on your record, a written reprimand, a fine, suspension without pay, or demotion."

I stared at him, mouth open, a lot of things passing through my mind. I was getting more and more outraged as this incredibly stupid, ignorant little prick droned on and on.

I wanted to say a lot of things, most of them obscene, but looking at the bland-faced man, I realized anything I said would be pointless. Since there was no way I could deny using the hollow-points, I signed the papers, which he quickly snatched back and slid into the pile.

"All right, Detective, that's all. Return to your division and see your captain."

He stood up, took one step, opened the door, and walked away without another word.

"Cocksucker," I muttered, turning the other way.

I drove down to Temper Street to talk to the captain. I wasn't looking forward to it and had no intention of going through another sleepless night worrying if I could get it over with now.

Most captains, in my experience, are nothing more than paper shufflers. The only time they concern themselves with crime is when the department is getting bad press for something particularly nasty and the brass jump on him to get it solved. He then jumps on the lieutenant or sergeant and goes back to his paper shuffling. Keep the paper piles turning over nicely, brownnose the inspectors and deputy chiefs, attend all the right parties, and maybe you'll get promoted and sent downtown. That's the way captains think.

There are exceptions, of course. There are always exceptions. My captain, Captain Todd, was not one of them.

Todd was the flowchart king. That was what everyone

called him, in fact: Flowchart. It seemed every day he was coming up with a new flowchart to show how manpower could be more effectively used and distributed. He was sure that one day one of them would come to the attention of someone who counted and he'd be yanked out of Temper Street and sent downtown, where he'd be under the eyes of the brass and have more opportunity for promotion.

Out on Temper he was out of sight, out of mind. The only time he came to the brass's attention was when something went wrong. That was why being a division captain wasn't considered a great career move.

I flashed my badge at the rookie guarding the parking lot and he waved me through. It occurred to me then that guarding parking lots was one of the career alternatives facing me. You only needed one good arm to wave cars through the gate.

I moved quickly through the lobby, hoping to avoid everyone for a bit. I didn't want to get into back-patting and welcome-backs when my future here was so uncertain. I said a quick hi to a couple of guys who noticed me, and trotted up the stairs to the admin offices.

Todd's office was in the rear of the building, as quiet a place as he could find on Temper Street. It also overlooked the parking lot, so he could catch those coming in late and leaving early. There was a little alcove in the hall before his door, and his admin sergeant had a desk there and a bunch of filing cabinets.

"Sergeant Dixon," I greeted him, "I need to see the captain."

" 'Bout what?" he asked casually. Dixon sucked up knowledge like a sponge, and delighted in being the division's prime source of gossip. As Todd's administrative assistant he opened most of the captain's mail and had access to the rest. Whatever Todd knew, Dixon knew.

"About the IAD thing," I said.

"Ahhhh," he nodded, not asking what I meant, not needing to.

"Go ahead in. He ain't doin' anything important."

I went past him and knocked on the frosted glass window of Todd's door.

"Come in," he called.

He stood up and smiled when I opened the door.

"Detective O'Neil," he said. "Come in, come in."

He came around the desk and took my hand, still smiling, and being a lot more friendly than he should be, especially under the circumstances.

Todd was a short man, just barely over the guidelines, the ones that'd been relaxed to allow more women . . . short ones, I mean, and minorities, like Asians, on the force. He had brown permed hair, a thin mustache, and wore a pair of round-lensed glasses, which, according to the rumors, taken from Dixon, were of plain glass, and were meant to give him a look of intelligence.

He led me to one of the chairs in front of his desk, still smiling and holding my hand.

"How are you? How do you feel?"

"Uh, okay, I guess, considering," I said warily.

"I was so relieved you weren't more seriously hurt. I went down to see you a couple of times, but you were still unconscious."

"Oh, well, that was . . . nice of you," I said.

"Not at all, not at all. How is your shoulder? Has it been evaluated for duty yet?"

"Not yet. I have an appointment tomorrow."

"How does it feel?"

"Pretty good." I pulled my hand away from his at last, waving my arm around to show him how well it worked. He smiled and nodded, his eyes flicking up and down, up and down. He sat down in the chair next to me, rather than behind the desk.

"Excellent, excellent," he said. His other nickname was Double-Talk. "Now, as to why you're here, oh yes, but first, I had other news. I was looking through your file recently, when you were shot, of course, and I noticed you'd passed the sergeants' exam. Congratulations."

"Well, uh, thanks," I said, now totally confused. I'd passed it six months earlier. "Not that it matters, since promotions are pretty much frozen."

"Not entirely, not entirely," he said, smiling, teeth gleaming. "You were aware that Sergeant Dixon was retiring at the end of the month?"

"Vaguely," I said. As if I cared. Dixon wasn't any friend of mine.

"Well, as it happens, he is, and of course I'm looking for a replacement. In fact, my own time here is almost up, hopefully, and when I go downtown I'd like to take my new administrative assistant with me, if that were you, of course."

"Me?" I stared blankly, totally unprepared for this.

"You've put in for reassignment."

"Well . . . well, yeah, but as a detective, maybe in Robbery or somewhere."

"Yes, yes, but as you've observed, other than the very highest qualified individuals, promotion to sergeant is unlikely for those on the list, unless of course they're needed for some specific duty, some duty that they are best qualified for."

"Like your assistant?" I asked, still confused.

"Yes, yes, exactly."

"But I don't know anything about how to do that."

"Nonsense, nonsense, Dixon would be glad to show you. It doesn't take long to learn and can't be terribly difficult. He does it, after all, and the man's not in the upper ten, now is he?"

29

He smiled conspiratorially, like we two smart people knew what a dummy Dixon was.

Jesus, the man had a phony smile.

"I still don't understand why you'd want me and not someone more . . . experienced."

"Someone old and fat and lazy and just waiting till he can retire, you mean?" he sniffed. "I want someone who'll reflect well on me, especially once I go downtown."

His chair was right next to mine and he slid his right arm up across my shoulders, smiling again. "We two could help enhance each other's career prospects, Caitlin," he said, smiling his phony smile again. He took my hand in his other hand again, squeezing and massaging it. I looked down at it, then at his phony smile.

"Think of how much faster you'd make the lieutenant's list with a rabbi downtown pulling for you," he said.

"Lieutenant?"

Then, as I was staring at him in near total confusion, he leaned over and kissed me . . . on the lips. I was so stunned I didn't react at all. I sat there frozen. Then I shoved him back hard and jumped up, furious. "You sleazy little—"

"Shhhhh! Shhhh!" He jumped up and held his hands out toward me, frantically patting at the air as his face jerked back and forth between me and the door. "It's not what you think! It's not what you think!"

"If you think I'm gonna sleep with you to be a sergeant, you're out of your fucking mind!" I snarled.

"Shhhh! Keep your voice down! You don't have to! I mean, that's not what I wanted! Well, not really! I just want you for my secretary."

"I'm not a goddamn secretary!"

"Think of how well it would help your career."

"Fuck my career, and fuck you too!"

I headed for the door, boiling mad, and he skipped over in front of me, putting his back against it.

"Just listen to me," he begged.

"You touch me again, I'll put you through that door, Todd."

"No, no, no. I won't. I won't. Please, just sit down for a moment."

I backed up a little, but didn't sit down.

"Look, O'Neil . . . Caitlin, can I be frank?"

"Try me," I said stonily.

"I'm trying to create a good impression here, both of my work, and of me, the man. You could help enhance that impression. And it would take very little effort. All I need for you to do, is, well, whenever a certain person was coming, if you could, say, oh, act very, uh, very friendly to me in his presence, smile a lot, you know, maybe speak a little suggestively."

He looked at me hopefully and I stared back in astonishment.

"You mean you want them to think you're screwing me?"

"Must you be so crude?" he winced.

"Forgive me. I've been in Vice playing hookers for six years. My etiquette has slipped."

"But that's it exactly," he said, excited.

"What's it?"

"Well, I mean, you've been acting like that for years, pretending, putting on an act, as it were, acting sexy for the suspects. All I want you to do is a much more toned-down version of that, and you wouldn't even have to wear anything more than a uniform. Oh, well, you could attend a few small functions with me, and dress up for them, but basically all you'd be doing would be administration."

"What was with the wet kiss then?" I demanded.

"Uhm, well, heh, heh." He grinned a little self-consciously. "You can't blame a guy for trying."

31

"Want to bet?"

"You can still have the job. I won't touch you," he said, holding his hands up and smiling hopefully.

"Forget it," I said bluntly.

"But think of how quickly you could rise in the department."

"As your whore? I don't think so."

"But it would only be pretend!" he said.

"I'm not an actor, I'm a cop. I want to continue being a cop."

"Well, then, perhaps you should consider the position you're in," he said, his face taking on a calculating expression. "Not only haven't you been approved for duty, but the case involving banned ammunition has been delegated to me for decision."

"What's that supposed to mean?" I demanded.

"Well." He smiled. "Most doctors these days like to cover their behinds. We all know a great deal about that," he said, smiling again. "I get his report, and it's up to me to . . . to interpret it. If I decide you're simply not fit for regular duty . . ."

"I'd rather quit than play some whore secretary," I said fiercely.

"You've been playing a whore for years! What's the difference?" he demanded.

"The johns aren't as sleazy as you," I snapped.

"You ungrateful bitch! I'm offering you sergeant's stripes years before you'd ever get them putting on those push-up bras and miniskirts! All I'm asking is a little bit of playacting for the brass!"

"Forget it!"

"Fine!" He scowled. "Then we'll get on with your discipline for the violation of ammunition standards!"

"Fine."

"Do you have anything to say in your defense?"

"No."

"I didn't think so." He sneered. "You're suspended without pay for two weeks. And when you come back, officer," he said, lowering his voice and spitting out the word, "I think you will find, regardless of the medical opinion, that the transfer you requested will send you into Watts or South Central, where you'll be handcuffed to a typewriter every day. Officer!"

3

Somehow I've managed to gain a reputation for a fiery, almost uncontrollable, temper. That's just plain untrue. I first got the rep when I was still a kid and threw a chair over a balcony at my brother below. Now granted it probably would have caused a deal of damage if it'd hit him, but he was looking up at the time, and the distance was more than sufficient for him to duck out of the way. I'd known that when I tossed it.

What I'm saying is that I never really lose my temper. That's not to say I don't get really angry, but I always calculate before I act, however quickly.

So slugging Todd was not, as it might have seemed to the casual viewer, an act of uncontrolled temper. On the contrary. In a very few seconds I decided that, not only did he deserve to be slugged, but was unlikely to be able to offer up any meaningful response, either physical or otherwise. He was out of shape and I knew I could beat the crap out of him without half trying. As for regulations, well, a captain with a desperate desire for promotion was not going to bring up a female officer on charges for slugging him in private, not even if she looked like Magilla Gorilla. In the macho world of policing that would carry a stigma. Everyone would laugh at him, "the captain who got beat up by a broad."

So slugging him, though it was a result of anger, was not the act of a crazy uncontrolled temper an observer might have thought. It was a reasonably calculated move.

Unfortunately, the calculation was thrown off by two things.

First, I didn't know how weak a chin Todd had. I'd heard the term "glass jaw" before, but hadn't ever run into one. So breaking his jaw was a straight-out accident. All I'd wanted to do was wound his dignity a little. Hell, I've hit plenty of guys harder and their jaws never broke.

Things still might have been okay. Like I said, in the world of policing, captains who wanted to be promoted didn't complain about getting beaten up by blondes (even fake blondes like me). Unfortunately, Inspector Cairwen was right outside the door at the time, having arrived for a meeting with the captain. He was the second flaw in my calculations.

When Todd went sailing backward he hit the credenza behind him, knocking off a crystal decanter and a matching set of tumblers, all probably waiting for the inspector's visit. They, and he, landed very noisily on the floor, and seconds later the door was thrown open by the inspector, a goggle-eyed Dixon right behind him.

Now, according to the strict interpretation of not only police regulations, but the criminal code, I was in deep trouble. Physically assaulting and breaking the jaw of a police captain would not only get me fired, but arrested too. And for a few days it began to look as if that was precisely what was going to happen.

Fortunately, politics reared its ugly head.

The LAPD was, to put it mildly, in the midst of a torrent of

35

bad publicity. Every brass hat in the department was trying desperately to prevent any more incidents from making it into the press. Without much difficulty, my union lawyer was able to paint a picture of how delighted the media would be with the story of a pretty blonde who'd slugged her captain after being physically assaulted (the kiss), and was then set upon by the full weight of the sexist, misogynistic police administration.

He even speculated on who would play me in the TV movie.

The brass, as usually happens, collapsed. No charges were filed, either by Todd or the department. My career was finished, of course. Bureaucrats never forgive and never forget those that made waves and gave them headaches. So with my chances of promotion or a decent posting about the same as that of *Architectural Digest*'s doing a layout on South Central L.A., I let my lawyer negotiate my retirement.

The disability pension would be barely enough to starve on, but then I wasn't planning on just sitting around the house for the next forty-odd years. I'd get another job.

That was the thought, anyway.

Unfortunately, there were people out there on the unemployment line clutching their masters' degrees, and I was suddenly what was quaintly termed "unskilled labor." I had two years of college and no useful job skills, unless I wanted to become a security guard.

It was Brooks who came up with the only viable alternative, going to Oregon to work for a buddy of his who was a county sheriff. It wasn't very appealing, and the pay didn't sound very good. We talked about it for a few hours while getting drunk on my couch. I turned him down then, but after thinking about it for a couple of days I changed my mind.

After all, I'd been looking for a transfer, hoping for a job that wouldn't be so scummy and hard-edged. Being a county deputy made me think of parking in a squad car by the side of a highway, listening to the radio and watching for speeders. I'd never had time to do anything like that in L.A., even in the few months when I'd been in uniform. It was always one call after another then. And later, in Vice, it had been a constant stream of scumballs and sleazoids in my face, guys who made me feel dirty even without touching me.

Maybe things wouldn't be so bad as a deputy sheriff. People probably wouldn't curse you every time they saw you, and you wouldn't have to worry about getting shot so much. The courts probably weren't so overloaded up there either. Maybe when you arrested somebody up there, he or she actually did some real time.

Two weeks after I'd retired I was on my way north to Oregon.

I wasn't really sure what to expect. I'd worked with county deputies before, from L.A. and Ventura counties. But those were large, modern, mostly urban forces. Loren County, Oregon, was a sparsely populated rural area with more cows than people, and more tractors than sports cars. It might bore me to tears. Maybe life as a security guard would be better.

On the other hand, although "Better to reign in hell than serve in heaven" wasn't an exact parable, it did hold the general idea. I thought it must surely be better to be a police officer in Loren than a security guard in Los Angeles. I decided to find out, anyway.

There wasn't much traffic on the interstate. Roads without major traffic hassles would take some getting used to. I pushed the Jeep (I'd traded in my Audi turbo, figuring Oregon was more Jeep country) up past seventy, enjoying the brightening day. The engine growled a little, but the Jeep managed to climb into the eighties with a little coaxing.

I almost missed the exit ramp for Madison. I braked

sharply, and the Jeep's rear slid sideways before I brought it back in line. I was back below sixty as I left the highway and turned south down a nameless two-lane road. I kept an eye out for more signs but didn't spot any for miles. The road stayed empty, with nothing on either side but trees, empty fields, and a few cows.

Finally I rolled past a sign that said "Welcome to Loren County," and right past that came a sign that said Madison was thirty miles ahead. I slowed down further, figuring it would be impolitic to get nabbed for speeding before I'd even joined the sheriff's department.

The odd house began to appear among the trees, nice little wooden places out of a Norman Rockwell painting. I turned east onto a wider highway, following a sign. Within a mile I passed a used-car dealership, then a Kentucky Fried Chicken, the first signs of retail life I'd seen since leaving the highway.

Farther along, a series of small businesses were spaced out along both sides of the road, along with a couple of motels, restaurants, some gas stations, and a big video store.

Then I was in Madison. Houses lined the streets just as in any other town or city. I drove aimlessly, looking for some sign to indicate where the cop shop would be. I passed into a commercial section, with lots of stores, and figured I was probably close to my objective.

I was looking for Durham Street. I didn't have a map but figured it couldn't be very hard to find in a town of nine thousand. I continued on straight until I was into another residential section. Cursing mildly, I turned around and drove back the way I had come, then took a left turn at the first road I found.

I slowed and rolled to a stop at the curb, then slid halfway out the door to confront a man walking past.

"Excuse me," I said. "Can you tell me where Durham Street is?"

"Just keep going two blocks, honey," he said.

I didn't much like the "honey," but the guy looked about a hundred years old, so I let it go.

"Thanks," I said, ducking back into the Jeep.

A couple of blocks down I found Durham, and saw something that looked likely a block down. It was a small single-story red brick building set back from the street. There was a flag in the middle of the little lawn, and a cop car sat parked against the curb.

I pulled up behind the cop car, slightly surprised that it was a nearly new Chevy Caprice with modern flashers. I guess I'd been half expecting ten-year-old rust buckets with those big old-fashioned single dome lights like you see in black-and-white movies. The colors were light green on white, and the traditional EMERGENCY 911 was on the tail.

I couldn't see into the building even as I moved up the walk. There were large windows but they were tinted. There was a backlit sign out front, surrounded by flowers. It proclaimed the building the headquarters of the Loren County Sheriff's Office. The building looked very modern, and my hopes started to rise that I wouldn't be spending the next few years with Oregon's version of hillbillies.

Inside was a twelve-by-twelve lobby. The floor was carpeted a pale blue. The walls were wood paneling, except for the one looking out onto the road, which was mostly tinted glass. There were two doors directly across from the front door, and between them was a wide brick-lined counter. The quiet hum of air-conditioning was the only sound in the room.

A uniformed woman sat behind the counter. She stood up as I approached, smiling inquiringly.

"Hi," I said.

"Hi there."

"I'm supposed to meet Sheriff Bradford."

"Sure thing," she said cheerfully. "I'll just call him." She reached down to the phone and I noticed the words "Auxiliary Police" printed above the pocket of her uniform. She looked to be about my age, though shorter, with curly brown hair and a round, pleasant face.

"Sheriff? There's a lady here to see you," she said into the phone. She paused a second then said, "Right away."

She hung up, smiled again, and pointed to the door on my right. "Just go right through there," she said.

"Thanks," I replied, pushing back from the counter and going around it to the door. It buzzed just as I reached for it, and I pulled it open, nodded at the woman, and went through.

I was in a narrow carpeted hallway, doors on both sides. A man stood at the end of the hall, maybe twenty feet down, apparently waiting for me.

"You O'Neil?" he asked as I approached.

"Yeah."

"Come on into my office. I'm Sheriff Bradford." He held out his hand and I took it as we sized each other up.

He wasn't what I had expected, but then neither was the station. He wasn't old and didn't have a beer belly. He had spoken precisely, in a clipped tone, was clean, well-shaved, and wore a perfectly pressed beige uniform. In short, he looked nothing like my concept of a small-town, or maybe I should say small-county, sheriff.

He was about six feet tall, an inch more than I was. He had short brown hair, though not military short, a narrow, smooth face, strong, maybe a little too-strong, jaw, which kind of stuck out a little sharply for my taste, large eyebrows and a long neck. Still, he wasn't an unattractive guy, with a trim body beneath what I guessed to be a tailored uniform.

"Sit down, Miss O'Neil," he said, motioning me to a chair in front of his desk. "Or is that Miz?" he asked, sitting down himself.

"Whatever you like." I shrugged negligently.

His office was small, but as neat as he was. Aside from the desk, there were a pair of chairs in front of it, one of which I was occupying; a credenza was behind him, under the window; a floor-to-ceiling bookcase covered the far wall; and a large couch and coffee table were along the side wall, away from the door. A computer sat on a side table, with a laser printer on a stand beneath it.

There was an in/out basket on his desk, along with a multi-line phone, a blotter, pen set and clock. Aside from those his desk was completely empty except for a single file, which lay open directly in front of him.

"You look pretty young for thirty-two."

"That's one of the reasons Lieutenant Brooks brought me onto his squad," I said. "Looking young is handy for a Vice officer."

"No doubt. I'm glad you decided to join us." He smiled. "Jack speaks highly of you."

"The lieutenant's a good guy," I said.

Brooks hadn't told him the precise reason for my leaving the LAPD. He said Bradford was kind of conservative and probably wouldn't appreciate my having assaulted my last boss.

"Your record with the LAPD is excellent, a lot of felony arrests, some undercover work, drug buys and such. You don't have a whole lot of time in uniform, but the first six months is always the most important, and you've done that. Most important, Jack speaks well of your communications skills. He says you've got great empathy and know when you're being lied to. I consider those the most important skills for a police officer to have.

"You won't be doing any drug buys or undercover work here. We're too small a department, so everyone involved in that kind of activity would quickly come to know you. We pretty much leave that sort of thing to the state police. They can keep rotating people so they aren't recognized."

I nodded, face bland.

"Tell me why you want to come and work for us, Miss O'Neil," he said.

"Why?" I thought about that for a second. "I like being a cop. I guess I've always sort of been one, even back in school. I was the schoolyard cop, keeping bullies from beating on the little kids. It's all I've ever really done and I don't know what else I'd do now. I'll admit I'd rather be back on the LAPD, but lately I've started to think being a deputy out here might be pretty attractive."

"Why?"

"I'd gotten really tired of things in L.A. It wasn't just dressing up as hookers and junkies, it was the whole rotten scene on the streets there. I have to say, looking back, that I never really accomplished anything. There's no way the police can ever make a dent in the crime there, not so long as they've got those damned slums. There aren't enough cops, prosecutors, judges, courts or prisons to take care of them. The whole system's broken down and I was really growing frustrated at having to deal with it. Making a good bust loses a lot of its satisfaction when the perp doesn't suffer any real punishment.

"I'd put in for a transfer before the shooting. I was sick of life on the street. I was hoping for something like Robbery, which I figured was a lot cleaner, you know. I don't know, maybe out here being a cop will be a lot easier."

"We're not exactly free of crime out here," he said.

"I'm not worried about crime. I'm just tired of working in a sewer where you watch the walls and roofs for roaches every time you go inside somewhere, and watch everybody you see for guns. I don't know, maybe I'm burned out a little. I'd just like to take things a little easier for a while."

"A lot of people feel like that after a while on the job."

"I don't know about that. I do like being a cop. I just don't like the feeling that I can't affect things. So what if I bust a few dealers? There's a thousand more, ten thousand more, selling up the street. And if you get all of them, there's a million more people waiting to take their place. The courts are too busy and bargain things down almost all the time. Hell, machine-gunning a house isn't even a felony anymore, unless you hit someone. We let them plead to unlawful discharge of a firearm, a misdemeanor. Can you believe that? Course, the jails are overcrowded and releasing people after a fraction of their sentence anyway. It was just all starting to seem like a colossal waste of time. That's why coming out here seems kind of appealing."

"You think you'd be more effective here?"

"I don't know. I hope so. I figure maybe you can deal with things one at a time here, handle them and move on. Maybe you don't have to keep a hundred balls in the air at once."

"Well, things are slower here. There's no doubt of that." He smiled. "But how do you think you'll handle the boredom?"

"I could use a little boredom."

"Sometimes police from cities, where they're constantly on the run, come out to a rural area and can't handle the hours of monotonous patrolling. You might drive around for an eight-hour shift here and only get a couple of calls, both of a very minor nature. That's especially true on the dog shift, where you'd be starting. That might sound nice at first, but how do you think it'll be after a month?"

"I'd like to find out."

"Well," he said, "okay then. We will."

"You mean I'm hired?"

"I wouldn't have Jack send one of his people out here if I wasn't almost sure of hiring them," he said. "All I wanted to find out for sure was that you weren't some burned-out veteran who was going to park under a tree, quaff down a six-pack, and sleep all night."

"I don't drink much anyway," I said with a brief smile.

"Well, good. I don't either. We're about the only ones here that don't, though. Most of the men like to live up to that hard-drinking, macho western image. Speaking of which . . ."

He made an odd face, then smiled again. "You will find the people, especially the men out here, sometimes kind of, well, backward in their treatment of women, as compared to the men in Los Angeles, at least. Many of them aren't very politically correct, and there's a lot of them that don't take to feminism at all."

I snorted. "There's a lot of them in L.A. too."

"Maybe so, but here they'll probably be less likely to keep their opinions to themselves. We're talking loggers, other lumbermen, farmers, and, well, I'd say about half the men on the department don't think there's any place for women police, other than to search female suspects and type out reports. These are blue-collar guys with blue-collar attitudes.

"Some of them aren't very educated either. They're the holdovers from decades back, when all you needed to be a deputy was muscles and a gun. Most of those ones were on the Madison police force before it was incorporated into the county sheriff's office. They've never been to a police academy and don't know much, nor care much about modern policing.

"I'd like to get rid of some of 'em, but the agreement with the city when we took over guarantees their jobs unless they really screw up. Don't get me wrong, now. Some of 'em are good, decent guys, and good deputies, but there's maybe six or seven of 'em I'd like to get rid of, and I doubt you'll get along too well with them."

"I'll avoid them." I shrugged.

"No, I'm afraid you won't," he said with hesitation. "You

see, midnight shift is not a really well-liked position. You gotta go on it to start because you're new. The guys with the most seniority get the best shifts."

"I know that," I interjected. He held up a hand to silence me.

"But seniority isn't all that counts. Those guys that, well, shall we say don't have the best social skills, and don't make much attempt to correct their . . . deficiencies, I put on the midnight shift so they'll have less opportunity to cause trouble. There ain't a whole helluva lot for them to do on the midnight shift, and not too many honest, decent, God-fearing Christians up at that hour for them to offend."

"In other words, most of the guys working the midnight shift are assholes?" I asked uneasily.

"I wouldn't go that far. These aren't really bad guys, Miss O'Neil. If they were, I'd have fired them by now. They're just not all that bright, and not all that . . . well, let's just say their method of solving problems tends to be more physical than most. They aren't a very graceful bunch, and they don't have much in the way of communications skills."

I pictured a group of Neanderthals in uniforms, grunting like apes as they swung their clubs around.

"Greeeaaat," I sighed.

"Really, they're not that bad," he said anxiously. "They do their job. They don't have a lot of style, maybe, but they get things done."

"Uh-huh."

"Anyway, they shouldn't give you too much trouble. They do, you let me know."

"Sure."

"Now, they're a little annoyed at you coming in from the city and taking over like this, but they'll get over it soon enough."

"Wait a minute. What do you mean, taking over?"

45

"Well, being made sergeant over them. Billy Masters thought he should be sergeant on account of his seniority, but—"

"I'm supposed to be a sergeant?"

"You'll be supervising officer on the dog shift."

"In charge of this . . . caveman squad?" I demanded.

His face cringed a little.

"Please, Miss . . . Sergeant O'Neil, we really don't need any more nicknames for these guys."

"But I don't know the area. I don't know the procedures. I don't know a damn thing!"

"You know how to be a good cop, and that's more than any of them know."

"I'll be getting lost all the time for the first couple of months."

"Not at all, we're a real easy county to find your way around in, once you get the hang of things. Besides, being shift sergeant isn't all that much here, not like in Los Angeles. You just patrol like any other deputy. If one of the other deputies has a problem, they contact you, is all."

"Have you given any thought as to how these good ol' boys are going to react to some young blond woman coming in and becoming their boss?" I demanded.

He snorted, his mouth parting in a wide grin. "Heck, O'Neil, it's been giving me chuckles for days. The whole department's been snickering about it since word got out."

"Great. I'm glad you're all amused."

"Don't worry, Sergeant." He grinned. "Really, the place pretty much runs itself on the dog shift. You've got six cars on the road, mostly doing nothing, and one volunteer at the station answering calls and handling the radio. There ain't much more to it than that. Besides, you're perfect. They can't hit you, seeing as you're a girl, and if they did I'd fire 'em right away.

"Remember, we are a paramilitary organization. They can't refuse your orders, and they can't be openly insubordinate . . . not all the time anyway."

"I don't know, Sheriff. It doesn't sound like the peaceful job I was hoping for."

"Ahh, it'll be fine, you wait and see. You won't have to stay on the dog shift forever, and these guys won't be with us forever. Most of 'em already have twenty-five to thirty years in.

"Besides, we need you. I need someone responsible for that job, and, to be frank, I need more women on the force. We've only got two of them and we're having trouble getting more. It isn't the kind of job local women think about doing, if you know what I mean. We aren't all that liberated out here, and the girls who are liberated want to go off to college and become doctors and lawyers."

I nodded, unconvinced.

"Look, what've you got to lose? Look around the county. You'll find it's a pretty nice place to live, with nice people. It's not a sewer, or anything close to one. Plus, things are a heckuva lot cheaper out here than in Los Angeles. The salary isn't all that great, but combined with your pension from Los Angeles, you can live pretty darned well here. You can buy yourself a nice little house and still put some money away."

He reached behind him to the credenza and lifted a heavy file, then turned back and put it on the desk near me. "Here's everything you need to know: procedures and departmental rules—most of which are a lot simpler than L.A's; city, town and county maps; and the papers you need to fill out for Joleen, she's our secretary."

He shoved it across to me and I looked at it, a little reluctantly.

"Look around, look them over, then get back to me. I'll give you a few days to think about it. In the meantime, there's a hotel up the street that's pretty reasonable."

He stood up and came around the desk. I stood as well and shook his hand as he held it out.

"I think you'll decide to give it a try, Miss O'Neil," he said with a smile. "And I think you'll like it here."

4

Madison was a pretty little town, pretty little city, really, though I had trouble thinking of it as a city. The hotel was an old two-story brick building only a block up the street from the police station. It was all polished wood and heavy furniture, no chrome and steel here, and I found it charming and beautiful.

The room had a big old wooden double bed, thick old wooden dresser, side tables and chairs, and a twenty-one-inch color TV. There was a blue rug—rug, not carpet—on the floor, and frilly flowery curtains and bedspread to add color.

I dumped my things on the floor, having forgone the services of a bellboy, supposing they had one, and flopped on the bed with the pile of papers Bradford had given me.

I scanned through the rules and procedures first. They seemed relatively straightforward and commonsense. There were a lot fewer rules than the LAPD manual contained, for example.

The department had thirty-seven deputies, some working

eight-to-four, Monday-to-Friday shifts. There were permanent four-to-midnight, and midnight-to-eight shifts, and rotating shifts that moved through the evening and midnight shifts. Weekends were twelve-hour shifts, and unless you were one of the few lucky eight-to-fours, you worked a shift of seven days on, three off, then seven on, four off, and so on.

That made an average of forty-three hours a week, with very little overtime. There were no detectives, as such. Small-scale investigations were done by the sheriff and a couple of daytime officers, but anything that was too complex was handled by the state police.

There were, according to the guidelines, six deputies on duty during the dog shift, eight during the evening shift, and ten during the day shift. The reason for the larger day shift was to account for officers on court time and transporting prisoners around.

The pay rate, as Bradford had said, wasn't great; even as a sergeant I would make less than two-thirds of what a cop makes in Los Angeles. On the other hand, adding in my pension, and what was likely a much lower cost of living, I would be nicely off.

Bradford had included a number for a real estate woman, along with one for a clothing store where I could buy uniforms.

I unfolded a map of the county. Loren was about eleven hundred square miles in size, dotted with several small towns and two small cities, Madison and Ashford. Most of the rest of the territory was divided between farms and forests. It was generally flat, the mountains being farther east, and the main roads crisscrossed it like a grid.

I studied the map intently, trying to memorize the locations and names of the main roads and towns. A phone call interrupted me. It was the real estate lady. Bradford had called her and told her I might be looking for a place.

"I don't know how long I'll be staying," I said. "I'm sure not looking to buy a place just yet."

"Oh, of course not, dear," she said. "But I've a number of lovely places to rent as well. Why don't I come over there and show you around the area a little, let you see a few places?" Since getting to know the county was what I needed, I agreed, and ten minutes later was getting into a large Buick with a frizzy-haired bottle blonde named Irene.

She was a font of information about the county and its inhabitants, starting with the mayor of Madison, the councilmen, then the sheriff. Bradford, she said, was a straitlaced, religious man, and, in her opinion, a politician to the core.

"You watch," she said. "Give him a couple more years and he'll be running for mayor."

"Think he'll make it?"

"Probably. He knows all the right words to use. Anyway, he gets things done. He's done a pretty good job as county sheriff, especially with the budget cutbacks. He created that police auxiliary thing, which is mostly answering the phone, but it saves a whole lot of money since he doesn't have to pay them anything."

She showed me a half dozen places, but the one I really liked was just on the edge of town, the edge of the city, I mean. It was off a main road, tucked in behind an auto-body shop, though well back from it.

"Fred built this place for his son Michael," Irene said, pointing at another house closer to the auto-body shop. "He and his wife live there, see, and he figured Michael would work for him and live just up here. Michael decided to move to Clearwater and start his own shop there, so this place has been vacant for a while."

It was a single-story house built on a low hill, with big windows looking out onto a wide grassy meadow. It had a big, elevated deck in the back, where the hill sloped sharply, and I could easily imagine myself sitting out there and watching the sun set, or rise, or whatever. It seemed peaceful and quiet and all alone. It was just around a bend of a dirt road from the other house and out of sight of both it and the body shop.

It was a modern, well-built place, attractive, and with central air-conditioning. There was one large bedroom, a large living room, dining room, and kitchen, with a dishwasher, and just off to one side a cupboard with a small washer and dryer. It had a two-car carport at the side, which was nice, since the manual said that supervisors drove their police cruisers home and were on call anytime, day or night. It was only four hundred a month. Try renting a house like this for four hundred a month in Los Angeles.

"It's actually a lot like Fred's house, except his has several bedrooms underneath and a swimming pool. Repairing cars is pretty good business around here."

"Or anywhere else," I said.

"Well, anyway, Michael doesn't want it. Carol, his younger sister, is off at college, and if you want my opinion, isn't too likely to come back, and her little sister is still years from living on her own. Fred still hopes one or another of 'em will live here eventually, though, so he's renting it instead of trying to sell. The view is nice, if you like grass. The problem is it's not big enough for a family place, and a lot of younger people want something that's either in town, or out in the country, preferably on a river or lakeshore."

"I think the view is fine." I shrugged. "You get tired of the view after a few months wherever you are."

"That's absolutely true." She nodded.

"Fred's pretty handy to repair cars and build houses," I said, running my hands over a corner beam.

"He is that, always has been. I guess it's all pretty much the same sort of thing, working with tools and such."

"Well, I'll take it, I guess, if it's okay with him."

"Oh, I'm sure he'll be delighted." Irene smiled.

Fred was delighted, maybe a little too delighted. He was a tall, cadaverous-looking fellow with a gaunt white face and oversized, sunken eyes. He smiled and looked me up and down repeatedly while Irene talked and told him I wanted to rent the house. He didn't exactly hang his tongue out the side of his mouth but I resolved to put curtains up first thing.

His wife, Shelly, a pudgy-looking middle-aged woman, was less enthusiastic, frowning a lot. I felt like telling her the thought of sleeping with her husband was only slightly more appealing than sleeping with a corpse. She glared at her husband, and at me, but didn't say a lot.

"You need any help with anythin', shiftin' furniture, or breakdowns or somethin', you come 'n' call on me," Fred said, bobbing his head.

"Oh, sure thing." Yick.

If I'd met Fred beforehand, I probably would have found someplace else. As it was, I couldn't think of any graceful way of backing out. I signed a lease and Irene drove me back into the city.

"Known Fred long?" I asked casually.

"Oh, don't worry about him. He stares a lot but that's all he'll do. Just keep your bedroom curtains drawn when you're changing."

My very thought.

"It's your hair, you see. Fred's always been daffy for blondes, ever since high school."

"That's nice."

"Is it real?"

"What?"

"Your hair."

"Nope."

"Didn't think so."

"Thanks."

She howled with laughter, slapping the steering wheel.

"Don't worry, hon, it's still a better-lookin' job than mine."

I diplomatically didn't comment.

"Here we dye our hair blond to attract the men, and look what kind of man we attract." She chuckled. "But don't worry, I've known him all my life. He really is harmless."

"I think I'll change the locks, anyway."

"Can't do that," she said. "Landlord's gotta have a copy of the keys. What you should do if you're worried is just drill a couple of holes in the doorframes, right through into the doors, see, then slide a couple of nails through them. That way nobody can get in while you're home."

"What about when I'm not home?"

"Oh, well, I think Shelly will pretty much keep him away, but if you're at all worried, put a lock on your dresser and closet. That's all he'd be interested in, anyway. He'd just poke around through your undies, nosy-like."

"Uh-huh."

Better and better.

"Really, hon, he won't do nothing. He's scared of the police, for one thing. He got himself arrested about twenty years ago for peeping into a woman's window. He's real careful now how he acts."

"You might've told me this before I rented the place."

"Hell, I been trying to rent or sell that place for over two years. You think I'd screw that up?"

"Your bleach job really sucks, you know," I said.

She laughed uproariously.

She let me off at the hotel, where I called Brooks and told him to have the moving company send my stuff down.

"I take it you were hired."

"Yeah, they loved me," I said without enthusiasm.

"Good, good."

"There's one thing, though. They want me to be a sergeant, to supervise the midnight shift."

"That's great."

"Yeah, but I gotta keep track of what sounds like a bunch of goon cops."

"You'll manage. Just sweet-talk them."

"From the sounds of these guys, sweet talk isn't gonna work nearly as well as a foot in the crotch."

"Whatever keeps them happy."

"Also, I rented a house off a guy who's a Peeping Tom and lives practically next door."

"Why'd you do that?" he asked, puzzled.

"Because I'm an exhibitionist and want to put on nightly shows. Why'd you think? I didn't know about that until after I'd signed the papers and given them two months' rent."

"Well, I'm sure a Peeping Tom won't give you too much trouble, O'Neil. You are a cop, after all."

"Yeah, so I'm told."

I gave him my address and hung up.

I went down to the clothing store Bradford had listed and ordered a half dozen uniforms, then went to a hardware store and bought chains for the doors, and a measuring tape. I went back to the house then and let myself in. I spent a good half hour measuring things, then went back into town and got blinds for all the windows. A nearby furniture store, providing you weren't picky, could supply curtains immediately. I wasn't picky. By nightfall they were in place and I went back to the hotel for the night.

The next morning I went back to see Bradford, giving him the application and employment papers I'd filled out. My picture was taken for an ID card and I was sworn in as a Loren County deputy sheriff.

From there I was handed off to Bradford's second in command, a tall blond guy in his mid-thirties with a gee-shucks look on his pleasant face. He was the department's sole lieutenant, as opposed to five sergeants like myself. His name was Patrick Goff, a local boy who'd always wanted to be a cop and seemed deeply satisfied as to his progress with the department.

He was not, however, the naive innocent he appeared at first impression, as I learned when we got into a patrol car for a tour of the area. A tour of the county, all eleven hundred miles, was out of the question, but he promised to at least show me around the Madison area.

"I can't wait until you meet the Monster Squad." He snickered as he looked behind him before pulling out.

"Are they that bad?" I asked anxiously.

He snickered some more, then stomped on the accelerator, jerking me back against the headrest as the Caprice lurched forward.

"They're also called the goon squad, the apemen, the trogs, that's short for troglodytes, and the newest, Gates's boys. That's because they've formed a Larry Gates fan club. You know, the L.A. police chief?"

"Yeah," I sighed. "I've heard of him."

"You're talkin' about a bunch of guys who love fighting, are racist, sexist, and everything else -ist you can think of, who'll pull over and piss—excuse me, ah, urinate—against the patrol car, and wave to traffic passing by. They come on to women, any woman, hell, any girl that strikes their fancy, and they are far from subtle. You know, like those construction workers in the city that whistle and yell obscenities at the women passing by? Half the complaints we get are from outraged women, or husbands or parents. It wouldn't surprise me if they took the occasional bribe from motorists, either. They're oversized, undertrained, and don't take criticism very well. In short, they're a supervisor's worst nightmare."

"Swell."

He laughed in amusement, turning onto what seemed to be the city's main commercial street.

"Did Bradford tell you to come to him with any trouble?"

I nodded and he snickered again.

"Let me tell you what he really means. What he wants is to never have to hear from or about these guys again, ever. Unless, of course, it's about one of them quitting or doing something outrageous enough to justify firing them. Don't expect a lot of backup from him. I should know. I was their supervisor until now."

"How did you handle them?"

"I didn't. I pretty much let them do what they wanted, and investigated every complaint we got about them in the hopes we could get rid of one or another. I did manage to fire two of them, but it took three years for that to happen. Hopefully, you'll do better."

"You mean I've been hired to get rid of these people?" I asked uncertainly.

"Oh no, but if you could arrange to fire a few, I'm sure the sheriff would be delighted."

"I'll see what I can do," I grumbled.

He laughed again. What a happy guy.

"Why can't he just fire them if they're so bad?" I demanded.

"Can't," he said, shaking his head. "The agreement with Madison was pretty specific. The mayor used to be the police chief and likes these guys. He's your original good ol' boy, even if this is a bit northerly for that kind of attitude. If you read the agreement, it says plain enough that the sheriff acknowledges their lack of training but will continue to employ them unless and until they violate their oaths as police officers or commit a felony. Being crude and ignorant doesn't count.

"We've had a lot of B and Es along this strip in the last couple of months, so check the doors and windows during patrols and stop any groups of kids wandering around. There's a curfew that says that if you're under eighteen, you have to be home by midnight. We enforce it here, so if you see any kids, pick 'em up."

"Uh-huh. How many B and Es you have lately?"

"Here? Five this year alone."

"Wow, a real crime wave."

He snorted, turning off onto another street. We drove over a river and past what looked like an old mill, but was actually a restaurant. He turned again and we drove through what seemed to be the undesirable part of town, with old, shabby-looking houses.

"Basically, our problems in Loren are B and Es, mostly from teenagers; vandalism, again from teenagers; general rowdiness and drunkenness, from teenagers; and traffic offenses, mostly by teenagers. Startin' to get the picture?"

"Yeah. Move the curfew to six o'clock and you could close down the department after dark."

"Pretty much," he chuckled. "There's some loud arguments to break up, and now and then a fight, usually between drunks. We had three murders last year, all domestics, and all solved right away without much effort. We also had six reported rapes, but we figure the ratio of occurrences to reportings is something like twenty or thirty to one, as opposed to about ten to one in Los Angeles, say."

"How come?"

"Small-town atmosphere. The victims don't want everybody finding out. The local paper helps that. Any rape happens they put it front page, naming the victim, and if they can, putting their picture on the front page."

"Great guys."

"Yeah, it really pisses Bradford off, excuse me, but the editor says the people have the right to know. He says rapes are just like any other violent crime an' there's nothin' for the women to be ashamed of."

58

"Easy for him to say."

"Yeah. But what can you do, freedom of the press and all that. Anyway, aside from that, our only real problem is a couple of bars just off Interstate Nine. The truckers and foresters go there and get a little rowdy sometimes, especially when the foresters are out in force. One, Eddie's, is just your normal blue-collar bar, only a little bigger. The other one, Shooters, has topless waitresses and strippers. You have any doubts about the girls' ages, make sure you get ID. The sheriff is real hot on that."

"What about hookers?"

"Yeah, we got a few. We don't have them parading up and down Center Street, but there's a few around. Mostly they hang around Eddie's and Shooters or work out of their houses. Unless someone complains we don't waste much time on 'em.

"This is Stewart's Lumberyard." He pointed to a tall warehouse with piles of boards all around it. An eight-foot chain-link fence topped by coiled barbed wire surrounded the yard.

"Get a lot of trespassing there, guys lookin' for some cheap wood. 'Less they're actually carting stuff, we just charge 'em with trespassing.

"Over here"—he pointed to a fenced-in plant on the other side of the road—"is the Coke bottling plant. All the Coke, Seven-up, an' . . . I think Sprite, is bottled and shipped from there for Loren, Peel, and Karrin counties. You see the trucks parked inside the fence? Half of 'em are loaded with full cases and they don't lock. So we got the same thing there as at the lumberyard, only there it's mostly kids. There's a security guard there but he's more trouble than the kids, a real nasty old man. Calls us more than anybody in the county. Real foul mouth on him, too."

He drove out past the city limits and picked up speed, climbing to seventy-five on a fifty-five highway.

"There's one other source of trouble," he said.

"Yeah? What?"

"Well, the city of Ashford decided against amalgamating with the county sheriff, and they have their own police department. At least, they call it that."

"They like the Monster Squad?"

"No," he said shortly. "They're worse. Or maybe they're just like the Monster Squad run by someone who encourages them instead of trying to tone 'em down. We get a lot of complaints about them. They're a lot less choosy about using force on someone than we are. Fact, some of them are downright mean. The so-called police chief is the worst of the bunch, and the mayor isn't any better. They're all a bunch of thieves and crooks if you ask me, but the sheriff says try and work with them." He shook his head in disgust.

"What kind of complaints do you get?"

"You name it, we get it. Unfortunately, we can never seem to get enough evidence to prove it. We had one girl, some tourist, came in said she was pulled over by an Ashford patrol car, then handcuffed and raped. She identified a picture of one of their officers, but police log there said he was working at the station at the time, and there were a dozen witnesses to prove it. They all say the girl came storming in to complain about a traffic ticket and threatened to get the guy if he didn't cancel it."

"But you believed her?"

"She was crying and hysterical. The doctors say she was raped."

"Get a semen sample?"

He turned and gave me a disgusted look. "The guy tossed her into a river afterward. Wasn't anything to get. The state boys nosed around for a while, then left.

"Most of the complaints aren't that bad; motorists extorted, people beaten up, sometimes robbed. Most of what

60

they do they do inside Ashford, and the people there don't dare report it. We mostly get things that happen outside Ashford. These guys like to poach on our highways, see, where there's more traffic.

"They can't even legally write a ticket for a county road but they like to threaten the motorists, get a bribe out of 'em. Sometimes they'll search the car and find some drugs that weren't there before, then they'll threaten to arrest whoever they've got unless they're paid off. We hear they extort sex out of female motorists too, though we haven't had an official complaint. We also hear there's some drug-running going on but we got no proof at all as to that."

"You never found proof on them?"

"Once or twice in the last ten years. Each time it was a single officer, once for assault, another time for theft. Both wound up in county jail for a few months, then they went back to work. Those guys stick together. Any complaint against one always brings a dozen witnesses to say something else.

"They're a real pain in the ass. Excuse me.

"Anyway, if you have any trouble with 'em, call in one of the monsters an' they'll convince 'em to stick closer to home. They're good for that much anyway. Don't go after 'em yourself," he said, glancing sharply at me. "These guys aren't above pitching you in a river, if you get my meaning."

"I think I can handle some flabby redneck."

"Well, good, then you won't have too much trouble with the monsters."

We drove through some very pretty country and half an hour outside of Madison came to the Ashford city limits. We drove all around the roads surrounding the city of five thousand, with Goff pointing out which roads were ours and which were theirs. Then we drove into Ashford, which he said I should do now and then, just to let them know the county was keeping an eye on them.

61

"It's not our jurisdiction, but they can't stop us from driving through. The state boys think they're a transfer point for drugs," Goff said glumly. "We don't have a big problem with drugs in Loren, but the feds say they're getting drugs here from Idaho . . ."

"Idaho?" I blinked in amazement.

"Yeah. You don't figure they have any drugs in Idaho?" He grinned.

"I'd almost forgotten there even was an Idaho. Do people still live there?"

"A few."

"Where in hell would they get drugs from anyway?"

"It rests up against the Canadian border. Smugglers are starting to avoid the southern states because they're so well patrolled. It's comparatively easier to get them into Canada because there's so much rugged, empty shoreline and so few patrols. Getting them across the border from there is pretty easy. The terrain is ideal in northern Idaho and southern British Columbia, all forest and mountains."

"But why would they want to?"

"Idaho borders on six states, in case you've forgotten your high school geography," he said. "They can move drugs across the whole Northwest from there."

"Idaho drug smugglers," I murmured. "Hot damn."

"Drugs are everywhere, Caitlin. You should know that."

"Yeah, I guess."

"Anyway, the FBI office in Idaho—"

"They have an FBI office in Idaho? Where is it, a farmhouse? Do they have cities in Idaho?"

"Boise. You aren't exactly a country person, are you, Caitlin?" he asked dourly.

"I like to drive in the country sometimes," I said defensively.

He gave me an odd look.

"You ever lived in a small town?" he asked.

"I've driven past a few, along the highways."

"Uh-huh. Anyway, keep an eye out for vehicles with Idaho and California registrations. When you're in Zone Nine, that's the one that covers Ashford and the surrounding area, watch the traffic to the northeast. It wouldn't surprise me, though, if they transferred the stuff into their own patrol cars out in the country."

"The Ashford police?"

"Yeah. There's only five of 'em, including the sorry excuse for a chief. They're all crooked and they're all mean. They've all got a lot more money than they should have, too. None of 'em's in very good shape, but watch yourself if you confront one. A sucker punch isn't all that unlikely. Real rednecks, the lot of 'em," he said.

Ashford was a gray-looking city, kind of run down and rusting. We passed the police station, which was exactly the kind of place I'd pictured when Brooks had first mentioned coming to a small town. City, I mean. It was a small one-story brick building that didn't look much bigger than a double garage. There were bars on all the windows, and a beat-up-looking Ford patrol car was parked in front.

"Sorry goddamn disgraceful-looking place. Excuse me."

"Stop that, will you?" I scowled.

"What?" He looked blankly at me.

"Stop all that excuse-me crap. I've been working in the vice squad for six years. I've heard a lot more swearing than you ever will. It doesn't bother me."

"Well, I don't like to get into the habit of swearing in front of ladies."

"Who says I'm a lady?"

"Excuse me. Woman."

I sighed and let my head back against the headrest.

"I guess you'll hear a lot worse from the monsters too," Goff said, putting on speed as we passed the city limits.

"What, you mean they'd dare swear at their supervisor?"

He chuckled and shook his head. The digital speed readout clicked upward past seventy.

"You know, everybody thinks they're a real dumb bunch," he said. "But some of the names they called me, well, you gotta wonder where they came up with them. I guess they do have minds if they want to put 'em to use."

"I've got a few choice words myself."

"Doesn't do any good. They like being cursed at, especially if it's real inventive. I think they'll like it even more being cursed at by a pretty blonde."

"Know any?" I asked sourly.

"Hey, you're not bad-looking."

"Thanks."

"I mean, you're pretty good-looking. Bit tall for my taste, but . . ." His eyes flicked up and down, and then he shrugged as he caught my scowl, halting his tribute to my looks.

"I'm sure the monsters will let you know too, in their own way."

"I'll look forward to it."

"Maybe that was one of the reasons Bradford put you in charge of them, to provoke them into saying or doing something stupid. Hell, Allen Sims is already threatening to resign."

"He's one of the monsters?"

"Uh-huh."

"Look, I don't get it. If these guys are so bad, why doesn't Bradford fire them? I know he promised to keep them on, but if they're racist and sexist and insubordinate, it seems to me that's plenty of excuse to dump them."

"He doesn't want trouble from the mayor, so he wants

more than an excuse, he wants something everyone will agree was way out of line. Calling a sergeant a dumb asshole, for instance, isn't good enough. As for racist, well, we don't have many minorities in the county, mostly Asians, and they never complain."

"What about sexist?"

"Well, so what? As long as they're not getting really obscene, the mayor'll just put it down to boys bein' boys. He's not gonna accept firing someone 'cause he whistled at a pretty girl or told her she had a nice . . . ah, that he liked her looks. Hell, he even argued about Joe Rothman. Bradford caught him screwing a sheep, for God's sake."

"A sheep? You're kidding!"

"Nahhh, was on duty too, up in the north end, around four in the morning. Bradford figured he was parking and sleeping half the night, so he poked around, found Rothman's car, and found Rothman in a field humping some sheep. Uh, excuse me for saying it."

"Yeah, yeah, I've heard lots worse. The mayor tried to defend that?"

"He said the sheep didn't complain, and neither did the farmer, so why should Bradford care? Said it was better than him taking money or somethin'."

"This is gonna be real fun." I shook my head.

"Oh, they aren't that bad. Rothman was weird but the rest of 'em are pretty normal, at least so far as sex goes. They all thought Rothman was kinda disgusting."

"It's good to know the sheep population is safe now."

"Yeah, now all you have to worry about are the human females." He grinned.

"Like me, for example?"

"Oh, sure, that'd be real convenient, too—if you could arrange to get yourself attacked, that is. I'm sure the sheriff would appreciate it."

"I'll run right out and get myself a sheep costume."

"Just be sure it's a white sheep."

¦5¦

We spent several hours driving around the county, with Goff pointing out areas they had trouble with. I thought the country around Loren was lovely. There weren't any real mountains this far west, but the land around the north and west side of the county was very hilly and covered in forest. Still, as Goff noted, the winding roads that looked so quaint and lovely in the daytime turned into utter blackness at night. Few had streetlights.

Interstate 9 was something else again. Where nature had done well by Loren, some of the things men had built were indisputably ugly, and Interstate 9 was one of them. It was a broad swath of asphalt cutting north to south along the western border of Loren. Cheap motels, gas stations, restaurants and used-car dealers lined the road, which was one of the main routes up to Washington.

We stopped at Eddie's so Goff could introduce me to the owner. As he'd said, the place was just a big beer bar, maybe three times the average, with country music playing on the stereo.

There were a half dozen men at the long wooden bar, and maybe twenty more sitting around in booths lining one wall or at wooden tables. The decor was decidedly low-brow, as were, at first glance anyway, the occupants. The conversations were almost all about trucks or cars, or somebody's crummy boss. There weren't any philosophical discussions on the origin of man taking place, none that I overheard, anyway.

There were several pool tables at the far end of the bar, and a pair of dart boards in the corner near a jukebox. The bar, and some of the tables, were deeply gouged in places, though the bar, at least, seemed reasonably clean and my shoes didn't stick to the floor.

The owner, Marty Newton, I liked right away. He was tall and thick-bodied, with red hair and a well-trimmed beard. I don't usually find men with beards attractive but Marty looked good in one, and well, he looked good in jeans too. He had a nice friendly grin as we shook hands and Goff told him I'd be around on the midnight shift.

"If you want to arrange to drop by around two-thirty, I'd appreciate it," he said. "That's when we close. Sometimes some of the customers are kind of surly about leaving."

"Yeah, and some of them are drunk too," Goff said. "So you can pick up a few DWIs then."

"Get a lot of fights here?" I asked, looking around. It looked like the kind of bar that had fights regularly. Breaking up fights was not something I was looking forward to.

"No more than most places. We get a lot of rough-edged characters moving through, but they're mostly decent guys who just want to blow off a little steam. They don't usually mean anything."

"That means if they want to go at it outside, Marty isn't very quick to call us," Goff said sardonically.

"Not true, depends on how serious it is," Newton said. "If one guy's a lot bigger, or the other one doesn't want to fight, then I'll call in right away. Usually, though, if I can't calm them down it's because they're a couple of surly bums and they want to go at each other. I figure better they hurt each other than some third party, like a cop, for example."

"That's what we get paid for," I said. Goff snorted.

"One thing you gotta remember, Caitlin, this isn't Los Angeles, where you can have a dozen two-man cars come back you up in two minutes. Sometimes the nearest car could be five, ten, or fifteen minutes away. And for any large backup, like a big fight here, it could be over an hour before you get any substantial reinforcements."

"Wasn't that a doozy back in September?" Newton grinned at him. He turned to me, leaning forward on the bar. "Bunch of loggers and truckers, traditional rivalry. Musta been sixty or seventy guys fighting it out. The whole place was trashed."

"We had to call in off-duty officers, the state police, and Peel County." Goff said. "Took us almost two hours to get enough people here to settle things down. Five cops were hurt, including two of your monsters."

"We had to close down for two days just to repair the damage," Newton said.

"You called us earlier, we might have calmed things down before it got that bad," Goff said.

"Hell, if it wasn't for Haggar tossing that trucker through the fuckin' window, things might never have got that bad either."

"Haggar's one of yours," Goff said apologetically.

"Haggar the Horrible." Newton grinned.

"No beard, though." Goff shrugged.

"It'd be an improvement on that guy," Newton said.

"That why you wear one?" Goff retorted.

"Absolutely." Newton smiled broadly. "Actually," he said,

turning to me, "I have to wear the beard to keep the women from going crazy. Before, they just kept jumping me, leaving their husbands and boyfriends, and even their children. It was making me real guilty. Tired, too."

"You're full of crap, Newton," Goff said. "He wears the beard 'cause he's ugly as sin. His customers were complaining they couldn't eat."

"You're just jealous."

"That'll be the day."

"I take it neither of you Gorgeous Georges is married," I said.

"I'm too young to get married," Goff said.

"That's what he keeps telling his mother, anyway." Newton laughed.

"What about you?" I asked.

"Hell, who'd have him?" Goff snorted.

"Half the women in the county," Newton said. "They just don't wanna keep me." He looked at me, grinned and shrugged. "What respectable woman'd marry a guy who's out till three in the morning every night at a bar?"

"What about the ones that aren't respectable?" Goff said.

"Hell, I have high standards, Pat, you know that."

Goff smiled and nodded knowingly.

"Seems nice enough," I said to Goff as we backed out of the parking lot.

"Oh yeah, Marty's a good guy. He keeps a pretty clean place."

"Why's it called 'Eddie's' anyway?"

"That was the name of the guy that owned it before Marty." He shrugged.

"What about Shooters? Who owns that?"

"Guy named Clubb, James Earl Clubb. He's never there, though. Manager is Dennis Whitelaw. He's short, pudgy, and

70

kind of a weasel. He doesn't mean any harm mostly, but don't expect any cooperation from him if it isn't in his interest."

"He use a lot of underage girls?"

"Nahhh, not really. He doesn't look for 'em, understand. Most of the girls are circuit girls. Their managers shift them around from club to club all over the western seaboard. Sometimes they aren't too careful about their age, so long as they have some kind of ID, real or not. See, they just claim they didn't know the girl was sixteen, or whatever. Not much we can do about it either, aside from taking in the girl and contacting the child welfare authorities."

"They hook? The strippers, I mean?"

"Some. It happens. We have a little trouble with local girls hanging around there and Eddie's looking for dates too, if you know what I mean. Some of the girls figure, what the hell, pick up some extra spending money here and there: who's gonna know? Most of these guys they go with aren't local anyway. We've got a list of names back at the station of local girls we figure turn a few tricks."

"What about boys?"

"None around here that I know of," he said, shaking his head. "We're only talking maybe half a dozen local girls and a few strippers. Most of that type are in Ashford. They've got a couple of real whorehouses there, and they definitely do have some underagers. It's outta our jurisdiction, though."

"The police involved?"

"We figure. Chief's brother owns one of 'em. Ol' James Earl owns the other."

"How young you think the girls are?"

"Oh, not real young, none of that kiddy stuff. Even they wouldn't go for that shit. 'Scuze me. Naah, I'm talking, oh, maybe a few sixteen-year-olds, maybe even fifteen- or four-teen- if they got good bodies. Most of them are older, though."

"Any rumors of coercion?"

71

"Hmmm? Not really. It's a poor area. Lots of girls there figure the money's pretty good at a place like that. Like I said, it's out of our jurisdiction anyway, so we can't go busting in to count heads and check IDs."

"The state police know?"

"Oh, I suppose. They aren't gonna get up a big group and come all the way out here to raid a whorehouse, though."

He pulled into the parking lot of a bar that had a big neon SHOOTERS sign blinking on the roof. There were no windows on the ground floor, which was circled by a wide porch. A few chairs and tables were scattered around on the porch, all empty at the moment. A pair of wide wooden doors were located in front, just up three short stairs to the porch, and we parked just in front of them.

I looked around the lot as we walked up to the porch. There were eight or nine cars parked out front, so the place wasn't exactly booming. That was good. I wasn't sure what the inside of this place was going to be like, but figured the fewer people around, the better.

I'd been to more than a few strip clubs in my time. Some of them were so sleazy you didn't even want to sit down for fear of catching something. Some were upscale, or at least tolerable. None had been the kind of place, even disregarding the strippers, where I would have cared to hang around.

Well, there had been that off-campus bar I and some friends had gone to when I was in college. They'd experimented with topless waitresses for a year, despite protests by some of the harder-edged feminists. The girls had mostly been college students themselves, working part-time. They'd seemed half-embarrassed, half-excited by prancing around with their boobs hanging out. I'd thought it funny as hell.

I put a bored look on my face as I followed Goff into the bar. It was darker than Eddie's, and at first I couldn't see much of anything but the lights on the tables, and those were cheap little things that didn't give off much light anyway. Goff went to the bar, which hugged the left wall, and I followed. The stage was on the right, but empty, lit by a purple light. A TV was perched against the wall behind the bar, showing a porno movie. The sound was turned down but that didn't seem to bother a pair of men who were eyeing it with bored expressions.

The bartender looked bored too. He was tall and thin, with short curly hair that looked to be going prematurely gray. He greeted us with a nod and an expressionless face.

"Where's Dennis?" Goff asked.

The man nodded toward the back of the room and Goff nodded back, heading that way. I followed, keeping closer to him than was strictly necessary. We passed what I assumed was a waitress sitting on a stool at the end of the bar. She was a curly-haired bottle blonde, maybe twenty or twenty-five. I thought at first she was naked, but actually she had on a G-string and a pair of high spiked heels. She ignored us as we passed, intent on draining the last bit of tar from her cigarette.

There was a padded door at the rear of the bar. Goff pushed it open without knocking and walked into a small, narrow office. It wasn't exactly luxurious, containing an ancient brown desk, a couple of filing cabinets, a pair of chairs and a low table. A small man sat behind the desk. His hair was oily-looking and combed straight back. His face was flabby, with small eyes and an unhealthy pallor. He wore a really bad green suit, without a tie, and looked up at us without surprise.

"What now?" he sighed.

"Nothing special, Dennis. Just doing the grand tour. This is Sergeant Caitlin O'Neil. She's going to be our new midnight-shift supervisor."

Whitelaw's eyes flicked to me, then back. He didn't seem impressed.

"Dennis doesn't talk much," Goff said. "How many girls you got working here now, Dennis?"

"Just one during the day, five more at night," Whitelaw replied. "Business is down."

"Yeah, the economy sucks," Goff said. "You have any trouble here, you come right to Dennis. He doesn't look like much but he is in charge of the place, and at least the bouncers and girls will do pretty much what he tells 'em."

"We're an honest business," Whitelaw said. "The only people here who cause trouble are the customers."

"Try running the place without them," Goff said.

"Yeah, well, that's true enough."

"You got any new girls since I checked the other day?"

"Not till Friday. The ones we got now leave then and a new bunch come in. They're all legal, Lieutenant. I told them you always check 'em out."

"So long as we keep checking them out, then things should be okay, right?"

Whitelaw didn't respond to that.

"You'll make sure your boys are real polite to Sergeant O'Neil, won't you, Dennis? I'm sure the guys would all be real upset if you gave her any trouble."

"We never give you guys trouble, Lieutenant. It's always the other way around."

"It's our job to give you trouble, Dennis. The sheriff says you're a blight on the community."

"How'd he like it if these guys went into Madison for their fun, screwed around with the local girls?"

"Madison's off the main road. If you weren't here, they'd just pass on by."

"They'd pass on down Elm Road to Ashford, you mean," Whitelaw said, looking sulky now. "See how much luck you have keeping underage girls out of there. And drugs. We run a clean place. It's legal and it don't hurt nobody."

"Two-thirds of his dancers are on coke or heroin," Goff said. "If we could come in and search the place every night, we'd find stashes in every purse."

"What they do is their business," Whitelaw said. "I catch them using shit in here, I kick their asses out the door. If they use it at the motel, there ain't nothing I can do."

"The girls stay at the Dunning Motel, half a mile down the road," Goff said. "It's about the cheapest place we got in the county outside Ashford. You're looking for your husband late at night, the Dunning Motel's as good a place as any to find him. That's where all the prostitutes take their tricks."

"None of my girls trick. I catch them screwing with the customers, I kick their asses out the door." Whitelaw scowled.

"He's sweet, isn't he?" Goff grinned.

"Have much trouble here?" I asked.

"Mostly the bouncers control anybody that gets rowdy, but sometimes they go a little overboard, right, Dennis?"

"They gotta protect themselves. Some of these punks got knives and guns. My guys gotta wear bulletproof vests," Whitelaw growled.

"And sometimes they put guys in the hospital who didn't have guns or knives," Goff said.

"Hey, a guy picks a fight, there ain't no way to control what's gonna happen. It's on their head."

"Yeah, a two-by-four," Goff grunted.

"My guys gotta protect themselves," Whitelaw repeated stubbornly.

"Uh-huh." Goff sounded unconvinced. "C'mon, Caitlin, we'll head back and I'll introduce you to your squad."

We left without closing the door. My eyes had adjusted to the dim light, though they could have saved the effort. The bar wasn't worth looking at. It was odd. The furnishings were better quality than at Eddie's. The bar was high-class and padded at the edges, the tables heavier, more stylish, the chairs padded and more comfortable. A lot of money had obviously gone into the place. Still, it seemed like a cheap, depressing dump, even in comparison to Eddie's with all its rickety furniture.

The waitress was standing at a table as we passed. With my improved vision I noted now that she was wearing a bow tie, in addition to the G-string. Her breasts were a bit droopy and I couldn't imagine someone, even a man, thinking she looked erotic. It wasn't that she was poorly built, just, well, kind of bored-looking. The girls at the campus bar had been cheerful, smiling and a little cocky. This one seemed dull, businesslike, and not terribly excited with her own nudity. Kind of like those documentary pictures of topless native women in Africa.

I noticed Goff eyeing her carefully as he passed, though. Men are all such cheap sluts.

We passed the bar, where the two guys were still staring at the porno flick. Two girls were groping each other, expressions of what I guess was supposed to be lust on their faces.

"Popular place?" I asked Goff on the porch.

"At night it is. Mostly it's through traffic from the highway, but he gets a lot of local forest workers too. It's a pretty nice place, really."

"You think so?" I was surprised.

"For around here it is. I mean, for a bar. There's a couple of bars in Madison that cater to what you might call a better cut of people, but if Whitelaw would show a little imagination, this place could really be something."

"If you say so."

"Oh, well, a strip joint isn't ever gonna be popular with you gals, but us guys like to get together now and then, and this is as good a place as any."

He got into the driver's seat. I waited for a moment for him to unlock the passenger door, then realized he hadn't bothered to lock it. I pulled it open and slid in beside him.

"I didn't much like the atmosphere in there," I said. "Too dark and hot."

"Well, with what the girls wear, it's gotta be warm." He grinned. "And the atmosphere picks up with the crowds and the stage show. Some of the girls get real inventive up there, swinging around the pole, doing somersaults and stuff. Got some nice costumes, too."

"You go there a lot?"

"Oh, well, no," he said, "not really. I gotta go in to check out the girls. In the line of duty, I mean."

"Sure." I grinned, drawing out the word. "Gotta check out the girls." The car's wheels spun a little on some loose pebbles as he accelerated out onto the highway.

"Now don't make it sound like that," he protested. "I'm a normal-enough man, is all. I can't claim to hate the sight of pretty girls."

"Specially naked ones."

"Well, no."

He turned off the highway and down a county road. We drove past the local high school, a wicked den of pot-smokers and underage drinkers, according to Goff, where God only knew what kind of sexual shenanigans were taking place in the nearby woods. Goff sounded half-indignant, half-jealous when he said that, and I wondered if hanging around with the monsters had affected him to some degree, or whether he just had the normal male fixation on teenage girls.

Back at the station, Goff presented me with the files of the guys who'd be working the midnight shift with me, and was kind enough to recite anecdotal evidence on each man that, I assumed, was intended to make sure I didn't trust any of them as far as I could throw them.

"This's Haggar, the guy Marty mentioned," he said, opening the first folder and pointing at the picture clipped to the corner. It showed a large-faced man with shaggy hair and an

77

unkempt uniform, at least what I could see of it. The file said he was six-three and weighed two hundred and sixty pounds.

"He's not a bad guy, really. He's just not too bright and he tends to get real angry whenever anyone disagrees with him. That's especially true if some citizen doesn't want to do what Haggar tells him to. He makes a lot of arrests for no good reason. If someone makes him mad, he arrests them. Make sure you check out the facts on any arrest he makes."

"He makes false reports?"

"No. If he did that, we could fire him, even arrest him. No, his problem is he arrests people and drags 'em back to the station, where he expects you to come up with some law to charge 'em with. He doesn't know the laws himself very well, see. What you have to do is pat him on the head, send him away, then release whoever it was he arrested."

"Doesn't that make him mad, later?"

"Sometimes, but what else can you do? He usually doesn't even remember rules of evidence, let alone the criminal code. Hell, the only reason he remembers to read people their rights is because all the cops do on TV."

He opened another folder, showing a happy-looking man with close-cropped hair, a big nose and huge forehead.

"This's a cousin of yours. Joey O'Neil. Call him Irish, or Ox."

"Six-six, two ninety. Ox is a good name for him."

"He's the dumbest cop you'll ever meet. Nice guy, though. He'll probably be the easiest of the bunch to handle. Doesn't like to use obscenities. Always polite. Drives real slow and careful," he said with a half-smile. "Dumb as an ox, though, maybe even dumber."

"Him and Haggar buddies, by any chance?" I asked cynically.

"Naww, Haggar isn't dumb, he's just stupid and lazy. He

could learn to do things the right way if he put his mind to it. He just doesn't bother. Now Ox, he's dumb."

I opened the next folder. A sullen-looking man looked out at me.

"Stanislaw Pczchornek. The amazing Pole. Not much more than six feet tall, but he makes up for size with lots of mean. As far as I've been able to find out, he hates everybody and everything. I've never seen him smile, never heard him laugh. If you want to hold a party, do not invite this man. He's incredibly depressing. It's like he's got a black cloud hovering over him."

I passed on to the next file.

"Billy Masters. He thought he'd be made sergeant after I left. Not likely. He's got the most seniority and the foulest mouth. He thinks he's God's gift to women, but he's incredibly crude. He is not happy about you taking over and he'll probably give you as much trouble as he thinks he can get away with. He's lazy, and half the time you'll find him parked up near Moss Road sleeping. If he's late coming in in the morning it's because he's parked over by the high school watching the girls on their way in. He actually drools sometimes when he's staring at pretty girls. It's real disgusting."

"Looks like a real charmer too." I sighed looking at the picture. Masters was in his fifties, completely bald, with big, really big eyes.

"Yeah, it's too bad he's so ugly. If he was better-lookin' he'd probably be able to get some teenybopper into bed and we could arrest him for statutory rape."

"He goes after young girls?"

"None of these guys are all that discriminating in their taste, Caitlin. If she's got breasts, they figure she's fair game. Some of the things you hear them saying about the girls in their miniskirts, well . . ." He shook his head.

79

"I can imagine." I turned to the next folder.

"Allan Sims. He's threatened to quit rather than work for some . . . rather than work for a woman. Hopefully he's not bluffing. We think he's been taking after the Ashford police, shaking down motorists for bribes. No proof, though, and he hasn't got too much opportunity after midnight anyway. He's the smartest of them, though that's not sayin' much."

I turned to the next file, and a picture of a big, square-jawed man, kind of handsome, really, if you liked older men.

"Mike Ford." Goff yawned. "He's got the most complaints of excessive force. He's big and kind of arrogant. Likes to throw his weight around. He's kind of stuck on that uniform and he doesn't react well to people who aren't impressed by it."

"He's got a complaint outstanding," I said, reading the first page of the file, which was a complaint form.

"Yeah, one of the strippers at Shooters claim he, uh, threatened to rape her with his baton."

"Said he tried to rape her," I corrected.

"He wanted to know where she bought her drugs, so he jammed his nightstick up against her crotch." He sighed. "Doesn't matter, anyway. It's going nowhere. The girl's gone on to another town and Ford denies everything."

I turned to the next file and for the first time found a face under forty.

"That's Jimmy Coogan, one of the newer guys. He's okay. The rest are the same, mostly they're new or on the swing shift, going between midnights and evenings."

"So there's just those seven?"

"Now. Hopefully six if Sims quits. If you could find yourself a miniskirt and act like a real bubblehead when you meet them for the first time, but a nasty bubblehead, I could almost guarantee he'd quit. Do you do a Valley Girl impression?"

"Not my style," I said.

"Too bad. Well, he might anyway. We'll cross our fingers."

6

I spent the rest of the day driving around the county trying to familiarize myself with the area I was soon supposed to be patrolling. It would be incredibly embarrassing if I got fired for not responding to a bank robbery or something because I got lost. I mean, if I couldn't even do the job of a deputy sheriff in a place like Loren . . .

So I drove slowly, with the map pinned to the dashboard as I moved around the county. It was aggravating. I kept getting lost and having to retrace my route. I just hoped there weren't any emergency calls in the first week or two. Of course, around here an emergency call probably meant getting a cat out of a tree.

By nightfall I was thoroughly sick of the Jeep and never wanted to drive a standard again. Still, I kept driving, going over some of the main roads twice to see what they looked like in the dark.

They looked dark.

I headed back to Madison, had a quick meal and went to

my room, where I called Brooks to let him know how much fun I was having.

"Are you settling in yet?" he asked.

"Settling in? I haven't even got my furniture yet. How am I supposed to settle in?"

"It should be there tomorrow."

"Good."

"How's the job going?"

"I spent the day driving around the county trying to keep from getting lost. Oh, and I read the files on the lovely people I'm supposed to be supervising. From the sound of them, their idea of modern policing is using clubs without the spike on the end."

"I'm sure you'll cope."

"One of them was fired for . . . for screwing a sheep!"

"Ahh, country people," he sighed.

"It's not funny! I gotta work with these guys!"

"Look at it this way. At least you're not a security guard."

"That's starting to look good. At least I wouldn't have to wear a cowboy hat."

"They wear cowboy hats? No shit?" He laughed with delight.

"No shit. I'm not gonna wear one, though."

"I think you'd look cute in a cowboy hat."

"Thanks."

"That's almost worth coming up there to see. Maybe I'll be up later on, once you've gotten settled, visit Bradford, see your new house, show you a bunch of inventive uses for handcuffs . . ."

"In your dreams, Brooks."

"Every night." He chuckled. "And now you'll be wearing a cowboy hat."

"Why are men all such horny perverts?" I sighed.

"It's our deprived upbringing. If we'd gotten enough sex

when we were younger, we'd be much more mature as adults. You should have thought of that when you were a teenager."

"Why, I did, Jack. I did so many . . . but you don't want to hear about that."

"I do too," he exclaimed.

"Naaaah, I wouldn't want you to think I was, I don't know, a nymphomaniac or something."

"I love nymphomaniacs. They're my favorite kind of women."

"I'll talk to you later, Jack."

"You're cruel, kitten." He sighed mournfully.

The phone woke me the next morning. I am not one of those people who normally jump out of bed all bright-eyed and bushy-tailed. I wake up groggy and confused at the best of times. And six in the morning isn't the best of times for me.

It was Shelly Cunnard. I had no idea who Shelly Cunnard was at first, but as she talked, telling me the moving truck was there with my furniture, I remembered old Fred's wife, Shelly, the overweight woman who'd been so pleased to have me as a new neighbor.

"They're there?" I groaned in confusion.

"Yes, right now. Fred's gone to let them into the house."

"Okay," I sighed, rubbing my face. "I'll get there as soon as I can."

"That'd be best," she sniffed, hanging up without saying good-bye. Nice people, these rural folks.

I lay in bed for a moment, yawning and stretching, turning my head to gaze out the window. Then I got a vision of Fred running his fingers through my panties and maybe appropriating a few souvenirs.

"Oh, gross!" I said to the room, sitting up straight. I tossed the covers back and stumbled across the floor to my clothes. I pulled on jeans and a tank top, then stomped into a pair of tennis shoes and hurried down the stairs to the Jeep. My stomach started to complain very quickly, so I stopped along the way at a place called the Golden Griddle for coffee and some rolls to go.

If I was going to be unpacking crap all day, I'd need at least something to eat. I was just sorry that something had to be rolls and coffee. A delicious wave of breakfast smells assaulted me as soon as I walked in the doors and my mouth practically watered at the scent of bacon, coffee, pancakes, waffles and toast, all mixed together. I promised myself I'd come back as soon as the truck was empty.

I got to my new home within twenty minutes of Shelly's call. By then they'd already carted out my bedroom set and were half finished with the boxes, courtesy of a big handcart that held a dozen at a time, and three big guys who'd come with the truck.

"You guys are early," I said to the first guy I came across.

"Nahh, we're late. We were supposed to be here yesterday evening, but we got lost."

"Oh well, as long as you got here," I said.

"You want anything moved around in the bedroom, let us know. We just put the stuff down where it looked like it'd all fit."

"I'll check it out."

I'd bought the bedroom set right after I'd moved to Los Angeles. There was a double bed with teak headboard, matching side tables, a tall dresser, and a wide one with a big mirror over it. The bedroom here was a bit larger than the one in my apartment had been, so everything fit pretty well. The far wall was the only one where you could sensibly put the bed against, and the rest of the room was laid out in a reasonable fashion. I didn't think I needed anything changed.

The tape running along the front of the dressers was still

intact, so I figured Fred hadn't tampered with them. Maybe Shelly had kept an eye on him, bless her.

I spent the next hour supervising the rest of the unloading, and the arranging of the living room, which, like the bedroom, was larger than my apartment's. After that the guys took off and I was left alone to unpack the boxes and take care of the thousand little details that moving entailed.

Among those details was a ten-shot semiautomatic shotgun called the Peacemaker, which I loaded and slid behind the headboard of my bed. A girl can't be too careful living alone in the country, after all.

I had a hard time finding a place for the TV. It was one of those giant-screen things, and took up a lot of room.

It was traditional to throw a retirement party when a cop left the force. Everyone in the division would contribute something toward a present. How much was contributed depended on how well-liked the retiree was, and how long he or she had been on the force. TVs and VCRs were popular choices for presents, since a retired cop would suddenly find himself with a lot of spare time.

I'd only been a cop for six years or so, and hadn't exactly been Miss Congeniality around the station. So under normal circumstances, if I'd really retired because of my damaged shoulder, I would in no way qualify for a big-screen TV. I had Dixon to thank for it. Within minutes of my knocking Todd on his ass, the whole station knew about it. The TV, and a shiny VCR, were more a thank-you from all the grateful cops who'd dreamed of slugging him than anything else.

I was putting away the dishes when the doorbell rang. For some reason the thought of pizza came to mind, which made my stomach rumble. I opened the door and found Fred there, along with a guy in jeans and a blue shirt. Fred's eyes moved immediately to my chest and I belatedly remembered I had no bra on. Well, screw him.

"I'm here to hook up your phone, miss," the other guy said.

"Oh yeah, okay, come on in," I said, ignoring Fred.

"Gettin' moved in all right?" Fred asked.

"Oh yeah, pretty good," I said. "Just unpacking boxes now."

"Well, you need any help, you just call. We're real neighborly out here, you know. Ain't like the city where you never know your neighbors."

Or want to, I thought.

"If I need any help, you'll be the first person I call," I lied, forcing a smile. It was lost on Fred, whose eyes were still on my chest.

I eased the door slowly closed and he looked back up at my face, smiling tentatively. " 'Bye now. Thanks for the help," I said, pushing the door firmly closed. Maybe I was supposed to have invited him in, but I guess I was just an unfriendly city girl.

"How many and where?"

"Huh?"

"The phones?"

"Oh, well, one here," I said, pointing at the corner between the chesterfield and love seat. "And another in the bedroom, on the night table."

I went back to the kitchen and finished with the dishes, then unpacked the things for the bathroom. It took the phone guy about ten minutes to hook up the two phones, for which he presented me with a bill for $135.

"A hundred and thirty-five bucks for ten minutes' work?" I demanded.

He shrugged. "That's the charge for your initial connection, plus there's a deposit on the phones in case you take off with them."

86

"I'm a cop."

He shrugged again, obviously unimpressed. Does anything impress the phone company?

By twelve-thirty I was starved, and headed back to the Golden Griddle for lunch.

There I overate, taking my time and enjoying every mouthful. When I was stuffed, I drove back to my house, only to find two pickups, two Jeeps, and a van parked out in front of it. I didn't have a clue as to whom they belonged. I couldn't get my own Jeep into the carport, so parked behind one of the pickups.

The front door was unlocked and as I pushed it open I heard male voices talking from off the hall. I doubted whoever it was was here to ambush me, so wasn't too concerned as I moved down the short hall and into the living room.

A guy was bent over behind my TV, his butt sticking in the air and an open toolbox beside him.

"Hey," I said.

He pulled his head around, bobbed it and smiled. "Loren Cable," he said.

"Okay," I replied. He immediately stuck his head back behind the TV.

Most of the voices were coming from my bedroom, just past the kitchen. Somewhat miffed, I walked over there, only to find half a dozen guys in my bedroom, including Fred.

Now I'd had fantasies about half a dozen guys in my bedroom, but this scenario didn't exactly match my dreams. There'd been no one like Fred in my fantasies, for one thing. Besides that, all the men were gathered around my Solo Flex exercise machine, not my bed.

I recognized Pat Goff, and then the big guy sitting on the bench shoving up on the bar, that was my namesake, the giant cop named Ox. He was wearing a tank top and his chest heaved, his huge arms bulging as he lifted. One of the other guys, whom I didn't recognize, stepped back a half-step and I saw a shorter, dark-haired woman standing beside him. All their eyes were on Ox and nobody had even noticed me yet.

"Having fun, people?" I asked, voice heavily laden with sarcasm.

They all looked over, including Ox. A couple of the guys looked a little embarrassed.

"Oh, hi there, Caitlin," Goff said, grinning and waving a Coke at me. "Coke's in the fridge."

"That's nice," I said questioningly.

"We came over to help you move, but it doesn't look like you need anything much done."

The woman pushed past him and gave me an apologetic smile.

"I'm sorry," she said. "I tried to keep them out but once they saw this thing . . ." She gestured at the Solo Flex.

"I bought it in a weak moment, after trying to jog in the rain."

"I hope we haven't offended you," she said, holding out her hand. "I'm Brin Chiari. I work the evening shift."

I took her hand, much of my annoyance fading. She was about six inches shorter than I, with bright brown eyes in a narrow face. Her black hair brushed her shoulders.

"We see these things on TV all the time." Goff grinned and shrugged. "I didn't figure you'd mind that much. And anyway, I'm a lieutenant, so there ain't much you could do anyway."

" 'Cept maybe kick you in the nuts," Chiari said.

"Now don't go givin' her ideas, girl," he protested.

"This's Bobbie Whyte," Goff said, introducing a thirtyish yuppie-looking guy. "He's the regular sergeant on evening shift. This is Gordie Brandt, the swing sergeant," he said of another man, this one about forty, with a beer belly and balding head. I shook hands with both of them. Then the giant presence of Ox loomed before me, shoving his hand at me. I took it uncertainly and my hand was completely engulfed by his huge paw.

"This is Ox," Goff said unnecessarily.

"Hi, Sarge," Ox said, grinning broadly. "Do you know we have the same name?"

"Your name is Caitlin?" I asked. He looked confused for a long moment.

"No. O'Neil. My name is O'Neil. We must be related."

"I don't think so," I said.

"But we got the same name."

"There's thousands and thousands of O'Neils around, uh, Ox," I said.

"Yeah, but they all come from Ireland, and somewhere back we musta been related."

"Well, I suppose, maybe hundreds of years ago," I said reluctantly, trying to discreetly tug my hand back.

"See?" he said enthusiastically. "We're like cousins."

"Kissin' cousins." Goff grinned.

"Up yours," I said, forgetting he was a lieutenant for a second. He didn't seem to consider it insubordinate, laughing happily as I finally got my hand free from Ox.

"Don't none of you guys give her any trouble," Ox declared stoutly, throwing a huge arm around my shoulder and jerking me in against the side of his chest. "You bug my cousin here and you'll answer ta me."

Brin winked at me and Goff and Whyte exchanged amused looks, which gave me the suspicion they'd put the stupid idea I was related to him into Ox's head. I pulled away from him as gracefully as I could, then shook hands with the other deputy, a guy called Ed Rice.

"Well, I'm sorry you guys all came out here for nothing," I said, "though I thank you for the thought."

"Aw, we didn't have anything much else to do," Whyte said.

"Anyway, now we know you got this thing, and that big-screen TV, we'll probably be over a lot."

"Yeah, so you better keep some beer in the fridge," Brandt said. "You didn't have anything in there when we came. Good thing we brought our own."

"You guys in L.A. must get paid a lot better than us." Brin sighed enviously.

"Yeah, but it's a crummy job," I said. "And I got tired of acting like a hooker or a junkie all the time."

"I wouldn't mind that," she said. "It sounds kind of fun."

"It gets old fast."

"Traffic's real bad, too," Goff said. "They gotta drive real slow."

I made a face at him and he grinned.

Shelly Cunnard showed up then, glaring at her husband.

"Are you still here?" she demanded.

"I hadda let the cable guy in," he said defensively, "and her friends here."

"You did that," she growled. "Let's go."

Fred smiled at me and then trailed his wife back down the hall.

"Keep your curtains closed at night," Chiari snorted.

"Yeah, I already heard. You have any trouble with him?"

"Nah, he just stares, is all. Well, c'mon, guys," she said, turning to the others. "Let's get out of the lady's bedroom."

I stepped back as they all filed out past me, a couple of the guys looking back reluctantly at the Solo Flex. I gave the room a quick once-over, then followed them into the living room.

"You got a really nice place," Goff said.

"Nice view, too," Whyte said.

"Yeah, but the real important view sucks," Whyte grumbled.

"What's that?" I asked.

90

The view when you open the fridge. I can't believe you ain't got no beer at all."

"Yeah. What kinda hostess are you anyway?" Goff demanded with a grin.

"A damned poor one," I said. "On the other hand, who the hell invited you anyway?"

They all laughed, and Brin put her hand on my shoulder.

"Really. We did come to help. You're just way too industrious for this crowd. We didn't figure you'd have much done by now."

"I couldn't bring myself to sit down until the place was set up," I said.

"Well, look, you must be exhausted, seeing as how you did all that work already. We should really clear out guys, and let her enjoy her new house."

"No, that's okay," I said, with a reasonable attempt at sincerity.

"Well normally I'd disagree with anything you said, Brin, just on general principles," Goff said, patting her on the head. "But since there's no damned beer in the place . . ."

"Hey, I'll buy some," I laughed. "Give me a few days and I'll have you all back."

"Well, maybe we'll take you up on that," Gordie said, hitching up his pants as he stepped toward the door.

"Real nice to meet you, Caitlin," Ox said with a huge smile.

He put an enormous hand on my shoulder.

"You need anythin' you just call me."

"I'll uh, do that, Ox," I said, shuffling back a bit.

They all filed back into the house, Brin just ahead of me.

"Glad to see another woman on the department," she said, her head turned back toward me. "There's too much damned testosterone there."

"Well . . ."

"Too much testosterone?" Whyte demanded, turning on her. "There ain't no such thing!"

He grabbed her around the mid-section and lifted her up into the air and over his shoulder, making what I assumed was cave man type sounds.

"Let me down, you asshole!" Brin shouted as he lurched toward the door with her.

She slapped at his back, then reached back and grabbed his hair. He yelped and hurriedly dropped her to the floor.

"You see what I gotta put up with?" she demanded with a grin, pushing her hair out of her face.

"I'll bring a whip and chair to work," I said, laughing.

Gordie stopped just at the door and turned to come back.

"Whoa. Do I hear kinky sex stuff? I don't wanna miss any kinky sex talk."

"Go," Goff said, shoving him back through the door.

I followed them out front and waved as they drove off, then went back in and closed the door with a sigh of relief.

7

There were two ways of getting ready to start working a midnight shift. The first was to go to bed early the night before, get up early that morning, then have a nap before your shift begins. The second was to stay up late the night before, get up as late as you can that afternoon, and stay up through to the following morning.

I'd never liked going to bed early, not even when I was a kid, and I liked getting up early even less. I elected to spend most of the night watching old movies on cable, finally turning in around four. I managed to sleep all the way through to one-thirty the next afternoon.

I went downtown and picked up my uniforms from the clothing store, trying one on first to satisfy myself that they actually fit. Then I spent a couple of hours doing a quick tour of the county main roads around Madison before heading home. After an evening of watching TV and rereading the departmental procedures manual, I still felt completely unprepared for a patrol that night.

I would have much preferred another week to familiarize myself with the county. Bradford didn't think it mattered much, saying the midnight shift was as quiet as could be anyway. Besides, the normal shift turnover was tonight, and he figured it best I start then.

At eleven I changed into my new uniform, shaking my head a little as I looked at myself in the mirror. Beige wasn't exactly my color.

Shift change was at midnight, but you were, according to the manual, required to be in by eleven-thirty for inspection and any information that was to be given out. It was just as I was looking in the mirror that it occurred to me that rather than being inspected, I was the person who was most likely supposed to be doing the inspecting.

I felt an instant's panic, a tightness in my stomach at the thought of how horrendously stupid I could look by screwing up something as simple as that. I dove back into the manual to reread everything relating to uniform dress and weapons; when you had to wear a tie and when you didn't, what kind of weapons you were allowed, what color shoes and socks, that kind of thing.

I felt even less prepared, especially knowing the men I would be inspecting had been doing this for twenty years or more. Of course the knowledge that they were probably all going to be pretty hostile and just waiting for a chance to make me look stupid didn't help either.

Goff was supposed to be there. I took off early in hopes of getting some tips from him. I lost some time by forgetting my gun at home and having to go back for it, but still got to the station by eleven-twenty. I parked in the small lot behind the station and hurried in, carrying the gun in a small bag.

Goff was hanging around the radio room and smiled a greeting when I showed up.

"Got here just in time," he said.

"I forgot my gun," I confessed. He blinked in surprise, then laughed.

"I've been off for months," I said defensively.

"Okay, okay," he chuckled.

"I need a holster too."

"Yeah, I know. Come with me."

He walked me to the equipment locker, where he found a Sam Browne belt, handcuffs, a baton, portable radio, and the other equipment of modern policing.

"This radio is different than the ones in the patrol cars," he said. "They have only two bands, the one for the base and communication between cars, and a second for the state police. This has three, an extra band for you to communicate with the base without the other cars' hearing."

I nodded, not particularly caring just then.

"I'm supposed to inspect these guys, right, this Monster Squad?"

"Course. You're the supervisor."

"Okay. I've read the book. Tell me how it's done in real life here. I mean, just how particular are you about them meeting the official requirements? I don't want to be lax, but I don't want to be a little by-the-book automaton if they're not used to it. That'll just make them hate me."

He snorted in amusement.

"You know what I mean," I insisted. "There's always written rules, and then the way things are actually done. I know the written rules; what about real life?"

"Well, like you said, officially they're supposed to look like recruiting posters. Unofficially . . ." He shrugged. "If they're not drunk, don't have too many stains on their uniform, and have shaved in the last twenty-four hours, I usually let it fly. But it's really up to you. You're their supervisor."

"Hi, there, Pat."

We turned as a white-haired man in his early sixties came in.

"Toby, just in time. This is Caitlin."

"Hello, Caitlin," he said, smiling and holding out his hand.

"Hi," I said.

"Toby's one of our auxiliaries. He'll be on the radio and phone tonight."

"You want anything at all, Caitlin, you just give me a call," he said.

"Maybe I'll want you to tell me where the heck I am," I said.

He laughed and bobbed his head. "It wouldn't be the first time, young lady."

"C'mon, I'll show you your troops," Goff said, leading me out the door and down the hall.

"What happens if I find one of them unsatisfactory?" I whispered.

"You tell him to go home. He loses a day's pay. Then you have to tell the evening sergeant and he picks one of his people to stay on and do a double shift. Needless to say, that makes you real popular with both the guy who's stuck and the guy you boot out."

"Great."

"You can also fine them up to twenty dollars for stains or something like that, wrong-color socks, for instance. But they have a way of getting back at you for that kind of thing."

We passed a couple of cops and Goff stopped to introduce me to them. They were from the evening shift, already in. They were pleasant enough, until Goff joked with them that I was going to be superstrict when inspecting my shift and boot anyone who wasn't immaculate. Then they looked at me warily and hurried away, no doubt wanting to be out of the station as fast as possible.

"I don't mean to be disrespectful," I said to the snickering Goff, "but you really are a prick sometimes."

"I know." He sighed happily. "Privilege of rank. Here's your troops."

We went into the squad room, a twenty-by-twenty windowless affair with chairs and tables scattered around. Ox was there and he stood up, smiling happily as he greeted me. No one else said anything.

I recognized a couple of them from their pictures. Pczchornek was slouching against the wall, next to Sims, who was slumped in a chair. Neither was looking particularly friendly. The hairy man sitting across from Sims was Haggar the Horrible, and the fifth man, who gave me a faint grin, was one of the swing-shift people, not a monster. I couldn't remember his name.

"Okay, everyone. Up against the wall," Goff said.

Ox moved quickly, and the swing-shift guy a couple of seconds behind him. Pczchornek got up after another few seconds and moved slowly across the floor to stand next to the others. Sims and Haggar looked at each other, then Haggar gave a snort and sauntered across too. Goff and I looked at Sims for a couple of seconds before he slowly got to his feet, scratched his ear, and took his time walking across to join the rest.

"You all know who this is," Goff said. "Sergeant O'Neil will be your supervisor from now on. "I know you're all as glad to have her take over as I am."

Haggar snickered at that.

"Sergeant O'Neil," Goff said ostentatiously, "these are Deputies O'Neil, Mason, Pczchornek, Haggar and Sims. They're all good men . . ." He paused, as if that were too much for his mouth to handle. "I'm sure they'll perform as well for you as they have for me."

97

"Just ask us, blondie." Sims grinned. "You'll see just how well we can perform."

He and Haggar snickered, Pczchornek glared, and I fought to keep calm, but knew I was losing and my face was turning red. Mason looked away and Ox looked confused.

"They're all yours." Goff sighed.

For a couple of seconds I was lost, but then Sims's smirk kind of got to me. I held my face steady as I looked him up and down.

"Like what you see, honey?" he taunted.

"Not much, no."

He shrugged, still grinning unpleasantly.

"Sims, you look like some kind of teenage punk. Try to stand up straight, or can you anymore?"

"Some rule says I got to stand up straight . . . baby?" he sneered.

"Probably is, but I was thinking more along the lines that an ugly motherfucker like you shouldn't have bad posture too."

He blinked in surprise, then glared angrily at me as the others snickered. I heard Goff sigh unhappily behind me.

Well, being lax and friendly hadn't helped him any with this bunch. Bradford's stiff-necked approach apparently hadn't worked either. The drill instructor I'd had back at the academy had been neither. He'd been a foul-mouthed, taunting bastard. I still cringe at the thought of some of the ripe oaths he directed at me. I figured he'd understand this bunch pretty well. Certainly they would understand him. So without really even consciously thinking it at first, I decided to run things the way he would.

"And the rest of you aren't a helluva lot better," I growled, raising my voice as I scowled at the others. "Try standing up straight, if you can manage that without falling over."

Ox and Mason straightened right away, though neither had

been slouching much. Haggar straightened a bit. Pczchornek glared at me and Sims turned to him and muttered something about loudmouthed whores.

"Lieutenant?"

"Uh, yes, Sergeant."

"Which of the six zones do you consider the least desirable?"

"Well, I think Zone Five is usually considered to be the, uh, emptiest. Nothing there but some farms and the Hutterites."

"That's your zone, Sims," I said. "From now on."

"What?" he demanded. "We rotate zones every night."

"Says who?"

"Says me."

"You aren't in charge, are you? You got a complaint, go to the sheriff. I'm in charge and I say it's your zone. Try and keep the cows from wandering off."

There was more snickering from the others. Sims glared at me furiously. "You fucking whore!" he snarled.

"Oh boy," Goff breathed.

Ox growled and started to move toward Sims.

"Ox!" I snapped. "Get back in line."

"But Caitlin . . ."

"Back," I ordered. He moved back unhappily and I turned to Sims.

"I understand how you'd make that mistake, Sims," I said coldly. "Fucking whores are probably the only women you've ever known, including your mother." He gaped at me in surprise.

"If you call me that again, though, I'm gonna take your baton and shove it up your ass."

"Bend over for the lady, Sims." Haggar snickered.

"As for you, Haggar, get a haircut. You look like some kind of wild man that's been raised by wolves."

"He was." Mason laughed.

"Fuck you, Mason." Haggar glowered.

"You're fined ten bucks, and you'll get fined the same every night you show up looking like that."

"Hey!" he protested.

"Pczchornek," I said, moving over in front of him.

"What?" he demanded.

"You stink. Take a bath or a shower or go stand in the rain. I don't care what you do; throw yourself in a lake or something. Just get some water on yourself so people don't need nose plugs around you. And find a clean uniform. You're fined ten bucks too."

He continued to glare, though he didn't say anything. There were snickers from some of the others, though.

Sims said something else to Pczchornek after I stepped back but I didn't catch it.

"Sims, you're fined twenty bucks."

"For what?" he demanded.

"For being an asshole!" I snapped.

"There . . . ain't no such fine," he spluttered.

"I just made it up now."

"You can't do that!"

"Yeah? Sue me."

I turned my back on him and went over to the pedestal where Goff had left the briefing notes. There wasn't much there, really, just a report of a B and E at a drugstore, where cigarettes had been taken, and a list of the available cars, along with any deficiencies in them. There was also an envelope with keys in it. I emptied them into my palm and tossed them one at a time to the deputies, giving them their car number. I gave Sims the one with the squeaky brakes and cracked side window.

I assigned zones to everyone but Sims. I took Zone 8, which was twenty miles east of Madison. Then everyone signed for his shotgun, including me.

"How come I gotta get Car Fourteen too?" Sims protested as he signed.

"Because you were mean to me, Deputy Sims," I said, widening my eyes and looking pouty. He frowned in surprise. "Since I've got to give it to somebody, it makes sense for me to give it to someone who's mean to me, doesn't it?"

"I don't fuckin' have to be nice to anybody!" he snarled.

"And I don't fuckin' have to give you a good car, you dog-faced, turd-eating cocksucker," I snarled back. "And you're fined another ten bucks for foul language, you shit-for-brains mongrel!"

He muttered obscenities under his breath and stormed out of the room. The others, who'd stopped to watch, moved out after him.

"Um, not exactly the best way to get them to like you," Goff said.

"Fuck Sims. He wants to mouth off, he can sit in a cow pasture all night."

"He'll try and get back at you. Pczchornek and Haggar too."

"Let them. I'm smarter than they are. Besides, I can be a real bitch if I put my mind to it."

"Yeah, I saw," he said, shaking his head. "And to think I was excusing myself for saying 'damn' in front of you."

"You don't work with pimps, hookers and junkies for six years without picking up a lot of sweet talk," I said.

"Uh-huh. Sweet talk, eh? Well, wait until Tuesday, when Masters comes on duty. You'll hear plenty of sweet talk then."

"I'll brush up on my bald jokes."

We went out to the parking lot. Sims's car screeched away, engine growling. Mason, then Ox, drove quietly out behind him. Haggar lit a cigar and blew several puffs out the open door before swinging his feet in, starting the engine and driving out. Pczchornek, after scowling at me, drove quickly out after him.

"Any rule says I have to stay in my zone, or can I drive around to keep an eye on these guys?"

"Uh, well, you're supposed to stay in your zone to answer radio calls, but . . ."

"But my zone's in the middle of the county and I should be able to reach it pretty quick from most of the other zones. Oh, I'll still patrol it, but I'd like to wander into the other zones from time to time, just to keep them wondering."

"I never did that," he said doubtfully.

"If they think I might show up without notice, they'll be less likely to pull over somewhere and fall asleep."

"No, they won't, they'll just hide better. There's a lot of places to hide out there, y'know."

"Well, I'd still like to try."

"It's up to you," he said.

"Good."

I got into the car, took off my baton and radio and put them on the seat beside me, then locked the shotgun in its holder. The engine started smoothly, and I slammed the door closed. Goff backed up and I waved, then started forward. He waved back briefly, shaking his head a little as he watched me drive around the corner.

The second I stopped at the sidewalk and looked both ways for traffic, it hit me that I was a cop again. Oh, I know that technically I'd been a cop since graduating from the academy, but those few months of inactivity had seemed like a lot longer than they actually were. Besides, it'd been years since I'd worn a uniform and driven in a marked patrol car.

Turning onto Durham made my stomach flutter a little. After all, a couple of months in uniform six years ago had not made me blasé about this kind of policing. No doubt I'd find it boring within a few weeks, but not now. My eyes scanned the radio, shotgun, and the switches for lights and siren, and I kind of straightened in my seat and looked around me as I drove through town.

"Base to Patrol Three, radio check," the radio crackled. I picked up the mike and held it up to my mouth. "Patrol Three, ten-two," I said.

"Roger, Patrol Three. Patrol Four, radio check," Toby said.

"Patrol Four, ten-two," Mason's voice said.

The zones were numbered four through nine. Each car had the same call sign as the zone it was in, except mine. The supervisor's car was always Patrol Three, no matter what zone it was working. Goff's car was Patrol Two, and Bradford's was Patrol One. There were no zones one, two, or three, so the numbers wouldn't get confused.

When he'd finished with the others I picked up the portable radio and called in on the private channel.

"Patrol Three to base, radio check," I said.

"Ten-two, Sergeant," Toby said cheerfully.

"Thanks."

"No problem."

I drove out the west end of town, carefully and dutifully watching any traffic I passed, looking down side streets and into store windows, really hoping to catch someone doing something.

Nothing happened, and there wasn't much traffic anyway. I hit County Road 5 and drove west for twenty minutes before reaching my zone, then slowed up some and started my patrol.

It occurred to me then that having all the cars change at the same time was kind of inefficient. The whole county was empty while one shift returned to base and turned their cars over to the next, and it could take an hour or more for the farthest car out in Zone 4 to drive to the station and then come back with a fresh deputy.

On the other hand, the county didn't have enough cars to

have the new deputies drive out to their zones first. And staggering the turnover times would be confusing and make it impossible for the shift supervisor to talk to all the people on his or her shift without putting in a lot of extra time every night.

I caught the strong aroma of skunk as I drove along, but I soon passed through it and the smell left me. Everything was incredibly quiet—and dark, for that matter. There was the occasional shadowy farmhouse or building, but they were all darkened.

I did a slow circuit of the zone, using the patrol route marked on the small plastic map that came with the keys. I decided not to go checking up on the other zones tonight. I'd already shown them I wasn't going to tolerate sloppiness and insubordination, and insulted most of them. I'd give them the shift to think that over. Tomorrow I'd start looking in on them.

Toby's voice came on the radio calling Patrol 7 about a domestic disturbance in Madison. I pulled over to the side of the empty road and checked the Madison map for the address, placing it in relation to the parts of the city I'd already seen. When I was satisfied I could find the place, I put the map back and started forward again.

Five minutes later Haggar's voice called in, checking on a license plate. It wasn't from Idaho.

The back of the plastic zone map had a list of things to check on. For Zone 8 that was the Cling-On tape factory on Rural Route 4, the empty Hurdman estate off Echo Road, Ed's TV and Stereo on Simpson Road, the Beechwood Cemetery on the same road, and the IGA food mart, also on Simpson.

I found the tape factory easily enough, and drove once around it as Toby radioed back on Haggar's license. A few seconds later Ox called in to say he was stopping to check in at Eddie's. I stopped the car near a set of doors and got out, taking the radio and flashlight with me. The doors were locked. I got back in the car and drove around to the next set of doors, checking them too.

It didn't take long to check all the doors and the couple of windows, then I drove out and headed for Echo Road.

Pczchornek called in a license and to say he was pulling the car over to see if the driver was drunk. I checked the Hurdman estate, Ed's TV and Stereo, and then drove slowly through the cemetery. Someone made loud, obnoxious noises on the radio. Who, I couldn't tell. Toby gave Haggar a traffic accident, just a fender bender. I checked the doors at the food mart. Mason got a call about a loud argument that was bothering neighbors. I drove around some more.

Then it was three in the morning.

I continued to drive slowly along the winding roads, being careful not to get lost. About a quarter past three I got my first call, a woman woken up by what she thought was someone at her window. After driving around in the dark for three hours I was glad to go and see anyone, even a paranoid old lady who'd mistaken a tree branch for a prowler. Maybe she'd give me milk and cookies.

For no justifiable reason I turned on the flashers as I sped down the empty road. But then, a couple of blocks from the address, I turned them off, feeling kind of stupid. I know that robberies and murders did happen in places like Loren, but I guess I was still finding it hard to take crime here very seriously.

The house was on Princess Road, set back from the road and separated from its neighbors by twenty or thirty yards of trees on either side. It was a fairly large house, and all the lights were on as I turned off the road and rolled up the dirt driveway.

I called Toby to tell him where I was, then got out of the car. The smart thing to do was to check all around the house and bushes first; however, practical experience had shown that it was more important to let the homeowner know you were there, so he wouldn't shoot you while you were poking around. If that gave the prowler time to escape, so what?

I was expecting a gray-haired old woman clutching her housecoat to her, but what answered the door was a pretty blond girl of fourteen or fifteen. I was so surprised I didn't say anything at first.

"Thank goodness you're here," she said breathlessly, eyes wide.

"You saw someone at your window?" I asked.

"I did, a guy peeking in through the den window," she said, pointing behind her.

"Show me."

She turned and hurried across the wide entry hall. I closed the door behind me and followed her through a luxuriously furnished living room and into what looked like a little library with a cluttered old oak desk. The girl halted just inside the doorway and pointed at a wide sash window. I crossed the floor and looked at it. It was unbroken, and the lock didn't seem to have been tampered with.

"You saw someone looking through here?" I asked, turning to her. She nodded, pale-faced.

"You were in here?"

"No, I heard a sound from my bedroom window. I came down here and looked out there because that's the best window on this side of the house. Just as I looked out, a man looked in at me. I screamed and ran away."

"What did this man look like?"

"I don't know," she said, shrugging helplessly. "Just a guy."

"Your parents home?"

"My mom's dead. My dad is away for the night."

"Nobody else is here with you?"

She shook her head.

"Okay," I said. "So this guy, was he old, in his forties, sixties, young like you or me . . ."

"He was old," she said, brow furrowing. "Maybe forty, and big, 'cause he could look in the window. His head was right there in the lower window."

"Where's the nearest door?"

"Over here," she said, leading me out of the den and down a hallway to a set of french doors that led out back. I went through, flicking on my flashlight as I walked around to the side of the house. I found the window easily enough, but didn't see any sign of anyone else having been there. It would have been convenient if there had been a broad strip of dirt around it, like in the movies, either with heavy footprints or something. Unfortunately, there was nothing but well-cut grass around the window.

I flashed the light around a little more, maybe hoping somebody had left his wallet or something, but I found nothing. Just to be sure, I walked all the way around the house, checking the doors and windows and flashing the light at the bushes around the place.

I knocked at the back door and the girl opened it. I moved in past her and she closed and locked it quickly.

"I couldn't find any sign of anyone . . . uh, what's your name?"

"Erika," she said, swallowing nervously.

"Erika, I didn't see any sign of anyone having been here."

"But I saw him!" she protested.

"I'm not saying there wasn't someone there. Maybe someone was wandering around looking for something lying loose they could make off with. Whoever it was, you scared him off. I doubt he'll be back again."

"You don't believe me, do you?"

"I didn't say that. If you saw a face, you saw a face. All I'm saying is that whoever it was is gone now."

"Okay," she said uncertainly, looking back at the door.

"If you're nervous, maybe you could call up a girlfriend and go spend the night with her," I suggested.

She shook her head slowly. "No, I'll stay here."

"If you see or hear anything else, don't worry about calling us. I'm just driving around out there and I don't mind coming back. My name's Caitlin, by the way."

She nodded again, still looking worried.

"Look, Erika, even if it was a burglar, he's sure not going to come back now. Burglars want empty buildings. At the very least they want places where everyone's asleep. No burglar is going to come back after he's been seen by someone."

"What if it's not a burglar?" she gulped. "What if it's some kind of . . . some kind of . . . pervert or something?"

"In that case he's probably still running," I said as reassuringly as possible.

She nodded, still unconvinced.

"Is this the first time you've been alone all night?" I asked.

"No, my dad has to travel a lot."

"When will he be back?"

"Not till Wednesday."

"Wednesday? You're alone until then?"

"I can look after myself," she said, frowning now.

"How old are you?"

"Fifteen. I'm not some innocent, virginal little girl, you know," she said huffily.

"Okay, I was just wondering. Look, I have to go. If you need me again, just call."

"Okay," she sighed. "Thank you for coming."

"No problem at all. Like I said, I'm just driving around out there in the dark anyway."

She smiled tentatively as we walked through the living room to the front door.

"I'll check around the house once more before I go," I said

at the door. "But I don't think you have anything to worry about."

"Thanks," she said, nodding.

I made another circuit of the house, checking the trees and bushes away from the house. There was a gorgeous-looking silver Jag parked in the driveway, which was a little odd. If I was going out of town, I'd have put my Jag in the garage, but then, maybe he had better inside. The license plate said FISHER. Nice to be proud of yourself, I guess.

I noticed Erika had closed all the downstairs curtains now. She was standing in the front window, holding one of the curtains open as I reached the cruiser. I waved to her and got in the car.

"Patrol Three to base," I called on the private frequency.

"Go ahead, Three."

"Do you know the people that live at this house?"

"That's Jake Fisher's place, Caitlin. He lives there with his daughter."

"Ever had any calls out here before?"

"Nope, not that I remember. I can check the logs for the past few weeks and see, if you want."

"No, don't bother. I looked around and didn't find anything. I'm heading back on the road."

"Ten-four, Patrol Three."

I pulled away from the house and Erika let the curtain close. I felt a little sorry I hadn't found anything, like maybe a balloon tied to a tree. I hated to think of her curled up in her bed scared stiff of some rapist waiting out in the bushes. I couldn't sit there and hold her hand all night, though, even though that would probably be the most productive thing I'd be doing on this shift.

8

B ase to Patrol Three."

"Go ahead, Toby," I said.

"Um, got a citizen here came in to complain."

"Yeah? What about?"

"Says he just got a ticket."

"So?"

"Says the cop that gave it to him, um . . . urinated on his car."

"What?" I blinked.

"Somethin' about his license plate being too dirty to be read."

"Who was it?"

"Haggar."

I paused to put myself in a supervisor's mode, and to avoid snickering.

"Does he, um, do this often?" I asked.

"Well, we did get that one other complaint about him. He

was urinating on his own car, though, on the side of Highway Eight. Wavin' to traffic as it went by, too."

So that's whom Goff had been talking about.

"Ten-four," I sighed. "I'll talk to him after the shift. I'm not driving all the way over there now to tell him to keep it in his pants."

"What do I do with the citizen?"

"If he wants to file a complaint, let him. I'm sure the sheriff will be delighted to see it tomorrow morning."

"Ten-four."

It's so great to work with professionals.

I spent another hour driving around in the dark, then returned to check the Fisher house. All the lights were still on, every one of them. I turned into the drive and parked, then went up to the front door and knocked. If the kid had fallen asleep upstairs I didn't want to wake her by ringing the bell. A few seconds after I'd knocked I sensed movement at one of the windows, but by the time I backed up a bit and turned my head, the curtain was closed again.

A few seconds later Erika opened the door, now wearing jeans and a shirt instead of her dressing gown.

"Hi. I just thought I'd swing by and see how you were doing?"

"I haven't seen him again," she said.

"That's good. I'm sure he's long gone."

"Yeah, I guess."

"But you're still not gonna go back to bed."

"I'm not really sleepy." She shrugged.

"At least school's done for the summer."

"Yeah, I'd be tired tomorrow if I had to go to school."

I nodded. "Well, since you're okay . . ."

"Um, you, uh, want some coffee?" she asked.

I hesitated, but really, what else did I have to do?

"Okay, if it wouldn't be a bother."

"No. I'd be glad to."

I followed her down the hall and into the kitchen, trying not to be impressed with the place. I'd always wished I had grown up rich. Erika's father must have a lot of dough. Even in Loren a place like this cost big bucks.

"How long have you lived in Loren?" I asked.

"All my life," she said.

We went through a pair of swinging doors and into a kitchen bigger than my house, with cupboards enough to store a year's food, one of those counter stoves set in a worktable in the middle of the room, and a pair of ovens built into the wall. Erika took a mug out of a cupboard and lifted a pot of coffee out of a machine.

"Oh, um, do you want decaf?" she asked.

"Whatever you've got is fine."

She nodded seriously and then poured.

She had a fine-boned, delicate-looking face, with a tiny nose and mouth and large blue eyes. Her complexion was very light and without blemishes. Her hair was lightly permed, kind of wavy, and fell around her shoulders like silk. She was probably a real blonde too. The jeans and shirt were both tight enough to see she had a well-developed body beneath.

Rich, blond, and beautiful. God, I'd hated girls like her in school. Why on earth did I feel sorry for her now?

She poured herself some coffee and we went through another pair of doors into another hallway, then into the living room. A stereo was playing low and a magazine was open on the couch. Erika sat next to it and I sat a few feet down from her, sipping the coffee to test its heat.

Erika was looking at me curiously when I glanced up.

"What's it like, being a cop?" she asked.

"It's a job like any other. I don't have to sit behind a desk all day."

"I'd like to be a cop," she said. "But I guess I'm not big enough."

"You're tall enough. What are you—five-five?"

"Six."

"You're tall enough. I doubt your father would be any happier than mine, though."

"Your father was mad at you?"

"To put it mildly."

"My father's always mad at me."

"That's what they do best. Getting upset, I mean."

"He wants me to be some virginal little princess with the perfect manners, the perfect clothes, the perfect grades, and the perfect looks, just so he can show me off to his friends."

"Parents are always showing off their kids. It doesn't matter to them what they look like."

"You don't know my father," she sniffed.

"True enough. But I'm sure there's a lot worse than him out there."

"Just because he doesn't beat me or screw me doesn't make him a good father." She frowned.

"No, but it makes him better than the ones that do those things. Wise up, kid. There aren't any Cleavers in real life."

"What's a Cleaver?"

"You know, 'Leave It to Beaver'? The Cleaver family? Perfect Mom, perfect Dad, perfect kids."

"I never heard of them. What were your parents like?"

"Oh, Old Country Irish, very old-fashioned. Very strict."

"Did they talk with accents?"

"Still do. I'm not that old, you know. They're both still alive."

"Oh."

"When'd your mom die?"

"When I was a little kid, four or five. I can hardly remember her."

"No sisters or brothers?"

"Nope, just me. I get it all when the old man kicks off," she said cynically.

"Going to go off to Harvard and become a lawyer?"

"Daddy wants me to marry some rich guy from a nice family and raise perfect little children."

"Yeah, mine was kind of looking forward to that too." I smiled. "It didn't work out that way."

"You're not going to get married?"

"I don't know. Maybe I'll meet some guy and get married. I'm not going to worry about it till it happens. I'm sure not going to marry to please my father."

"I thought about marrying a black guy, just to give my old man a heart attack," she said. "Maybe a Jewish black guy."

"Make it a Muslim, one of those fundamentalist types."

"Then I'd have to wear one of those black sheets."

"Imagine showing up for a party at your father's house dressed like that." I grinned. She laughed. She had perfect teeth too. I was feeling a little jealous, jealous of a kid. Must lead a nice life, if a trifle lonely.

"Your father goes out of town a lot? And leaves you alone?"

"I'm not a little kid." She frowned indignantly.

"I know a lot of full-grown women who don't like being alone in the house all night."

"Well, I'm not afraid. I like it here by myself. There's nobody to bug me. Anyway, I'm not always alone. Sometimes I have a guy over for the night."

She gave me a challenging look, as if I was supposed to be shocked or something.

"Make sure their wives don't find out," I said.

She blinked in surprise, then flushed. "I don't . . . I'm not a whore or anything . . ."

"I didn't say you were."

"I'm just not some little innocent afraid of the dark."

I nodded agreeably.

Toby came on the radio then, calling Mason to a possible B and E in Madison. That reminded me that the closest backup, should he need one, was me. I sipped some more coffee, then put the mug down and stood up.

"I have to get going, Erika," I said.

She got up too.

"It was nice of you to come by," she said, trailing me to the door.

"No problem. It was nice talking to you, and thanks for the coffee."

"Come back again, if you want."

"Try and get some sleep," I said, "it's almost dawn now. All the perverts are in their beds."

"You saying I'm a pervert?" She scowled. I halted briefly but she laughed in amusement.

"Funny kid," I snorted, getting into the car.

" 'Bye," she called.

I waved and started the engine, then backed down the drive. She watched for a few seconds, then closed the door.

The coffee had stirred up hunger in my stomach, so I headed for the only place in the area that was open all night. You guessed it, a doughnut shop. Country Style Doughnut was just across in Zone 6, outside Madison. It was a small place, and seemed overly bright after the darkness. Any jealousy I felt with Erika was more than offset by the crummy job and crummy life of the waitress there. Her name was Ann-Marie. She was forty-seven, overweight, divorced, poor, and miserable. I was the only customer, and after listening to her whining for five minutes I began to realize why. No doughnut was worth listening to her.

It did make me glad I wasn't a doughnut-shop waitress, though.

I got to write my first traffic ticket around six, to a surly middle-aged man who'd breezed through a stop sign in the mistaken belief there was nobody else around. After that I did a report on a minor fender bender, then stopped in at the Golden Griddle for a dinner of bacon and eggs. I patrolled a little more, then headed back to the station.

There I wrote out a long, carefully written and very complete report on the night's activities. The other guys came in one by one and dumped their reports on the desk in front of me. It was only after finishing my report that I glanced at them and saw how short and to the point they were. I looked at my report, then theirs. Even Mason's was half the size of mine and he'd had a B and E and a domestic fight to break up. I tore mine up and rewrote it, using a lot less ink.

"Still writing?"

I glanced up at a short, wiry man with sergeant's stripes on his sleeve, then shook his hand as he held it out.

"Paul Mitchell," he said.

"Caitlin O'Neil."

"Yeah, I know. You should bring one of those with you and fill it out in the car. That way you can just drop off your stuff, gather in the others' reports and head home."

"Yeah, I wish I'd thought of that last night."

"Now you know." He grinned. "How'd you find the shift?"

"Just opened my eyes and there it was."

He snorted in amusement.

"Actually, it was okay. Kind of strange driving around all night without a lot of calls."

"It's usually like that, depending on which zone you get. Six and Seven are the only ones with much action."

"Madison and the highway."

"Yup."

"Too bad we don't patrol in Ashford. From what I hear, that's the only place with any real crime."

"Yeah, but it's the cops doing it," he said.

"You're right. If we took over there, they'd probably all be put on my shift too."

"How'd you find the monsters?" he asked, giving me a warning look. He needn't have bothered. I never used the same dumb pun twice in a row.

"Sims was a smart-mouth. I gave him Zone Five in perpetuity."

"He must have loved that."

"I hope not."

"You fine him for foul language?"

"Uh-huh."

"You have to fill out a report whenever you fine someone, you know, Form Fifty-five-A."

"Oh, great. Where are those?"

He showed me where they were stored and I pulled out several, drawing an odd look.

"I fined a couple of other guys too."

"Okay," he said blandly.

I turned over the keys and other equipment to him, filed all the reports, dropped the disciplinary forms on Bradford's desk, and drove home to bed.

I slept through the day, waking after six, had coffee, then worked out for half an hour on the Solo Flex before taking a shower. After that came breakfast. By then I had a little over two hours before I had to be at work. I checked the answering machine, though the light wasn't blinking, and found I hadn't hooked it up. Oh well. I fixed that, then I watched the big-screen TV. It was an easy toy to get used to. I felt as if I were in a movie theater, a little one anyway.

I hadn't thought to check the mail, since it'd only been a

day ago that I moved in, so it wasn't until I was about to leave that I found a note pinned to my door. It was from Goff. In a slightly annoyed tone it reminded me I was a supervisor and couldn't lock myself away and turn off my phone while I slept. It also said I should have taken the Caprice home.

I hadn't thought about that at all. I'd driven the Jeep to work anyway. How was I supposed to drive both home? In any case, the cruiser was parked in the carport now, unlocked, with the keys in the ignition.

Feeling stupid, I got behind the wheel and started it up. Here I'd thought I'd gone through the first day without screwing up.

It took less than ten minutes to get to the station. Just before I got there I slid a portable radio under the front seat. It was against the regulations to have a civilian radio in the car, but I'd longed for one all last night and didn't intend to go through another shift without. So long as I didn't blast the music I didn't see how it was going to distract me from anything, supposing there was anything to be distracted from.

Pczchornek was just getting out of an old, dirty Ford pickup when I pulled into the lot. He gave me a sour look, then continued on his way to the door. I parked, then followed him. I found Goff in the front lobby chatting with one of the auxiliaries.

"Hi," he said. "How was your first shift?"

"Pretty slow."

"That's the way things are here. I tried to call you this afternoon."

"I was asleep. Sorry about turning off the phone. Force of habit."

"Break the habit. If we need you we don't want to have to send someone over there.

We went back down the hall toward the squad room, passing a couple of the evening people who'd just returned.

"What time you go to sleep, anyway?" he asked.

"About ten. Why?"

"Oh, really. Well, most of the midnight people don't sleep until the afternoon. That's why I figured you'd still be awake when I called."

"No, I used to go to work around eight in the evening and get off at four or five, so I'm used to going to bed in the morning. I found it better to sleep right away, then get up around five or six. I find it easier to shift from day to midnight times like that."

"Well, if you say so. Anyway, I never tried it that way. I used to go to bed around three and get up at ten, then come straight in. That's the way most of the guys do it."

"There's nothing to do at ten in the morning but sleep. At least there's something on TV in the evening."

"Well, that's true, though with VCRs the time doesn't really matter."

I shrugged.

"I see you had a call at the Fisher house last night."

"Yeah, Erika was alone and she thought she'd seen a Peeping Tom in the window."

"I read the report. What'd you think?"

"Of what? She didn't sound like the type to make things up."

"No, not exactly."

"Well then?" I waited expectantly. He seemed reluctant to continue, looking around to see if anyone else was nearby.

"Jake Fisher is a very influential man in this county," he said. "He has a lot of money and a lot of friends."

"So?"

"There've been some reports about Erika that nobody's ever really checked up on."

"Such as?"

"Remember how I mentioned some local girls hang around Eddie's or Shooters looking for dates?"

"Hookers, you said."

"Yeah."

"Are you saying Erika . . ."

"I'm not saying she is for sure."

"She's loaded."

"No, her father is loaded. There's a significant difference. He's known as a real tightwad, and she's got a reputation for loose pants. It wouldn't be inconceivable for her to pick up some extra money that way. She's got the looks for it, and a real attitude."

"I didn't notice any attitude."

"Well, she hangs around with punks. She dresses in tight clothes and short skirts, and she's been seen, at night, with adult men of dubious reputation."

"That still—"

"Remember I mentioned the whorehouses in Ashford use underage girls? We think Erika is one of them."

"But she seemed like a nice kid," I said, dumbfounded.

"She might be trying to run a con on you. It's hard for me to believe Erika Fisher was afraid of a Peeping Tom. She'd be more likely to strip naked and parade around in front of the windows for him."

"Even prostitutes can get raped," I said.

"Can they?" He grinned sardonically. "More like theft of services, isn't it? Just watch yourself around that girl."

"I think you're wrong. What could she possibly gain from reporting a Peeping Tom?"

"She had no way of knowing you were going to answer." He shrugged. "Maybe she was horny and wanted some big cop with loose morals to come and visit her. I doubt any of your monsters would hesitate to jump her if she asked for it."

"I just don't believe that. She seemed scared."

"What was she wearing?"

"A robe."

"What'd she have under it?"

"How would I know?" I scowled.

"Well, it might have been some lacy black teddy, or something like that. Maybe she was waiting to see what the cop looked like. When it turned out to be a woman she kept the housecoat on. Send Sims or Pczchornek next time and then see what happens."

"I'll keep it in mind," I said.

"Okay, don't say I didn't warn you."

I gathered up the things I needed and went to the squad room, where the same group from yesterday was waiting. Sims, Haggar and Pczchornek all stared at me with varying intensities of distaste. Ox smiled happily, while Mason glanced up, then back at a magazine.

Sims scowled in stony silence as I inspected them. He might have wanted to make snotty remarks but had probably decided it wasn't worth the money. Haggar had cut off some of his hair. Most likely he'd done it himself with scissors, though I wouldn't want to bet he hadn't used a knife. It was shorter, but, if anything, worse-looking than before. Pczchornek didn't smell quite as bad as the other day and had a clean uniform on, though it wasn't pressed.

"Well, here we all are again," I said.

I sat on the edge of a table and looked over the vehicle and information reports.

"Pczchornek, the P and G drugstore was broken into again last night. That's the second night in a row. I'm giving you Zone Six, so keep a close eye on it tonight."

He grunted in reply and I looked up over the top of the clipboard.

"I'll take that as a yes. Try and get that uniform pressed for tomorrow."

"Pczchornek's idea of pressing his uniform is to lay it down on the road and drive over it a couple of times." Mason snickered to general laughter. Pczchornek glared at him but then he always glared all the time anyway, so that wasn't really any way to judge his mood.

"Haggar, did you cut that hair off with a meat cleaver, or what?"

"What's wrong with it?" he demanded indignantly.

"It's ugly as hell."

"Any rule says I gotta be beautiful? And you guys shut the fuck up," he snarled, scowling at the others to forestall any comments.

"You look disreputable. That's against the rules."

"Fuck the rules. And fuck you, baby."

"That's a twenty-dollar fine for obscenity," I said automatically, glancing down at the report again. "And I'll fine you another twenty dollars if you don't get a proper haircut by tomorrow. And fuck you too."

"Fuck this shit," he muttered angrily.

"I'm not asking you to look like a male model, Haggar. Just cut your hair so it looks reasonably neat, so you don't frighten the citizenry."

"Fuck the citizenry."

"Spoken like a true civil servant. Mason, you've got Zone Seven tonight. Keep an eye on Shooters. There was another brawl there earlier this evening."

"No problem." He grinned.

"Yeah, he'll probably keep an eye on it from the bar," Sims sneered.

"Sims, you have Zone Five again, of course. Try and stay awake."

"This ain't fair." He sulked.

"Be a good boy and maybe I'll send you somewhere else

next week. Okay, that's it. Sign for the shotguns and disappear."

There were a lot of other things I could have called them on but I decided not to be too much of a bitch right away.

I took Zone 9, which was the one along the main route to Idaho and covered the territory around Ashford. Six years of Vice had left me with a bad feeling about drug dealers, users and smugglers. I would've liked busting a few Idaho drug smugglers.

9

As soon as I got to the zone I pulled over to the side of the road and stopped, then examined the plastic card for Zone 9. I decided to check the area around Ashford first, looking for Idaho drug runners. I spent a couple of hours driving along the eastern border with Karrin County, then, bored, drove into Ashford.

The town, for after L.A. I just couldn't think of this place as a city, didn't look any better than it had when Goff had driven me through it.

"Radio to Patrol Three," Toby called.

"Go ahead," I said.

"Go to Channel Three."

I turned to the private channel and called him.

"I think you oughto get over to Madison," he said.

"Why? What's up?"

"Haggar and Pczchornek are snarling at each other over the radio. Seems Haggar's in Pczchornek's zone. Pczchornek's yelling at him to pull over and I think he wants to fight."

"What? Where are they?"

"Not sure. My guess is Center Street. That's where the bars are. Most likely Haggar's just driving around looking at the girls on the street. Pczchornek gets real possessive about his territory sometimes."

"You don't think they'd actually fight over it, do you?"

"Pczchornek would fight over anything, and Haggar isn't a lot better."

"Give Haggar a call, a prowler or something in his zone. You can cancel it in five or ten minutes, when he's away from Pczchornek."

"Good idea," he chuckled. "Hang on."

I turned the portable radio on and heard him calling Haggar several times. I wouldn't be able to hear Haggar at this distance but I guessed he wasn't answering. Toby called Pczchornek a few times then, and he didn't answer either. I turned on the flashers and stepped on the gas, headed for the east-west highway.

"Neither one of 'em answers, Caitlin," Toby called.

"I'm on my way," I said. "Keep trying to raise one or the other."

"Ten-four."

The very idea of two uniformed cops fighting with each other on a public street was ludicrous. It would be embarrassing to the entire police profession. Neither Bradford nor Goff was likely to be very happy about it either. No matter how badly Bradford wanted the Monster Squad to screw up, I was sure he didn't want to see something like that.

At eighty-five I managed to get to Madison in about ten minutes. Just as I hit town, Toby came on the radio again.

"Caitlin, got a telephone call from Jacob Manley over at Ralph's steak house. He says they're goin' at it right out front of his place."

"Shit," I cursed. "Where the hell is Ralph's?"

"It's on Sherman, half a block up from Center. That's right near the Madison Inn."

"Ten-four."

I dodged in and around the traffic on Center, not that there was a lot of it, then slowed at the Madison Inn. I found Sherman and halted in the middle of the street, looking both ways. North looked clear, but there was a small crowd on the sidewalk not far to the south. I turned down there and quickly spotted the two patrol cars, both half on the sidewalk, looking as if one had forced the other off the road.

The brakes squealed, causing some of the crowd to turn toward me as I jumped out of the car. They eased aside as I hurried through them and I caught sight of Pczchornek and Haggar rolling together on the ground, snarling and cursing at each other. Haggar was on top, both hands wrapped around Pczchornek's throat. Pczchornek managed to pry one hand off as I approached and bit it hard.

Haggar roared in anger and pain, drawing his hand back and punching down at the smaller man, but Pczchornek blocked it and got a weak straight-fingered jab into Haggar's throat. He managed to knock him off, then rolled over on top, his hands tightening around Haggar's throat.

"You two stupid fuckers knock it off right now!" I yelled.

They both ignored me. I bent and grabbed Pczchornek's scraggly hair in one hand, then shot my other hand in between his legs and grabbed his crotch, squeezing as hard as I could as I pulled him backward off Haggar.

He made a strange strangling sound as I slung him backward, but I turned to Haggar as he quickly tried to rise. I put my foot against his chest and shoved hard, throwing him back onto the sidewalk again. I turned quickly to Pczchornek, but he was still lying where I'd thrown him, clutching his groin, his chest heaving as he scowled at Haggar.

"The first one of you stupid ignorant fucking apes that gets up I'll shoot his balls off!" I snarled.

"He . . . he was in my . . . zone," Pczchornek panted, still clutching his groin.

"I don't give a fuck! You don't have a zone. They're all my zones! I'm the one that decides who goes where. Not you, you ignorant moron!"

"I wasn't doin' nothin'," Haggar said resentfully. "He's the one that jumped me."

"And what the hell were you doing here? You're supposed to be up near Aliceburg. Why aren't you?"

"I forgot somethin' at the station," he said sulkily.

"What? Your brain? Get your ugly face into that car and get out of town before I forget I'm a lady, reach into your filthy mouth and tear your lying tongue out! Go! Get out!"

He got slowly to his feet, glaring at me and Pczchornek beneath hooded eyebrows. He shuffled over to his car, tucking in his shirt as he went, and muttering angrily under his breath.

"As for you, you simpleton," I said, turning to Pczchornek, "if you have a problem with anyone you come to me, you don't run them off the goddamned road and jump them! What kind of a dickhead are you!? Bradford is going to love this, I'm sure."

"Fuck Bradford," he panted, getting slowly to his feet.

Haggar's tires squealed and his engine revved as he stomped on the gas and bounced back into the road. He raced up the street, engine growling with acceleration.

"Yeah, right. Tell him that tomorrow when you see him."

His hair a tangled mess, he staggered over to his car and got in.

"Absolutely unbelievable," I said, shaking my head. I looked around at the crowd then and scowled at them.

"What the hell are you all looking at?" I demanded. "The show's over. Go home!"

I shoved them aside as I went back to my own car. Pczchornek pulled away, his engine roaring. I slammed my door, turned off the flashers and pulled out after him, still muttering and cursing quietly. How had I managed to find myself with a group this ignorant and unprofessional? I could pick any stranger off the street to be a deputy and wind up with better than these idiots.

How the hell was I supposed to explain this to Bradford? Maybe he would be happy they'd screwed up enough to get fired, but I was sure he wouldn't appreciate them making a public spectacle of themselves right in the middle of Madison. A place this size, half the town would be abuzz with it tomorrow. Bradford would not be pleased, and I just hoped he'd focus his anger on them and not me.

As I came to think of it, in fact, neither would likely be fired at all. From what Goff had said, they had to do something criminal, something totally unforgivable, to get fired. I'd never heard of two uniformed cops getting into a public fight in L.A., but even with their stricter standards I doubted the guilty parties would be fired for it. Suspended, definitely, but probably not fired. That would make Bradford even more angry.

I needed this crap like I needed another hole in the head.

Life would be a lot simpler as a security guard.

10

The intersection between County Roads 6 and 31 held a big Subaru billboard, and Pczchornek was parked just behind it. I did a three-sixty and pulled off the road, swinging around behind his patrol car. He was sitting on the hood and looked back at me briefly before turning away again.

"So play hard to get," I muttered, getting out of the car.

The grass and weeds were knee-high, except for twin dirt wheel ruts. This was obviously a favorite place to catch speeders. I walked through the grass and around in front of Pczchornek's car. He scowled at me resentfully.

"Come to check up on me?" he grunted.

"No, I missed your sweet disposition and kind face."

He snorted, unimpressed.

"I had a rape call. I guess Toby figured I'd be more sympathetic than you would."

"You got that right, lady. Some little slut puts on tight jeans and wags her ass around, then complains when someone gives her what she's been askin' for. I don't call that a crime."

"Why are you such a hard-ass anyway, Pczchornek?"

"Because people are assholes," he growled.

"All of them? Every last person out there on the face of the earth?" I sat back against the side of the hood, looking at the tree line and a pair of birds wheeling above it.

"Most."

"What about you? Are you an asshole?"

"Depends on who you talk to."

"Why'd you jump Haggar?"

"Haggar's an asshole."

"Yeah, I know, but so's everyone else, remember?"

"He was on my turf."

"Turf?" I turned toward him in disbelief. "What are you, some gang-banger from L.A.?"

"Haggar should keep his ass in his own zone."

"Yeah, but so what if he doesn't? What's it to you, anyway?"

"Shouldn't you be off somewhere powdering your nose, lady?" he growled.

"I never was one for makeup, Pczchornek, though you could probably use some yourself."

He didn't answer.

"Why are you such a fuckup?"

"I do my job," he scowled, turning to face me.

"I meant as a human being, though you aren't much of a cop either."

"Hey . . . kiss . . . my . . . ass," he barked, pronouncing each word carefully and distinctly.

"Not my idea of a tasty meal, thanks. You got a real attitude, Pczchornek. What is your problem, anyway?"

"You."

"Me? From what I hear, you've been a jerk for as long as anyone can remember. I've only been here a few days. Why'd you ever become a cop anyway, since you hate people so much?"

"I get to kill people," he said, drawing his lips back in a big snarling smile.

"With humor, no doubt." I sighed, shaking my head and turning back to watch the birds again.

"Think you're really something, don't you?"

"Me?" I asked. "I'm something else again."

"Think you're better than everyone else 'cause you're from Los Angeles."

"Chicago, actually."

"The only reason you got hired is because of your tits."

"Pardon me?" I asked, turning back and staring at him.

"The women's libbers been on the sheriff to hire more broads, so he found you, after the cops in Los Angeles said you wasn't good enough for them anymore."

"Pczchornek, I'm ten times the cop you are."

"Yeah, sure," he snorted. "Just wait till you haveta handle some drunk at Shooters."

"You think I can't handle a drunk?"

"Lookit you," he sneered, looking me up and down. "What do you weigh anyway, hundred twenty, maybe thirty? You ain't got the weight or the muscle for it."

I leaned over the car and put my elbow on the hood, holding my hand up.

"Are you kiddin'?" he snorted.

"Come on, let's see how strong you are, bigmouth."

He turned around and shook his head in disbelief.

"You're nuts, blondie."

"Chicken? Afraid I'll hurt you? Come on, little boy, I promise to take it easy on you."

I was taking a gamble, of course. I was willing to bet Pczchornek had never bothered much with actual exercise.

He wasn't exactly out of shape, and was probably reasonably strong. But there was flab on him, and though his arms were twice as thick as mine, I'd spent an awful lot of time power-lifting on the Solo Flex, doing push-ups and chin-ups and every other exercise I could that would increase my upper-body strength. When you worked in an area that required physical strength, and were by nature weaker than most of your antagonists, you couldn't afford not to have a strict work-out regimen. And as I said, with the damage to my shoulder I'd been doing a lot more work lately to get myself back in shape. Still, I was glad it had been my left shoulder that had been hit . . . and that I was right-handed.

Pczchornek leaned forward and his elbow hit the hood as he extended his hand. He had a smug smile on his face as his big hand folded around mine.

"Ready, little girl?" he taunted.

"Sure," I said calmly.

He slammed his hand forward, exactly as I knew he would. He was weaker than I'd thought. I held him easily, my hand going back only a few inches. I eased his hand back then until we were even, then slowly but steadily worked his hand backward. He frowned, then scowled, exerting more pressure. My arm started to ache as he put his shoulder into it, but after a few seconds' halt, I managed to ease his hand backward again.

He clenched his teeth as he tried to hold his hand up but I gave a sudden burst of power and slammed his knuckles back into the hood.

"Fuck!" he snarled.

"That's what happens when you work out regularly, Pczchornek," I said.

"I don't haveta work out." he said sullenly.

"You do if you want to arm-wrestle me, sweetheart," I taunted, moving back toward my car.

"Two out of three," he demanded.

"Some other time, honey. Gotta get back to work."

"You was lucky."

"And strong. Don't forget that," I called, pulling open the car's door and sliding inside.

He watched me back up and I knew he was wishing he could think of a way to tell me to keep my mouth shut about this without further embarrassing himself. I almost laughed. They were all so much alike, the older cops. They never worked out, had various sizes of pot, yet found it humiliating when a woman could beat them in arm-wrestling . . . or running, or shooting, or anything else.

A twelve-hour shift doesn't give you much time to do anything between shifts. I showered, watched TV for about an hour, then went to bed. I got up eight hours later, had a coffee and instant breakfast, tied my hair back, put on a fresh uniform and headed out the door.

Or at least I tried to. The door that led down to the carport wouldn't open.

I pulled on it as hard as I could. It was stuck as if it were part of the wall. I spent long minutes trying to figure out what the hell had happened to it in eleven-odd hours, then decided to go out through the front door. That was stuck too. Now I smelled a rat, probably one in uniform. I went to the sliding patio doors and tried to open them, but they too were stuck tight.

"Son of a bitch," I snapped at the air.

I tried the front windows to no avail, then managed to open one of the back windows. The problem with that was there was a fifteen-odd-foot drop to the long grass at the base of the sloping hill out back, and I didn't much feel like chancing what was below in the dark.

"Fuck," I said.

I picked up the phone by the bed. It was dead. I went into the front room and that one was dead too. Not only that, but my portable radio was missing. Someone had come in here while I was sleeping. That made me mad and gave me the creeps too. I figured Sims, Haggar and Pczchornek were the most likely suspects, and they were about the last people in the world I wanted in my house while I was sleeping. Hell, to get my portable radio they'd have had to come right into my bedroom. That really gave me the creeps. I usually slept in the nude, as I had today. I had a sheet and blanket over me, since I slept with the air-conditioning on full, but that didn't mean one of those filthy bastards mightn't have sneaked a peek.

I went to the one window that opened and looked down again. If it was soft there, I should be able to manage a landing without any damage. I reached to my Sam Browne belt and pulled out my flashlight.

Only it wasn't my flashlight. Someone had removed the hard-rubber flash and inserted something of a similar thickness, but softer. And it had no light.

It was a very large black dildo.

I tossed it out the window, really pissed off now and starting to think seriously about taking out the shotgun and blasting my way out.

Then I remembered the cellular phone I'd gotten. I'd figured it would be a good idea to have one out here, in the countryside, so to speak, where I thought the phone could fail easily enough. That was before I knew I'd be taking the portable radio and cruiser home with me every night. I'd put it away in one of my dresser drawers.

A few seconds' search turned it up. I heaved a sigh, remembering how the man had offered six months' free service with it. If it hadn't been for that, the phone wouldn't be worth crap because I never would've gotten it hooked into the system.

I hesitated, wondering whom to call. I didn't particularly want Bradford, or even Goff, to know I'd managed to let myself get locked into my own house.

I could call Pczchornek, and tell him I'd keep quiet about him losing at arm-wrestling if he kept his mouth shut about this, but he was one of my prime suspects and I couldn't give him the satisfaction. I looked up Ox's number instead. I was in luck, he was just about to head in to the station.

"Drop by my house first, will you?" I asked.

"Why?" he asked, confused.

"I need your help with something here. It should just take a second."

"Well, okay," he said, obviously puzzled.

While I was waiting for him I wrote out a note to Fred, asking him if he'd look at my stuck doors and windows, and have someone check the phones.

Ox rang my bell about ten minutes later.

"Ox?"

"Yeah?" he asked.

"See if you can push the door open, okay?"

"Huh?"

"The door's stuck. Push it open. I'll hold the knob."

He pushed experimentally a few times, then began to throw his shoulder against it. I stepped to the side, holding the knob by the deftest of grips, ready to tear my hand back if the door flew open.

Which was exactly what it did. Ox threw his considerable weight at it and with a terrific ripping sound it shot open. I jerked my hand back as it flew open and Ox fell into the room.

"Thanks," I said as he picked himself off the floor.

"Wow, that's some kind of stuck door!" he exclaimed. "I never saw one that stuck before."

"They're all like that."

"All of 'em?"

"I think somebody put superglue or something around the edges."

"Why would anyone do that?" he demanded, baffled.

"Just to bug me, Ox."

"Oh. Who'd do it?"

"Probably Haggar or Sims or Pczchornek."

He looked at the door, then back at me.

"Want me to kick the shit out of them?"

"No, Ox, I'll take care of them. All I want is for you not to mention this to anyone."

"Why?"

"Because whoever did it is waiting at the station snickering, wondering how I'm gonna get out. When I walk in and say nothing, he's going to be confused. He might give himself away by asking something stupid."

"Ohhhh. I get it," he said happily.

"So you won't mention anything about my calling you over and you busting the door in?"

"Okay," he said.

I was a little wary of the car, but it opened all right and there didn't seem to be anything wrong inside it. I checked the engine to be sure, not that I knew a whole lot about engines. Finally I started it up. It turned over smoothly and I backed up out of the carport after Ox. I stopped at Fred's house and taped the note to the door, then went on to the station.

I had long ago developed an expertise in watching people, especially men, surreptitiously. Sims was my leading candidate, followed very closely by Haggar, then, at a distance, Pczchornek and the other monsters I had yet to meet.

I kept my eyes focused on Sims as I entered the squad room. He was talking to Pczchornek at one of the tables. Pczchornek answered as Sims turned and watched me. Haggar sat slumped in his chair, scowling, while Ox and Mason talked with one of the evening-shift deputies in a corner.

"Have a nice sleep?"

I turned and looked suspiciously at Sergeant Whyte as he handed me the clipboard and keys to the units.

"I've had better and worse," I said.

"You'll get used to sleeping during the day," he said. "The first day is bad, the second worse, but from there it gets much better."

"I didn't have much trouble, really," I said. "I've done it before."

"Yeah, I guess you keep pretty weird hours in the vice squad." He nodded.

"To say the least."

"Well, good luck." He cast a doubtful gaze at the deputies, then headed out of the room. His deputy followed, leaving the room to me and the night shift.

"All right, children," I said. "Nothing major to report on, except the state police have a bulletin out on a brown van seen heading south in Bening County. It's a late-model Chevy with Washington plates, so if you spot it, call someone. The occupants are supposed to be armed and are wanted for a series of bank robberies in Washington and northern Oregon.

"Two males, mid-thirties, no real descriptions except they're white.

"Pczchornek and Haggar, unless you two have kissed and made up since yesterday, you'll get Zones Four and Nine. Haggar, you're in Nine. Mason, you're Seven, Ox Eight. I'll take Six."

"That's not fair," Sims exclaimed. "Mason had Seven Friday."

"I know that, Sims, but what can I do? You have to have Five, and I have to keep these two away from each other."

138

"I don't have to have Five!" he snapped.

"Until you learn a little respect, you do."

"For you?" he sneered.

"For the supervisor who can keep you wading in cow patties until you retire."

He scowled fiercely but kept his mouth shut. Maybe Sims wasn't a total idiot after all.

In fact, I'd considered shifting him tonight; I had to keep the other two at opposite corners of the county. But since he was my prime suspect for the break-in at my house, I was going to leave him where he was for now.

I went to the lectern at the end of the room to get the zone cards and found a long, thin box with my name on it. I opened it. It was another dildo. Cops were nothing if not predictable. I'd gotten a dozen dildos in the past few years, all but one in a public fashion meant to embarrass me.

So if I was expected to scream and drop the box like a hot coal, someone was disappointed. I calmly put the cover back on and set the box down, going back to them with the cards. I eyed them discreetly as I handed them out with the keys, hoping someone would give himself away, but aside from Ox, they were all looking at me oddly. No doubt whoever'd planted it had told the rest. That didn't tell me who'd done it, though.

Until Haggar opened his big mouth, the dummy.

"What . . . ah, was in the box, Sarge?" He grinned broadly.

"Hmmm?" I asked calmly.

"That box on the uh, lectern. We were kind of wondering."

"Erasers," I said.

"Huh?"

"Erasers." I shrugged, handing Ox his card and key.

"It was not!" he said indignantly.

"It wasn't?"

"You know it wasn't," he accused.

"Oh?"

"We got you a little present. We figured you needed it." He leered.

"Is that so?" I scanned the rest of them. Ox looked confused, which seemed normal for him. Mason looked away. "So I should fine you all then?"

"I didn't do nothing. That asshole put it there," Pczchornek said.

"Yeah, you can't fine us. It was Haggar put that dick there for you." Sims protested, no doubt worried his shrunken paycheck would shrink further.

I walked back to the pedestal and picked up the box, taking the dildo out of it. Haggar and Sims snickered as I carried it back to them. I tossed it to Haggar, who caught it awkwardly.

"Here, Haggar, I guess you need this, since you bought it."

"I bought it for you." He grinned wolfishly, tossing it back.

"But I don't need it, Haggar, and from what I've heard about you"—I tossed it to him again—"you do."

He stared at me in confusion.

"Congratulations. You've finally got one that works," I said.

"You wanna find out how good mine works, baby . . ." he scowled, tossing the dildo on the floor.

"And you're fined twenty bucks for insubordination and another twenty bucks for not getting your hair cut like I told you to."

"Wait a minute, that's . . . that's eighty bucks you fined me so far!"

"It's only seventy, Haggar, but unless this is from your personal collection"—I pointed at the dildo lying on the floor—"you're out another twenty or so."

"She knows how much a dildo costs at least." Sims grinned.

"Of course I know what a dildo costs, Sims," I said. "You dumb assholes are all the same. That's about the tenth dildo some idiot has given me trying to embarrass me. Half of you don't even take the price tag off. Maybe if you guys knew what to do with your real dicks you wouldn't keep showing me plastic ones."

Several of them scowled at that.

"I mean . . ." I laughed, shaking my head. "Do you think it's gonna scare me or something? I've been on the L.A. vice squad for six years. I've seen and heard worse than you can imagine. I've seen hookers and strippers of both sexes screwing and blowing johns in alleys, live sex acts, some of them with whips and chains, some using animals, snuff films, kiddy porn . . . You guys are not going to embarrass me with a FUCKING DIL-DO!

"So give it up," I said in a quieter tone. "Start acting like grown-ups and I'll treat you that way."

I signed for my shotgun, then headed to the door, turning back just inside.

"And Haggar, you should take that. An old guy like you probably needs one now and then."

I didn't wait for his answer.

I'd have preferred not to take Zones 6 or 7 just yet. Zone 7 was the busiest and Zone 6 was the next busiest. Zone 6 had Eddie's and Shooters and the north-south interstate. The state police patrolled the interstate, but it carried a lot of people through Loren and some of them stopped off for a time.

The three main areas to watch for, unsurprisingly, were the Dunning Motel, Shooters, and Eddie's, each requiring three visits per shift, according to the card.

The first place I stopped was Eddie's, figuring there'd be at least one friendly face to talk to tonight.

My previous visit had been in the early afternoon. At just past midnight the place was really hopping. Music was pounding inside and out, cars were going in and out of the lot at a fast pace, and I had to search hard to find a place to park. There were about twenty or so people in the parking lot, some standing and talking, most moving either toward or away from the bar.

Loud country music was blaring from speakers set in the corners of the bar as I pushed my way in through a small crowd at the door. Country was the definite theme tonight, both with the music and the dress of the clientele. A cleared area near a big fireplace was packed with dancers, the bar was elbow-to-elbow along its whole length, and every table seemed taken.

Eddie's was doing a booming business.

A lot of laughter mixed with the music and rolled through the air along with clouds of cigarette smoke. It was a happy crowd and nobody seemed to pay me much mind as I moved among them. I kept an eye out for kids but wasn't going to bother with someone unless they looked really young. Besides, though I'd only met him once, Marty had struck me as a decent guy.

I spotted him at one of the tables, standing over a half dozen people sitting around there, talking. He waved, his face lighting up happily, left them and hurried over.

"How does the old place look?" he yelled above the music.

"You must be making money hand over fist," I yelled back.

He held his finger in front of his lips, grinned and looked around.

"We don't do too bad," he said.

"Sure is loud," I yelled.

"Hey, it's Saturday night. People come to have fun. They want to sit around quietly, they can do that at home. Can I get you a drink?"

"I'm on duty." I smiled.

"Oh crap, that never stopped the rest of 'em, including Pat. Loosen up, honey. Things aren't so strict out here."

"I don't drink much, anyway," I said.

"Well then, if you won't drink, you'll have to dance."

"I couldn't, not dressed like this!"

"What's wrong with the way you're dressed? You look fine to me."

"I'm working, Marty. I don't think the taxpayers want to see their police out dancing when they're supposed to be working."

"Hey, you're keeping an eye on the place. What's it matter if you do that standing still or dancing? C'mon."

He took my arm firmly and hauled me toward the dance floor, ignoring my protests, and there wasn't a damned thing, short of getting violent, that I could do about it.

And it was hard to hit someone who was obviously just being good-natured, no matter how stupid he was making me feel.

He started dancing, luckily to a reasonably slow song, and with his hands on my shoulder and waist I really didn't have much choice but to join in. I was really self-conscious dancing in full uniform . . . well, almost full. I still wasn't wearing the damned cowboy hat. Anyway, we danced for several minutes, then the song ended and a much faster one came on. I held my hands up in surrender and backed away, despite his protests. I'd never been much for country music and wasn't going to experiment dressed like this.

"Nobody's gonna care, Caitlin, I promise," Marty said, following me off the dance floor.

"I can't stay and dance all night, Marty," I said. "I'm sure somebody would be upset at that."

"Just a couple of dances. What could it hurt?"

"I feel stupid dancing in this uniform."

"Hell, the others've done it."

"You telling me Pczchornek dances?"

"Well, maybe not Pczchornek, but most of the others."

"If you got Pczchornek dancing I'd pay to see it."

"Me too."

"I gotta get moving. I'll be back later."

"I'll be waitin'."

I made my way through the crowded room to the front and spotted a familiar face coming through the door. Brin Chiari was dressed in a tight spandex top with no bra and jeans so tight she must've had help getting them on.

"Hey, Caitlin!" She waved happily.

"Hi," I said.

"Marty get you to dance?"

"A little," I admitted.

"Feels stupid dancing in uniform, doesn't it?"

"Yeah." I laughed.

"This's Jack Cooper, from my shift," she introduced a tall thin guy with curly brown hair and a mustache.

"Hi," we both said.

"I gotta get over to Shooters. Have fun," I told her.

"You bet!" she said, then let out some kind of country whoop that confirmed my initial guess that she'd already started drinking somewhere else. She darted through the crowd clutching Cooper's hand as she made her way to the dance floor.

I went out into the lot, got my car and carefully made my way out the crowded parking lot and down the highway toward Shooters.

Several cars were going at a quick clip as I drove along, but the county line ended at the side of the road. The highway was state turf and everything on the west side was Peel County.

Shooters wasn't as busy as Eddie's but the parking lot was nearly full and there was a big crowd inside. It was a more subdued atmosphere, with the lights much lower and the music aimed at the girl on stage rather than the people in the audience. Most of the audience were men, though there were a few women with clothes on scattered around the place.

I stood to one side of the doorway, letting my eyes adjust to the dimness and scanning the room. The woman on stage was dressed in a schoolgirl's outfit—plaid skirt, blue jacket and white shirt and socks. Her hair was in pigtails and she was coyly rolling up one sock while grinding her behind in the air as the crowd watched.

The waitresses moved quickly through the room, dodging the occasional hands that moved toward them. The bar was crowded, with few of the men there watching the stage. I walked slowly through the room, eyeing the customers for signs of underage drinkers. I was prepared to be a little more stringent than I'd been at Eddie's but didn't see any likelies.

"Hey, baby, wouldn't you rather be up there?" a voice said nearby.

I turned and saw a large bald man leering drunkenly at me. I recognized the blunt face from the picture in his file, Billy Masters, one of the monsters who was off duty now but would start work Tuesday morning.

"Masters, isn't it?" I said coldly.

"That's me, baby. You know, that uniform'd make a great costume. Why don't you give it a try. Go up there and shake your tits for us. They look big enough to shake and bounce pretty good."

"Fuck you, Masters," I growled. "That mouth of yours is looking for trouble."

"Hey, I'm off duty, sweets. There ain't no regulation about being polite to people while yer off duty."

"Be nice to the lady, Billy," a guy next to him drawled. "Maybe she'll be nice ta you too." He tried to leer but was too drunk to accomplish it very well.

145

"Yer right, Mario, hell, she must be a real hot ride to get made a sergeant like that. Ain't that right, blondie? You a hot ride?" He leered very well. But then, from what I'd heard, he was a virtual professional at it.

"I don't know why you'd care, Masters," I snapped. "From what I've heard of you, little girls are more your speed."

"Nothing like popping cherries." He snickered. "I love the way they squeal when you rip 'em open," he growled, putting his face up next to mine and grinning nastily.

"You're a big dumb asshole, Masters," I said. "I think I'll make you my pet project starting Tuesday. I'm going to concentrate on making your life as miserable as possible."

"You won't be the first, pussy," he taunted.

"No, but I'll be the last, shit head."

I turned and stalked away.

"Lookit her swing that ass!" Masters yelled, then laughed uproariously. I didn't turn or stop. I was seething, and as much as I would've loved to ram my fist down his fat face, I couldn't legally do a thing. If I stayed much longer, though, I was the one who was going to get fired, for assault and battery most likely. Masters would love that. He'd also love getting a chance to hit me legally. And though he'd acted very drunk, I wasn't convinced he wasn't faking it.

Regardless, I was determined I was going to get that bald son of a bitch one way or another, even if I had to plant something on him.

The tires spun on gravel as I jammed my foot down on the gas. I turned sharply onto the highway and accelerated. I'd had plenty of worse insults directed my way as a Vice cop, but then it had all been pretty much a game, acting, playing a part. You never cared what insult was directed at you because it was really aimed at the character you were playing. Being forced to take that kind of shit while in uniform, in the midst of a crowd of people, and from another cop, made me furious.

If we'd been alone I think I would have gone for him, despite his size.

It probably dated back to when I was a tall, gawky, self-conscious twelve-year-old, but I loathed anyone who deliberately embarrassed me in public, loathed them with a virulent passion.

Billy Masters was going to be sorry he'd ever heard my name.

12

With the windows rolled down, the cool night air started to calm me down a little, and I tried to put Masters out of my mind.

I turned into the Dunning Motel parking lot and did a slow cruise. The place didn't look like a dump, just your average two-story, L-shaped motel, with a little office out front. There was nothing to indicate whether the guests inside were sleeping soundly or humping away like bunnies. I didn't hear any cries of passion as I cruised through the small parking lot, and people weren't chasing each other naked up and down the stairs or along the balcony.

With nothing going on there, I headed down the road to the small bedroom communities that bordered the highway. They were little more than a few blocks of houses set among the trees. Some were dirt-poor, some were middle class. All were dead quiet.

I headed back to Eddie's, glad of the well-lit highway after all those narrow, pitch-dark roads. It was about one forty-five when I got there. The place was still busy, though it seemed to have eased off a tad since midnight. I found a place to park easily enough, then moved up the stairs and went inside.

The crowd seemed a little lighter, and somewhat younger than before. It occurred to me that just about anyone leaving now, unless he was a designated driver, was probably over the legal limit.

That definitely included Brin Chiari. She was sitting, or maybe I should say lying, across Cooper's lap, an arm around his shoulders. She was laughing loudly, kicking her feet and plucking at his mustache. He kept turning his head away and slapping her hand down. He seemed amused, though.

I passed them by and walked along the bar, keeping my eyes open for underagers, or obvious drunks I could catch outside later. I didn't see either, except for one old guy who was slumped forward across the bar, apparently asleep. The bartender caught me looking, gave a sort of half-shrug and smiled.

I passed them by and went to the back of the bar. There weren't as many dancers now, and through them I could see some men gathered around the pool tables at the rear. Marty was one of them. He didn't see me. He was talking loudly as he lined up what looked like a difficult corner shot. He was lean-ing far over, his butt sticking out, and I had to resist the urge to goose him as I came up behind.

The ball bounced off one side of the table, hit a second and then struck the seven ball a glancing blow, sending it into the corner . . . where it promptly bounced back into the center of the table.

"Damn!" Marty shouted.

"Ahhh, a girl coulda made that shot," said a troublemaker on the other side, seeing me come up behind Marty.

"Yeah? Your wife maybe, seein' how she spends all her days here," Marty shot back.

"Maybe he meant me," I said.

He whirled quickly. "O'Neil," he said. "You think you coulda made that shot?"

"Nope. But then I'm not a girl."

There were several snorts from the other men gathered there.

"Look like one to me," the troublemaker said.

"This here's a woman," Marty said righteously. "You boys mind your manners or no cookies at recess."

There were some snickers, but most of them concentrated on another guy who was lining up a shot at the seven ball Marty had missed. He had a much simpler shot, and it snapped into the side pocket. Marty backed away, putting a hand out to back me off as well. The guy came around our side of the table and lined up another shot.

"You losing?" I asked.

"Well, let me put it this way. If you were wearing a low-cut top, I'd have you go stand in front of him," he grumbled.

The eight ball rolled off a side and into the opposite corner pocket, landing inside with a slight click. The shooter moved around to the other side of the table.

"You could always get Chiari over here," I said.

"Too noisy."

"She's sure flashin' 'em, though," a guy beside us said. "If she had a dimple on one of 'em, we'd see it."

"Yeah, well, you look too close an' Connors'll belt you one," Marty said.

"You need to get you some of them half-naked waitresses like they got at Shooters," a redhead said with a wide grin.

"Not bloody likely," Marty snorted.

"You think Maudie would come in here then?" some guy asked Red.

"If there was a buncha half-naked girls wandering around, wouldn't need Maudie here, now would I?" Red demanded.

"So go to Shooters." Marty sighed, trying to watch the other guy lining up his next shot.

"Ahh, they's all whores. I don't wanta see whores. I wanta see nice pretty girls."

"Naked," someone else added.

"Yeah."

"What about nice pretty naked boys?" I suggested.

Red looked offended. The others rolled their eyes.

"Well, why shouldn't us women have something nice to look at?" I demanded.

"You can look at us, little lady," one of them said.

"Ahh, you're all whores," I said. "I want nice handsome young guys."

"What'd she call us?" a guy in a baseball hat demanded.

"Whores," Marty said, not taking his eyes off the shooter. "You are all whores."

"All men are whores," I said.

"That's bullshit," Red said. "You don't see guys selling themselves for fifty bucks, or takin' our clothes off for money."

"That's 'cause we're all free." An older guy laughed.

"And worth every penny of it," I said.

There was a mixture of laughter, boos and catcalls from them. Then another ball shot into a corner pocket and the guy stood up with a grin.

"You got lucky," Marty said.

"Yeah, yeah, pay up."

Marty slapped a bill into his hand, then turned and put his arm over my shoulders, leading me away from the pool table.

"I hope you aren't disappointed in me, losing like that," he said.

"Why would I be disappointed?"

"Well now, I know you ladies all think of me as an example of the perfect man, and I do my best to live up to that."

"Uh-huh. What size hat you taking these days, Marty?" I sniffed.

We passed the dancers. A slower song was playing and they were all in each other's arms. In Chiari's case that was literally true. She and Connors were in a lip lock, her arms around his shoulders and her legs around his waist. He was still kind of dancing along as they kissed.

"Now that's one way to make sure he don't step on her toes," Marty said as we passed them.

"Does she get drunk a lot?" I asked.

"Ahh, don't worry about her. She's just blowin' off a little steam."

"The way she's acting she'll be lucky not to get gang-banged on one of those pool tables back there."

"Hey, she's safe here, just like any other woman. Believe me," he said seriously.

"I didn't mean that," I said. "But she is sauced to the gills."

"Yeah, well, we all get that way sometimes. She'll go home and do a little horizontal dancing with Connors, then wake up with a hangover. She's young and single. Ain't nothing wrong with that."

"What kind of guy is Connors; you know?"

"He's okay. Don't worry about her. She ain't no innocent virgin. She knows what she's doin'."

He led me over to a quiet corner of the bar and ordered a Coke for me. I had shrugged off his arm as we walked, but he put it back on again now. I shrugged it off again, giving him a dry look. He grinned in reply.

"So tell me, Caitlin, how does a guy get to know you better?"

"Maybe he asks me out sometime I'm not working," I said with a casual smile.

"Well, now. If I remember the schedules right, you're off Friday night."

"I might be," I said.

"Well, seeing as how this is the best place in the county to go out and have a little fun, maybe you could sort of drop by here, as my . . . special guest, you might say."

"If I have nothing else to do." I shrugged.

Connors stalked past then, to much applause. Chiari was draped over his right shoulder, giggling madly. He made for the door and used her butt to push it open. I wondered if I should do something about that. I doubted she'd welcome the intervention now, but tomorrow morning . . .

"Don't worry about Chiari," Marty said as if reading my mind.

"She's really drunk," I said.

"Connors won't see anything he hasn't seen before. Now, tell me, do you ever get drunk?" He grinned.

"Not that drunk. If you've got some idea of carting me over your shoulder like a bag of potatoes, think again."

"I like my women sober, thanks anyway. I want them to remember things the next day."

"Presuming there's anything worth remembering."

"Presuming that."

My radio squawked and I pulled it out of its holder and held it up to my ear, trying to hear better. "Go ahead," I said, speaking loudly above the music and laughter around me.

"You better get over to Zone Nine," Toby said. "Got a call from a citizen reporting a cop shot, and I can't raise Haggar."

"Where?"

"South end of Beckle."

"On my way. Who's closest . . . Ox and Mason, right? Send them too."

"Okay, Sergeant."

"He's probably just asleep," Marty said.

"Maybe not," I called over my shoulder, hurrying to the door.

I trotted down the stairs and ran across the lot to the car, then dropped the damned keys as I was taking them out of my pocket. I cursed, squatting down to reach under the car where they'd dropped, then rose and jammed them into the lock. I swung in and started the car with a rush of gas. The tires spat out dirt and stones as I took off.

I turned on the lights and siren and pushed down on the gas. The car surged forward onto the highway, accelerating rapidly. I turned down Melton and headed toward Zone 9. I didn't know if the thing was a gag or not. Maybe Haggar had set this up to get back at me. I guess it was possible a guy like him would think it was funny to make me speed halfway across the county for nothing.

Barreling down pitch-black roads, almost none lit by street lamps, and few of which traveled in a straight line for very long, was a bizarre experience. Even with the brights on I couldn't see very far ahead of me, and at the speed I was traveling, if some loon had parked a hay wagon or something across the road, I wasn't going to be able to stop in time.

On the other hand, if Haggar had been shot, shot bad enough that he couldn't answer his radio, he might not have a lot of time left. When I'd been shot there'd been a lot of other cops around, and I'd thought about the possibility of being shot out here . . . alone and in the dark, miles from help. It wasn't a pleasant thought, and even though Haggar was a bonehead, I didn't wish it on him.

I turned onto Highway 31, accelerating on the wider, straighter road. Five minutes later I was doing almost a hundred, and slowed down fast as I approached the intersection with Highway 6. I was just making the turn when I caught a flash behind the big Subaru billboard. The tires squealed as I jammed on the brakes and the Caprice swung its tail around hard, crossing onto the mercifully empty northbound lane before swinging completely around and stopping.

There was a cop car behind the billboard. I reached for the radio and called Toby.

"Toby, this is Caitlin. Have you raised Haggar yet?"

"Nope, not yet."

"Where's Ox and Mason?"

"Hang on a second." I waited impatiently, watching the parked car for signs of movement as Toby called the other two.

"Caitlin? Ox is just about there. Mason is a little behind him."

"I'm at the corner of Six and Thirty-one and I'm looking at one of our units parked behind the billboard. I'm gonna check it out."

"Want any help?"

"Negative. I'll get back to you. Out."

The citizen's report had come from the south end of the zone, and this was the north end. I didn't know what the hell was going on but wasn't going to take any chances. I pulled the Caprice out of the road and parked, then took out the shotgun and flashlight and headed carefully up into the low grass.

I swung the barrel of the shotgun from side to side, keeping the flashlight off as I moved forward, the partial moon illuminating the area enough to see by. Unfortunately, the other car was in the shadow of the billboard. I moved slowly, stopping every few feet, crouching and looking around. I didn't see or hear a damned thing.

My hands were sweating on the shotgun as I clicked on the flashlight. The beam flashed against the rear window and made the reflective paint on the cruiser shine. Nobody was standing near the car and I couldn't see anyone in it. I moved forward again, my head swiveling back and forth repeatedly.

I eased up to the car and warily peered over the edge, the shotgun ahead of me, ready to fire. If something had moved suddenly, I know I would have blown it apart first, without stopping to identify it. A sudden sound from the car made me jerk back, my heart rate shooting upward. I waited a second, then eased forward once again, this time staying low and reaching for the door handle.

It wasn't locked. I positioned myself carefully, then jerked it open fast, holding the shotgun with one hand. If I had to fire I wouldn't be able to hold on to it, but then at this range anything in front of me would be dead anyway.

Haggar's head fell out of the open door when I ripped it open, and his eyes jerked open fast as he yelped in shock. He looked up into the barrel of the shotgun, the light from my flash blinding him to anything else.

"Holy shit," he gulped.

I let out the breath I hadn't been aware I was holding, easing my finger off the half-pulled trigger and turning the barrel away.

"You dumb fuck," I said.

He continued to stare into the light, eyes wide.

"Get up, you asshole!" I screamed.

He scrambled up, then twisted around and staggered out of the car, rubbing his face and trying to smooth down his messy hair. I took out my radio.

"Toby, this is Caitlin. I found Haggar. He was asleep."

"I was just about to call you, Sergeant," Toby said in a soft voice. "Mason called. They found Sims dead."

"Sims!?"

"I don't know what he was doing on Beckle, but he was shot in the head," Toby said.

"Fuck," I sighed. "All right, call the sheriff and Lieutenant Goff, and whoever serves as a coroner around here."

"Right away," he said.

"Sims is dead?" Haggar blinked. I turned the light on his face again.

"I don't suppose you'd know what he was doing here in your zone?" I demanded.

"Uh, no."

"Uh, no," I repeated. "He must have come right through this intersection, Haggar. If you'd been awake you'd have seen him."

"He might not've," he said defensively. "If he didn't wanna be seen he coulda took a back road."

I turned away, then turned back, flashing the light in his face again. He shaded his eyes with his hand.

"Had a good sleep, Haggar? Think you might be able to do a little police work now?"

He glared but didn't answer. I stomped back to my car, got in and turned it around toward the south again. Haggar pulled out from behind the billboard and followed as I headed toward Beckle.

13

eckle was a quiet, almost deserted road halfway between Ashford and the border with Karrin County. Heavily leafed trees and thick brush lined it on both sides. There were about half a dozen homes clustered together on the north end of the street. The south end, where Sims's car was parked, was empty of any type of human habitation.

There were no lights on the street except what was coming from the patrol cars and their flashers. Mason and Ox had parked behind Sims's car. Their flashers were still rotating, swinging blue and red beams across the trees and brush. I parked behind their cars and Haggar slid in behind me.

Mason and Ox were leaning against the first car behind Sims's. They moved toward me as I got out of my own car.

"Didn't see anything obvious, Sergeant," Mason said. "And I didn't want to risk poking around on my own in case I messed something up."

"No, you did right, Mason," I said, moving past him toward Sims's car.

"There's no sign of anyone else around," he continued, walking beside me. "No shells or tire marks or anything like that."

"Either of you have any idea why he was down here?"

Mason shook his head. I turned back to look at Ox, who was following. He shook his head too.

"Is this zone attractive for some reason I don't yet know of?"

"Nahh, it's better than Five, unless you want to sleep, but not near as good as Six or Seven," Mason said.

"Sims didn't have a girlfriend out this way?"

"Sims didn't have a girlfriend at all, not so I knew," Mason said. "And I think he would've mentioned it."

"Does he have friends around here, or maybe in Ashford or Karrin County?"

"He coulda got to Karrin easier from his own zone," Mason said. "And as for friends, I don't think so. He lived over near Belmonte, and that's in Zone Four."

I stopped alongside the driver's window and focused the flash in, bracing myself for a mess. Sims didn't look that bad. He had fallen inward and lay half on his side, his feet still on the floor. The window was open and from his position the shot had been fired through it. There was a dark round hole in the left side of his head just behind the ear. Blood was pooled beneath his head and I knew the other side of his skull had probably been blown out. I had no great desire to look.

I pulled out a pair of gloves and carefully reached into the car, opening it from the inside. In L.A., I would have just waited for the Homicide guys to arrive. They were the pros, after all. Here, where the investigation would be done by Bradford and Goff, I didn't think I was really out of line in poking into it myself. I doubted either was much of an expert.

I bent forward and fished out Sims's notebook from the dash, then carefully looked through it. The last marks on it were a license number, but I doubted we'd get that lucky. Still, I pulled out my radio to check.

"Patrol Three to Radio."

"Go ahead," Toby replied.

"Did Sims check a license with you earlier?"

"Yeah, a couple."

"Was one of them LC7T45?"

"Lemme check," he muttered. A few seconds later he came back. "Yeah, he checked that earlier, Sergeant."

"How much earlier?"

"Maybe twelve-thirty."

"Ten-four."

"How long you think he's been dead?" Mason said very softly.

"Don't know for sure."

"Couldn't have been an hour and a half?"

"Could've been, I suppose. I wouldn't count on it."

I noticed the hole in the opposite door then.

"Aha," I said.

"What is it?"

I went around to the other side of the car, watching my footing, then opened the door and looked at the hole closely.

"This is where the bullet ended up," I said.

I left it where it was. I didn't know if Bradford had anything approaching a crime-scene team, probably not, but I wasn't about to try digging the thing out with my pocket knife and maybe scratching it up. I popped the glove compartment, taking out the papers there and examining them, then shoved them back. I looked under the seats, finding some *Hustler* magazines and a candy wrapper.

I gingerly slid my fingers into Sims's breast pockets, pulling out a few papers there and holding them up to the light. One had several license numbers, another had a string of numbers.

"Any ideas?" I asked, holding them up to the others.

"Uh, that one's his lottery numbers," Haggar said diffidently.

I nodded without speaking and went back around to the other side, the three of them shuffling along behind me. With Sims lying over on his side, I had no problem tugging his wallet out of his back pocket. Mason and Ox pointed their flashlights over my shoulder as I looked inside. There were eighty or ninety dollars in cash, half a dozen store cards, two video cards (one from an adult video store), a library card (that was sure a surprise), and a paper card (no picture) identifying Allan Douglas Sims as a member of the Christian Brotherhood.

"Was Sims religious?" I asked doubtfully.

"The Christian Brotherhood is a white supremacist group," Mason said.

"Oh." Well, that figured. The Northwest was heavy with them, and Sims was a likely enough candidate. Hell, so were the rest of the monsters.

"Any of you know of anybody who had a fight with Sims lately, someone who might want to kill him?"

They all murmured no. I didn't find anything else in the wallet of interest. I put the card back in and laid the wallet on the hood of the car, then removed the keys from the ignition and went around to the trunk. I wasn't expecting to find anything much, which was why, when I opened it, I was so shocked when something moved.

I let out a yell, reaching for my gun as I fell back. The other three were just as startled, and two of them had their guns out before we realized what was in there. It was a girl, Asian, maybe fourteen though it was hard to tell. She was crouched down in the trunk looking at us in fear.

"Holy shit!" Mason gulped.

"Yeah," Ox breathed.

The girl was naked. I gingerly stepped forward again, shoving my gun back into the holster.

"Come out of there," I demanded.

She didn't move. I repeated the order, waving her out, my right hand still on my gun.

She looked terrified. She rose and carefully climbed out of the trunk. Once I saw she didn't have anything in her hands I let go of my gun and helped her down. She clasped her hands in front of her groin, hiding it while scrunching a little to cover her breasts with her arms.

"I never looked in any of the trunks before. Wonder if they all got these in 'em."

I turned and glared at Haggar, then looked back at the girl. "What's your name?"

She didn't answer and didn't seem to have understood. I heard a distant siren and looked up the road, then back at the three men.

"One of you get a blanket from your car," I said.

They looked at each other silently, then Mason moved off. The other two just stared at the girl.

Mason hurried back with the blanket and I unfolded it, giving it to the girl. She took it awkwardly, still trying to cover herself.

"No Chink girl in your trunk?" Haggar whispered.

Bradford's car drew up then, siren still wailing as it stopped alongside us. He had an unmarked car, with a light in the windshield. He turned off the siren and got slowly out of the car, face grim. He didn't get any happier-looking when he saw the girl.

"Sergeant," he said, moving forward. I followed.

He stopped alongside Sims's door, looking in at him for a few moments, eyes flicking around the car's interior.

"Well?"

"This is how we found him, except both doors were

closed. Whoever it was shot him through this window. The bullet's lodged in the far door there. Found a license in his notebook." I nodded at the book sitting on the hood next to the wallet. "Toby says he called it in around twelve-thirty, didn't say why. Nothing in the wallet out of the ordinary except a card for the Christian Brotherhood, some kind of—"

"I know what it is," he said brusquely.

"I found the girl in the trunk, naked. She doesn't appear to speak English. Or if she does is pretending not to. There's no footprints around the car except ours."

"Not anymore."

"Ox and Mason didn't go anywhere but right here. It's bare pavement here anyway. I checked the dirt carefully before going around to the other side. There were no marks."

"All right," he sighed. "I've called the state police. They'll send over a crime-scene van to vacuum and check for fingerprints, all that crap. For now, just have the men check the houses at the other end of the road and see if anyone might have seen or heard anything. You talk to the guy who called it in yet?"

"No, sir. He wasn't here."

"Your radio," he said, holding out his hand. I quickly took the radio from its holder and gave it to him.

"Patrol One to Radio," he called.

"Radio to Patrol One. Go ahead," Toby replied.

"Who called this in?"

"A guy named Tabler, 23 Beckle Road, Sheriff. Said he was coming home from work when he spotted the car. He stopped, since it was odd it being there. He looked inside and saw the . . . Sims was shot."

"All right, I'm going there. Tell Goff. In the meantime find somebody who speaks Chinese and get them down to the station."

"Chinese?"

"That's what I said. Call Ping Leung, he speaks several dialects."

"Right, Sheriff."

He handed the radio back to me, then walked back to where the girl was standing in front of the three men, head down.

"You speak English?" he demanded of her.

She looked up at him but didn't reply.

"Take her back to the station and wait for Ping Leung to come, then see what you can get out of her," he said to me.

"Right."

"Come on, you," I said, motioning the girl forward. She had her head down again and didn't move. I reached out and gripped her upper arm and she quickly jerked her head up. "Let's go," I said, thrusting my head aside. She followed meekly, head dropping forward again.

She shuffled along beside me back to my cruiser, then stepped inside as I held the door for her. I closed it and got in the front, glancing in the mirror. She was looking down at her feet again.

I pulled out of the row of green-and-whites, turned, and headed back toward town.

The girl shuffled along quietly behind me as I led her into the station. She made no sound and kept her eyes on the floor. For want of anywhere better, I put her into one of the cells. She didn't hesitate, and almost seemed to expect it. I went out front and checked with Toby for some clothes.

"That Leung guy is on his way in," he said. "What the heck do you want him for?"

"Found an Asian girl in Sims's trunk," I said.

"What? What the heck was she doing there?"

"That's why we want Leung, Toby." I raised my eyebrows. He nodded.

"All we know is she's young, Asian, and naked."

"Naked?" He looked past me with interest and I remembered suddenly that he was just a volunteer. Maybe I should've kept my mouth shut.

"Is there someplace around here where I can get some clothes for her, to replace the blanket she's got now?" I added the last so he wouldn't run down the hall as soon as I was gone.

He gave me the key to Lost and Found. The only things there that seemed likely were a few old prisoner's jumpsuits, an old uniform shirt, and a raincoat. Nobody had been obliging enough to have left a skirt or a pair of pants lying around the place.

I took one of the orange jumpsuits back to her and shoved it through the bars. I had to call her several times before she looked up. When she did she looked at the bundle of orange, then slowly rose, shuffled over to the bars and took it. I went out into the squad room and started typing my report.

Five minutes into it the phone rang. I picked it up out of habit.

"Caitlin? Mr. Ping Leung is here."

"Send him back, would you, Toby."

I got up and went out to the hall to greet a slight, stoop-shouldered young Asian man, probably Chinese from the name. He had round glasses and wore a checked shirt and jeans.

"Hi, I'm Caitlin O'Neil," I said.

"Good morning, Sergeant O'Neil," he said, smiling shyly.

"The girl's in here," I said, leading him across the hall and into the booking office.

We went up to the bars and the girl looked up at us. The jumpsuit was way too big for her. She'd rolled up the sleeves and ankles, but she was still drowning in it.

Leung asked a brief question. He got no answer, so tried

165

another, then another. Finally the girl said something. Leung's face scrunched up and he talked again, very slowly. The conversation didn't appear to be enlightening either of them, and sure wasn't getting me anywhere.

He stopped finally and turned to me with a frown.

"I'm sorry, Sergeant O'Neil," he said. "She does not speak any dialect I am familiar with. I do not believe she is Chinese, in truth. I think most likely she is Thai."

"Thai?"

"She does not seem to be Chinese, and I have heard Vietnamese and Korean before. I do not think she is Korean or Vietnamese. Thai is most likely."

"Why?"

"The majority of Asians who come to this country are from Vietnam, Thailand, Korea, and China." He shrugged. "Besides, Mr. Carter said she was found naked in the trunk of a car. Many prostitutes are brought here from Thailand. It is, unfortunately, a widespread occupation there."

"Do you know anyone who speaks Thai?"

He thought for a moment. "Yes, I do know a man. If I can use a phone I will call him."

"Sure, just this way."

I led him across to the squad room, then went up front to see Toby.

"Mr. Carter," I said.

He looked up in surprise. "Huh?" he said.

"You shouldn't have told Leung about the girl being in the trunk naked."

"Why not?"

"Because he's a civilian, Toby. This murder is going to be sensational enough around here without that getting out. The sheriff might want to keep that quiet, especially if she's some kind of witness to what happened."

"Oh, I'm sorry. I wasn't thinking."

"Just don't tell anybody else. Can you get the sheriff on the radio for me?"

"Yup. Radio to Patrol One," he said into the mike.

There was a brief pause.

"Patrol One. Go ahead, Radio."

I took the mike from him. "Sheriff, this is Sergeant O'Neil," I said. "Mr. Leung couldn't understand her. He figures she might be Thai. He's calling someone he knows that speaks Thai."

"All right, O'Neil," he said. "Get back to me as soon as you get anything from the girl. I'm going to wait here for the state crime boys."

"Ten-four."

I handed the mike back to Toby and went back to the squad room again. Leung was just getting off the phone.

"He did not like to come in so late but agreed anyway."

"Great. How long till he gets here?"

"Perhaps twenty minutes, perhaps thirty."

"I guess I'll just have to wait. Uh, I guess you can go home if you want, Mr. Leung."

"Oh no, thank you, Sergeant. Mr. Kaien would not be pleased to find me gone when he arrives."

"Can I get you a coffee, then?"

"Thank you."

So I put off my report to entertain Leung, who wasn't a bad guy really, though I'd have much preferred he disappear somewhere. He was a systems analyst, and from what I could understand his work was incredibly boring, though apparently not to him. The conversation only started to get interesting when we started talking about how he could design a computer system that would cut police paperwork by eighty or ninety percent.

That's when Kaien showed up, of course. He was about fifty, short and stocky, with a brusque manner. He was a little surly, and scowled at Leung a lot, but spoke politely and listened in the same manner. Leung waited in the hall as I took him into the booking area and he looked in on the girl.

He directed a question at her, and she raised her eyes. He spoke again, the same words as far as I could tell. The girl answered and they began what I hoped was a conversation. Kaien remembered me after a minute and halted to turn and clue me in on things.

"Her name is Kao Shaiyen," he said. "She is eighteen years old, from Sanghon Province in Thailand. She has been a prostitute for some years now and was sold to some man who brought her here from Thailand. She does not know who the man was or where she was to go."

"Who put her in the trunk of the car?"

He queried the girl, then turned again to me. "She was in the trunk of another car. It stopped and she was taken out and put into the back of another car by a man with a uniform like yours."

"Ask her what happened after that."

Again he questioned the girl. "They drove away, then, after a time, stopped. The trunk was opened and she was taken out by the man in uniform. They . . . had sexual relations and she was put back in the car again without her clothes. She waited for some time until she heard the sound of another vehicle driving near. There were some words spoken between the first man and another, followed by a shot. The other vehicle drove away and she heard nothing more until sirens came."

"She doesn't know what the words were, of course."

"She speaks no English words that you would care to hear. Only very few words were required in her . . . her profession." He wrinkled his face in disgust. Whether the girl could understand or not, she seemed to get the idea and bowed her head again.

"Does she know what kind of man was speaking, whether he sounded young or old, or anything like that?"

He asked her and then shook his head at the answer.

"The voices were very low. Even if she knew the language, she would not have known what they said."

"Could she tell if the words were angry?"

He asked her that. "She says they did not seem so."

"Does she have any family, or anyone else she wants us to notify?"

He shook his head before even asking, then again afterward.

"She says not. She knows nobody here. As far as her family is concerned . . ."

"Yes, I know." Asian cultures placed a very, very high importance on virginity in women. A daughter who had been raped might well be ostracized by her family. One who was a prostitute would be better off dead as far as her family was concerned.

"We'll notify the Thai Embassy," I said.

"They will no doubt provide for her return." He nodded.

Where she'd no doubt return to whatever whorehouse she'd been working at before she was sold. It was frustrating knowing it and not being able to do anything.

On the other hand, it happened all over this country too. I couldn't count the number of girls who'd had the crap beaten out of them by their pimps. Their normal reaction was to refuse to testify, run away from whatever home they were placed in, and go right back to work for the guy.

It made me want to find every pimp in the world and blow his head off. Busting pimps had always been the most rewarding part of my job. Seeing the girl there made me realize how much I missed it.

"She has no idea where she was going, heard no names mentioned, not of towns or people or anything?"

He shrugged and tried again, asking her several questions.

"She was going to a whorehouse, she thinks, but as far as a name goes, she never heard one," he said. Then he yawned.

I felt like yawning myself. The girl, if she felt anything, didn't show it. She kept looking down at the floor.

14

I called the sheriff and let him know what I'd gotten out of the girl, basically nothing. Then I tried to write my report while being constantly interrupted by a stream of phone calls from off-duty cops wanting to know everything that was going on.

The sheriff had set up a command post down in Zone 9, and called in a bunch of off-duty guys to canvass the whole area looking for anyone who might have seen anything. They were also rousting local scumbags, especially any associated with pimping. I thought drugs were more likely, but who was I to say? I'd only been in this county, hell, in this state, for about a week.

Besides, the sheriff didn't seem to want any help from the Monster Squad. He'd already sent Ox, Haggar and Mason back to their patrol duties, using his own people to conduct the rousts. With nothing better to do, I went home around four-thirty for lunch, watched TV for an hour, then headed back to my own zone.

I was finding it hard to work up the usual outrage I felt when a cop was murdered. That was a little odd in that Sims was the only guy who'd ever been killed that I'd actually known beforehand. On the other hand, Sims wasn't much of a cop, and I'd thought he was a slimeball before finding out he was involved in slavery.

Hell, if he'd gotten hit by a semi I wouldn't have been put out at all. However odious he was as a person, though, I didn't much like the idea of someone putting a bullet into a cop, especially one of my cops. I felt a lot of indignation at that. I wasn't outraged, but I was put out.

So I couldn't help thinking about it as I patrolled the tree-lined roads of Zone 6. The bars were closed, and there didn't seem to be any action at the hookers' motel. It was that quiet period just before dawn. It was light enough out to see without the headlights, though the sun wasn't up yet. The birds were making a lot of cheerful noise as they woke. The world was not ringing with alarm at the death of Allan Sims. No doubt a few would hear it on the morning news and tsk, tsk before the announcer went on to the baseball scores. I wondered if it'd be any different if I'd been the one who got killed. Most likely not.

I was passing Blackburn Hamlet, a little village of sorts, when a car flashed its lights at me. It was a patrol car parked in a parking lot facing the road. I turned in and pulled up alongside it and saw Mason rolling down his window. I did the same.

"Hear anything new?" he asked in a subdued tone.

"Uh-uh. Sheriff has his own people working on it. I don't think he wants anybody else in on things."

"I thought you might've heard something on the supervisor's channel," he said, shrugging.

"Not a thing, really. Goff is out rousting people out of bed, but they haven't got a clue as far as I can see."

"My guess is it was someone from Ashford," he said.

"Why?"

"He was driving that Thai hooker somewhere, wasn't he?"

"How'd you know that?"

"I, uh, heard it, is all."

"Toby?"

"No, called another guy." He grinned a little.

"So you figure he was taking her to Ashford."

"That's where they've got the whorehouses. I don't know of any others in the county."

"Might've been taking her to Karrin County. They must have their own whorehouses."

"Ashford gets most of the business from Karrin County. I bet Sims was gonna turn her over to one of the Ashford cops. I bet it was one of them that killed him."

"Yeah, but why?"

"I don't know."

"Whoever it was couldn't have known the girl was in the trunk."

"No, I guess," he said thoughtfully.

"Probably it had nothing to do with her at all. He might have been delivering her to someone, but they either didn't show or they came, found him dead, and ran off."

"Well, then why would someone kill him?"

"Maybe he was involved in other things, like drugs. He was on the route they'd take between the Idaho border and Ashford."

"Maybe," he said, shrugging.

"He sure wasn't happy about being in Zone Five again, was he?"

"Nobody likes Zone Five."

"Why not? If all you guys do is sleep, one's as good as another."

"I don't sleep," he protested.

"I bet Sims did."

He shrugged again.

"What about those Christian Brothers of his? You know anything about them?"

"Bunch of guys who dress up like soldiers and play war games in the woods." He snorted disparagingly.

"Ever been involved in any trouble around here?"

"Naah, they send out racist leaflets and pamphlets warning about the yellow peril, or how blacks and Jews are wrecking the country. That's about it. Far as I know, they're all mouth."

We went our separate ways.

Nothing much happened for a couple of hours, though I did get to write a few speeding tickets for people taking advantage of the clear morning and lack of traffic.

I had just stopped in at a coffee shop around ten when Mason got a call from neighbors complaining about some kind of domestic dispute. Great for him. Unfortunately, just a minute later Toby called me in on it, after another complaint, this one having to do with a naked woman. I'd already dealt with one naked woman this shift, but couldn't see protesting. Toby and the other dispatchers were going to hand me anything having to do with sex and women anyway.

I was willing to bet all the other cops on the road were irritated it hadn't happened in their zone, and wondering how long it would take them to get there. Even in L.A., naked-women calls would bring a dozen cars pretty quick. Funny, women cops didn't see the same attraction in calls about naked men.

Sheffield Road was a residential street not far from Madison. Most of the trees had been cleared and replaced by a long line of cookie-cutter houses facing a field and baseball diamond on the other side of the road. Policy was to check with the complainant, who was at 274, but I could see what looked like someone hiding in a bush at 272, which was the house they were complaining about. Mason wasn't there yet, but I pulled into the drive and got out of the car there.

I could see pink flesh moving behind the bush. It seemed to move back as I walked toward it. I turned and saw a man looking out through his window from 274, with binoculars yet.

"Hello, there," I said to the bush. "You wanna come out of there?"

There was no answer. I stepped forward carefully, took out my baton and eased some of the branches aside. A very white round face looked up at me. It was a girl of maybe sixteen. She was squatting on the ground, knees drawn up against her chest, arms hugging them tightly as she looked up in fright and embarrassment.

"Uh, hi," I said. "What are you doing in there?"

I thought she might be a nut or something. She had a lot of scratches on her, probably from the bush, and her face looked tear-stained, as well as a little bruised. She had shoulder-length brown hair, now in a tangled mess.

"I . . . I haven't got any clothes," she said, almost in a whisper.

"What happened to them?" Now I instantly regretted my first assessment, figuring she'd likely been raped. I pushed my way farther into the bush and eased down next to her. She scrunched up a little more.

"My . . . my dad took them," she gulped, her lip quivering.

"He took them?"

"He said . . . he . . . he said he paid for them," she half-sobbed. "He threw me out of the house. He said he . . . he owned them."

"Why did he do that?"

She looked down then. I reached out and eased some of the tangled bangs away from her forehead. She jerked back, looking away.

"What's your name, honey?" I asked.

175

"Ginian Tyler," she said.

"Ginian. My name's Caitlin. You wait here and I'll get you a blanket."

I strode quickly back to the car, opened the trunk, and took out the blanket, then went back to her. This was a really weird night. Two naked teenage girls on the same freaking shift was unusual even by L.A. standards. You saw a lot of flesh working Vice, but it was seldom parading around completely bare.

I pushed through the bush and opened the blanket, putting it around her shoulders. She pulled it in tight, sniffling and wiping her face with her arms and hands.

"I'm pregnant," she announced.

"Oh, yeah?"

"I told my dad," she said, looking up at me. "I didn't have the money for an abortion."

I squatted down beside her again.

"Did your dad hit you?"

She shrugged and wiped her face again.

"Ginian?"

"He knocked me around a little." She reached up and patted her hair. "He pulled my hair," she sniffled.

I turned at the sound of an engine and saw Mason's cruiser pulling up. Well, about time. Still, I couldn't ride him for it. Hell, if it'd been any of the others, they would have floored it to get there for a naked-woman call.

"Why don't we go to my car, honey. It's a lot more comfortable than sitting on the ground." I straightened, taking her arm and pulling her up gently. She was enshrouded in the blanket, and keeping it tightly closed occupied both her hands. I forced the branches aside and eased her out through the opening.

She blinked her eyes rapidly, squinting to see as I led her toward the car. When we got there she bumped into the side.

"Is something wrong with your eyes?" I asked.

"I . . . can't see very well," she said softly. "My dad took my glasses."

"Because he paid for them," I said.

"He said I . . . wasn't his daughter anymore," she said, swallowing rapidly and rubbing her face.

I opened the front passenger door and put her inside, then closed it firmly as another cruiser pulled up.

I started toward them when an elderly woman marched up and confronted me.

"Officer," she scowled. "Don't you dare arrest that child!"

"I'm not arresting her, ma'am," I said.

"Mrs. Sullivan," Mason said, coming up beside her.

"Oh, Peter, thank goodness you're here," she said, turning to him and ignoring me.

"What happened, Mrs. Sullivan?" he asked.

"That awful man, calls himself a man of the cloth, he just flung that poor child out the door naked, threw her right down the stairs!"

"Reverend Tyler?"

"That's the one," she scowled. "Held her by the hair, just like this"—she held a clawlike hand down low to demonstrate—"and just yanked her out the door and threw her down the stairs naked. I couldn't believe my eyes! Why, if I hadn't been doing my gardening I never would have believed it at all."

Mason nodded in agreement.

"I called the police, of course. You know me, Peter, I wouldn't dream of interfering in people's personal affairs, but really, that was disgraceful, the way he treated that child."

"Yes, ma'am."

"And the filth he was saying, well, my stars, you wouldn't have believed a man of the cloth knew such words! Practically turned the air blue, he did. I think those Baptists are all crazy, flinging their arms around and wailing like nigras," she snapped. I wandered over, and then another cruiser pulled up.

177

"Mason, tell everybody to get back to wherever they're supposed to be," I said. "You stay here to transport a prisoner."

"Uh, you want me to go up with you, Sergeant?"

"No, no. I think I can handle it. You just get rid of the sightseers."

I walked up to the door and rang the bell. There was no answer. I rang it again, then a third time. Then I took out my baton and slammed it heavily into the wood. I heard sounds behind the door, then it was yanked open. A glowering, red-faced man looked out at me. He was about six feet tall and weighed maybe two thirty, most of it flab. He was in his forties, with a black crew cut and a big nose.

"What do you want?" he demanded.

"You Mr. Tyler?" I asked.

"I am Reverend Tyler," he said in a heavy growl.

"Get your ass back in there. I want to talk to you." I prodded him back with the end of the baton, shoving him indoors, away from Mrs. Sullivan's prying eyes.

"How dare you!" he hissed. "I happen to be a personal friend of every member of the County Commission! If you value your job at all, you will treat me with the respect I deserve!"

"If I did that I'd be spitting on you. Now back up, asshole," I snapped, poking the baton at him repeatedly. He tried to fend it off with his hand as he stumbled backward into the living room.

"Get away from me! Stop that!" he demanded.

A middle-aged woman rose off the couch, alarm on her face. I stopped poking him, though I held the baton ready.

"You want to tell me what happened with your daughter?" I asked tightly.

"I have no daughter," Tyler snapped.

"What about you?" I looked at the woman. She started to

178

speak, then looked at him. He glowered at her and she looked away, saying nothing.

"What about that naked girl I found in your bushes then?" I said.

"Some cheap whore, no doubt," he sneered. "You'd do best to cart her off and put her with the rest of the whores."

"And would you have assaulted this cheap whore by any chance?" I asked.

"What I do in my own house is none of your business," he snapped.

"A learned man like you must know it's against the law to beat up children in this state, against the law to throw them down stairs too."

He glared at me and said nothing.

"Turn around and put your hands against the wall. You're under arrest."

"I will do no such thing. What I will do is call Sheriff Bradford right this minute!" He started toward the phone and I stepped in front of it, blocking him.

"No, you won't. The sheriff has more important things to do right now than talk to child abusers. Now get against that wall right now!" I prodded him with the baton again.

"When I talk to Sheriff Bradford you will be FIRED!" He actually screamed the last word. He shoved his hand out and pointed a finger under my nose. I gripped his wrist and twisted it around hard, drawing a yell of pain from him. I jerked it up behind his back, spinning him around and shoving him into the wall as hard as I thought I could get away with.

I kept an eye on the wife but she just stood there wringing her hands and looking miserable and upset. I kicked Tyler's legs apart and snapped at him until he pushed both his arms out wide.

"You'll pay for this! You'll pay!" he said, fairly frothing with rage.

"Just don't move, child abuser."

I patted him down, roughly, and paid careful attention to his crotch, knowing it would humiliate him. I put a cuff on his right wrist and was just starting to pull it down when he let out a bellow of rage.

"You get back upstairs!" he howled.

Two small boys with white faces pulled back from the staircase and Mrs. Tyler hurried over to the stairs.

"This is your fault!" he snarled at her, jerking back, shoving me away almost incidentally as he raised an accusing finger to her. "You've raised them with no respect for God! You're useless!" he hissed.

She burst into tears and rushed upstairs after the boys. I pulled back on Tyler's wrist, the one with the cuff on it, twisting him around toward me. He started to shout something at me but I slammed my knee up into his groin. His words turned into a low "urk" and he staggered back, then dropped to his knees.

I shoved him down on his face and pulled both hands behind his back, having a little difficulty prying them away from his crotch. I cuffed them behind his back, then tried to get him up. I wished he had more hair so I could pull on that like he had on his daughter's.

There was a knock on the door, which opened a few seconds later. Mason peered in.

"Uh, need any help, Sergeant?" he asked.

"Take this asshole out to your car." I sighed, most of my anger and outrage going as limp as Tyler.

"Charge him with assaulting a juvenile, child endangerment, and resisting arrest, to start. I'm gonna go talk to his wife."

He nodded and struggled to heft the still gurgling Tyler to his feet. I went upstairs after Mrs. Tyler. I found her in the first room, crying.

"Mrs. Tyler?" I said.

She snatched some tissues from a box beside the bed and wiped her eyes.

"I'd like you to tell me what happened here earlier between your husband and your daughter," I said.

"It's . . . it's nothing. Nothing happened," she gulped.

"I know Ginian told him she was pregnant. Was that what set him off?"

Her face turned red and she closed her eyes briefly.

"I suppose everyone will know soon," she said with a groan.

"You really think everyone cares?"

She sighed and shook her head.

"What happened?"

"Like you said," she murmured. "She told us she was pregnant and Mr. Tyler was furious. As he had every right to be," she said, her voice strengthening as she looked up at me.

"Then what happened?"

"He demanded to know the name of the boy who did it, of course. When Ginian wouldn't tell him he became enraged. He . . . he called her names, said she . . . said she didn't know the name because she was . . . because she'd slept with so many boys."

She looked away again, her fingers twisting around and around in her lap.

"And then he hit her?"

"He did not hit her!" she said indignantly. "He slapped her a few times, that's all. Said she wasn't any daughter of his to act like that, and who could blame him?"

"And he stripped her clothes off and threw her out the door?"

"Said he paid for her for sixteen years and wasn't going to pay anymore, not for a stranger like her. Said he'd give the clothes to a good Christian child in need."

"Where's her glasses?" I said.

"He, I um, he smashed them," she said slowly. "Are you going to arrest him?"

"Already done." I pointed out the window to where Mason was leading the man toward his car. She stood up and looked out, eyes wide.

"Where's Ginian's room?"

"What?"

"Where is Ginian's room?"

"Uh, across the hall," she said, pointing.

I moved to the door, crossed the hall and went into Ginian's room. I opened some dresser drawers and took out some clothes for her—jeans, a shirt and some underwear and shoes. Mrs. Tyler came in and watched silently.

"In . . . in that cabinet," she said quietly, pointing. I looked at the cabinet, a small chest, probably for jewelry. I opened it and found a pair of round eyeglasses.

"Those are her spares," she said. "She can't hardly see at all without glasses."

"You know," I said, "we could force him to stay away from here if you wanted Ginian back. He'd have to keep paying for the place, too."

"Stay away?" she gasped in shock. "A wife's place is by her husband, a husband's by his wife!" She looked at me as if I'd just suggested she fly to the moon.

"What about a mother's place?" I asked.

She scowled resentfully. "She disgraced herself and us. She's old enough to do filthy things like that, she's old enough to be out on her own."

I nodded and moved to the door.

"Wait a second," she said, rushing past me. She opened one of the dresser drawers and pulled out a green shirt, handing it to me. "That one you got's too small. She outgrew that. This's her favorite." Her hand shook when I took the blouse.

I dropped the other and moved down the hall. She followed at my heels.

"What . . . what'll happen to her?" she asked at the door.

"Do you care?" I asked angrily.

"I . . . yes," she said.

"They won't throw her into the streets naked. The county has a bit more compassion than that. They'll find someone to look after her. Her and your grandchild," I added somewhat cruelly.

Okay, so I was in a bad mood. It'd been a long night, and as far as I was concerned she wasn't much better than her scummy husband. I trotted down the stairs and over to my car. When he saw me, Mason gave a wave, then got into his own cruiser and pulled out.

I took Ginian to the hospital, despite her protests. The doctors found more than scratches and bruises on her. There were welts all over her back too, so the good father had been at her with his belt before disowning her.

I was afraid of what would happen to her. From my experience with the overloaded L.A. system, kids like her were in big trouble. I remembered trying for hours to find some place for a teenage hooker a few years back. They'd finally had to send her to juvenile hall for want of anyplace better.

Brin was at the station, sober, but with a hangover. She offered to take the girl in for the weekend if we couldn't get anyone from child welfare. The child welfare person agreed to come in to work, though, and claimed she'd have no trouble finding a nice place. But then Ginian called an aunt, her mom's sister, and she and her husband showed up to drive the girl back to their place. They didn't seem to care a damn that she was pregnant either. We got half a dozen other offers to take her in that day as word got around her neighborhood.

I guess some things work a little different in the country.

15

One thing that seemed to work pretty much the same in a small county as in the city was that when people with clout get arrested there is a big fuss. That meant you had to justify yourself pretty damned clearly to superiors who wished the whole thing would just disappear.

To his credit, Bradford didn't appear mad, or even upset. He asked me a few questions, and that was it. I'd been expecting trouble from him, being religious, but nothing came of it. I did find out from Goff that old Tyler did have a lot of friends, everyone from the mayor to members of the County Commission and local church men. They made their outrage known to Bradford but he didn't pass any of it on down.

I did hear from a few of these people, the ones who took the time and effort to get in touch with me personally.

It's always surprising how people can overlook outrageous behavior in friends that they'd never tolerate in strangers. These people figured tossing his daughter out of the house was certainly the good Reverend's right, considering her behavior, and as for a little whopping with a belt, well, she deserved it, and more. It was all her fault.

In my younger days people like that had left me speechless. By now I was used to it and pretty much ignored them and hung up as soon as possible. One persistent preacher actually showed up at my door, ranting something about fallen women and feminism and Eve getting Adam kicked out of Eden. I looked at him for a minute, then just closed the door and went back to bed.

The local paper played Sims's death as its number-one story, but you could tell the newspaper people didn't really have their heart in it. What they were really interested in was Reverend Tyler's arrest for child abuse. It seemed the Reverend was pretty well known in the community beyond his church, being politically active in the fight against abortion, pornography, drugs, anti-Christian television, and other demons of godless secularism.

I was awakened Monday morning by a persistent pounding at my door. I looked out the window and found a TV truck parked there. I went back to bed. No way was I going to do interviews with the press, especially not right out of bed. Eventually they went away.

Tuesday was trouble. It was shift rotation for those who did split shifts. That meant Jefferson (the guy who'd replaced Sims), Mason, and Ox (who'd been doing split shifts this month replacing a guy recuperating from a hernia operation), went off for three days while Jimmy Coogan, Billy Masters, and Michael Ford came on.

"Kiss my ass, you bald freak!"

"Anytime, baby! Pull 'em down an' I'll plant a big one!" The voices were familiar as I walked into the back of the station. The first was Brin Chiari, the second, unforgettable, was Masters, apparently being his usual self.

I rounded the corner and saw a furious Chiari confronting a grinning Masters.

"The only way you'll ever get a woman, Masters, is by raping her or paying her," she snarled.

"Or maybe getting her drunk and fucking her out of her socks." Masters leered. "You know all about that, don't you, baby?"

They both turned as I walked up.

"Making friends again, Masters?" I asked.

"All the girls love me, baby." He snickered.

"I just thank God it's you that has to work with this pervert and not me," Chiari growled.

"Hey, you work with me, baby, I bet I'd have you out of your panties in two days."

"At gunpoint maybe," she snapped.

"Yeah, right. You had a lot of guns pointed at you, haven't you, Chiari," he taunted.

"Why don't you go into the squad room for briefing, Masters," I said. "I think you'll find it very interesting."

"I'm sure I will, Sergeant O'Neil," he said mockingly. "Hell, even if the words ain't worth listening to I can just watch you breathing."

He looked down at my chest, and I shrugged at Chiari. "Ignore him. You don't argue with retrogrades like this, you just wait for them to die of liver disease or something."

"The sooner the better," she said, turning and marching off.

"What color do you suppose her panties are?" Masters asked, watching her go. "Do you suppose she wears those little string bikini things, maybe black and lacy?" He turned his big eyes to me and smiled smugly.

"You'll never find out, Masters. Even she has standards."

"You could tell me, I bet." He grinned, easing closer. "I

186

hear a lot of women cops are . . . what do they call themselves now . . . queers?"

"If all men were like you, Masters, all women would be queers," I said, smiling at him. Then I turned and strode into the squad room.

I went over to the podium and took the keys and clipboard from Gordie Brandt, who told me about a bad accident on County 9, and a cigarette robbery at a 7-Eleven. He left then, eyeing Masters as he sauntered in, then looking back and giving me a grin.

"All right, everybody line up for inspection," I said.

Masters was first in line, grinning broadly. His uniform was immaculate, he'd shaved close, hell, he'd even polished his shoes. He obviously wasn't going to give me an excuse to fine him or send him home. Coogan was a youngish guy, tall and stringy, with a narrow face and glasses. Ford looked like a big goon, his face too wide and forehead protruding. His hair was close-cropped and his arms bulged with muscles.

"I've instituted a new procedure," I said. "From now on, the dispatcher will call you for a radio check every hour on the hour. You will also inform him of your position at that time. If you don't answer, you'll be fined twenty dollars. That's twenty dollars for every time you don't answer. So if you miss four radio checks it'll cost you eighty bucks."

"What the hell's that for?" Ford demanded.

"Ask Mr. Haggar," I said, smiling sweetly at Haggar. He flushed slightly, then scowled and looked away.

"That's a real good idea, Sergeant," Masters said, nodding approvingly. "Keep these deadbeats from sleeping all night."

"Yeah, look who's talking," Ford snapped. "Every time you're in Zone Four, we get complaints the sawmill is working all night."

"I do not snore," Masters said calmly. "You can come over to my house anytime, Sergeant, and I'll prove it to you."

"Not worth the effort of getting all those shots," I said. "In any case you'll be in Zone Five tonight." And every other night, I added silently.

"You can keep the cows awake with your snoring." Ford snickered.

"Anyone caught sleeping will get a fifty-dollar fine and a day's suspension," I said. "I just cleared that with the sheriff today." What I didn't add was that Bradford said I needed either a witness or some other proof.

"Coogan, you'll take Zone Six."

"Nice luck, Coogan." Masters grinned down the line at him. "Maybe that Tyler girl'll be parading around in her birthday suit again. I'd love to catch a look at that sweet body of hers."

"That will do," I said. "You'll have to continue to settle for magazines, Masters."

"Hell, from what I heard you got a coupla naked girls the other day. You sure are lucky, Saaargeeaant." He smiled broadly.

I assigned the rest of the zones, taking Zone 4, the only one besides Zone 7 I hadn't patrolled yet, for myself. Yesterday I'd taken Zone 5, spending much of my time specifically looking for places where a person could park a patrol car and catch some sleep. I wouldn't have to look very hard for Masters, though. I'd "borrowed" a bug from the locker they were kept in and planted it on the car I was going to assign him.

I'm a vindictive bitch sometimes.

I spent a little more than an hour patrolling Zone 4, then moved over to Masters's zone and turned on the little radio locator. The bug he had didn't have a lot of range, but when he reported his position at two, I'd be able to get closer. Radio check came. I reported a false position to Toby, then Masters came on and said he was on County 14. I headed over that way but couldn't pick him up. I drove along the normal patrol route for almost an hour hoping to pick up a trace on the machine, but nothing.

At three Masters called in saying he was going down Jaimeson. I headed that way, wondering if he was playing games with his position as I was. He was close enough for me to hear on the radio, so he was at least somewhere in the zone. I finally picked up a beep on Vancouver Road and followed it north. I turned off the headlights when I got real close, then parked and searched out Masters's car on foot.

I found it parked behind a clump of trees on County Road 2. I moved in very carefully. It would've been embarrassing to get caught sneaking up on him. Fortunately, the crickets were making more than enough noise to cover the slight shuffling sounds I made as I slid through the grass.

I moved up behind the cruiser and peered through the back window, seeing nothing. I walked slowly and softly along the side, watching the inside of the car very carefully. Masters was in the front seat, his feet propped up on the dash above the steering wheel. I dropped low and moved around to the driver's side of the car, then rose, my autofocus camera in hand.

Masters hadn't moved, and as I watched, he began to snore. Waking up every hour for the radio wasn't giving him much REM sleep, but then I guess he didn't really care. He was just a shadowy figure through the camera lens, but the thing focused itself anyway. When it beeped I closed my eyes and snapped the shot, opening them an instant later.

Masters didn't stir. I considered waking him as I had Haggar, but didn't really want a conversation with him, especially out here where there were no witnesses. I moved back to my car, then drove it up next to the clump of trees, closed the windows and picked up the mike.

"Patrol Three to Patrol Five," I called. He didn't answer. I called him twice more and he still didn't answer. I called Toby on the private channel and he called Masters. Masters answered right away.

"What's your twenty, Patrol Five?" Toby asked.

"I'm on County Four, Radio," Masters grunted.

"How come you didn't answer the sergeant?" Toby asked.

"Well, hell, Radio, I guess I'm out of range," Masters drawled.

I could hear him clearly on the main frequency. I still had my portable tuned to the supervisor's frequency and called Toby again.

"Toby, tell him the sergeant is parked about twenty feet outside his window, and tell him she says he's fined fifty dollars for sleeping, and twenty dollars for giving a false position. Tell him not to show up for work tomorrow either."

Everyone else would hear that too, of course, whereas they wouldn't have been able to hear my radio.

I rolled down my window as Toby delivered my message on the main frequency, and when Masters poked his head up above the dashboard I hit him with the high beams. He scowled and gave me the finger. I backed away and went down the road, then drove back to my own zone. I figured he'd be too aggravated to sleep further tonight anyway.

Besides, I could only use the bug to find him so many times before he wised up to it. Masters was an idiot but he wasn't a fool.

I was hyped up as I drove back into Zone 4. Hell, that'd been the most fun I'd had since coming here. The thrill of victory was extra sweet when it was over someone like Masters.

When I got home that morning my Jeep had four flat tires.

The locks on the front and side doors had keys shoved in and snapped off in them. And there was a note stuck to the door with a knife that said, rather poetically, "DIE, DYKE!" and underneath, in smaller letters, "The next one goes up your hole!"

I knew who'd put it there, of course. And he knew I'd know. The problem was I couldn't prove it. And he knew that too. If he was hoping it would scare me he was wrong. I knew Masters wasn't a total psycho. He wasn't about to do anything physical over a minor disciplinary measure. He was probably off somewhere having a beer and snickering, imagining me shaking with fear.

I went back to the car and radioed Jacklyn, the daylight dispatcher, and told her to call Madison Locks (the people I'd called to put on dead bolts after my last visit), and have them send someone over right away. I also had her call a mechanic.

Then I sat in the squad car for an hour, fuming, and trying to think of what to do next. I'd cost Masters seventy bucks and a day's pay. He'd just cost me four flat tires and the cost of a locksmith, which was likely to be higher. I was just glad he hadn't (apparently) been able to get into the house.

I'd already thrown the knife and note in the garbage. They didn't worry me. What I was worried about was Masters's repeating this anytime I caught him at something, or even if I didn't.

The locksmith arrived and deftly worked the broken keys out of the locks with little wires. He left a bill for $57. The mechanic arrived and changed my four tires to four new ones he'd brought. I was ready to hit the sack, but instead drove downtown and went to the electronics store. I picked up a camera and mount for a hundred bucks, and some wire to run it into my VCR. Then I went to the hardware store and picked up some floodlights.

I spent the next two hours installing them, putting the camera high up on the side of the front wall, just under the eaves trough. With the cost of the camera, floodlights, wiring, mechanic, and locksmith, Masters had cost me about $300. I'd cost him about $170, but then he at least had gotten a day off out of it.

Still, with my pension I could afford it a lot more than him, and if I had to outspend him to get rid of him, that was damned well what I was going to do.

I didn't have to wait long for results. When I woke up that night my locks were blocked again, glued this time. My car had four flats once more. There were obscenities painted on the sides of my house too, none of which bear repeating. He'd noticed the camera, and smashed it, but not before it had taken some sweet pictures of him jamming my front-door lock.

I didn't care. I was gleeful. I called the locksmith and mechanic again, then took the tape with me as I headed downtown. Gordie Brandt seemed surprised to see me so early. I showed him the pictures, though, and he shook his head in disgust.

"What an imbecile," he said.

"I want to swear out a formal charge against him. I also want to file a separate report about the incident this morning to have it on the record." I couldn't prove it had been Masters the first time, and a judge wasn't supposed to take that into consideration, but they were humans. A judge wouldn't have to be a genius to figure out it'd been Masters the first time too.

"Uh, you sure you want to do that, Caitlin, charge him, I mean?"

"I know, cops don't charge other cops. What the hell else am I supposed to do, Gordie? He's slashed eight tires and made me get the locksmith over twice now, and he'll probably do it again tonight."

"I could have a talk with him," he said doubtfully.

"He's not afraid of you," I snapped. "This guy doesn't give a shit about anything. The sheriff wants him fired. I'm all for it, and maybe this will be enough cause."

"It's not a felony," he said, shaking his head. "You're looking at trespass and malicious damage to private property, at best. He'll get a fine—"

"And almost surely be forced to make restitution," I interjected.

"Well, yeah . . ."

"Fine. If he has to pay for his damage maybe he'll stop causing it."

"Or maybe he'll cover his face next time," he said. "And maybe he'll burn the place down instead of painting it."

"I'll worry about that then. I'm not going to back off this creep because of what he might do."

"Okay," he sighed. "Your funeral."

"Or his."

Brandt would have much preferred to leave it to the day people, but I kept prodding him until he finally agreed to send over a guy to bring Masters in. He refused to let me go with him, though, and since it was his shift I had to relent.

Masters showed up in a jovial mood, an arm around the uncomfortable-looking deputy as though they were best buddies. He couldn't have been surprised at the summons, having known the camera had taken his pictures. And I was betting he was putting on an act.

"Well, hell. Hi, there, Gord," he said to Brandt.

"If you quit now we can forgo the charges," I said.

He turned to me and smiled. "Fuck you, bitch," he said pleasantly.

"Watch your mouth, Masters," Brandt growled.

"Hey, I'm off duty, Gord. My language is my own."

"Take him into the booking room," Brandt said to the deputy.

"How did he ever get to be a deputy?" I demanded.

"You didn't know?"

I shook my head.

"His brother-in-law was the chief of police."

"Ohhh."

"The chief that's the mayor of Madison now."

"Swell."

"Madison has almost half the seats on the County Council that pays our salaries."

"So you don't think Bradford will fire him?"

"As much as he'd love to, I don't think so, no."

"Well, if he gets caught a few more times, he'll have to."

"It's gonna cost you a lot of money before that happens. Don't think he'll fall for the camera again. Next time he'll be wearing a mask or something."

I caught Brin before she left and told her what had happened. She grinned happily at the thought of Masters's being arrested, but agreed with Brandt that he'd get back at me.

"That's what I wanted to ask," I said. "Would you mind staying at my place tonight? I don't want him breaking in there and wrecking the place before I can put in an alarm."

"Uh, well, the thing is, Caitlin, I was kind of expecting company tonight myself, uh, friendlier company, if you know what I mean."

"Oh."

"If you don't mind me having a, uh, friend over, I'll stay there tonight."

I weighed the idea of her screwing some guy on my bed with what Masters was likely to do if he got in there. It didn't come close.

"No problem," I said.

I gave her the keys and asked her to park her car near the Cunnards' place. That way Masters wouldn't associate it with my house.

"Maybe we'll catch the bastard," she said. "Wouldn't that be a treat."

I drove slowly along Rural Route 5, slumped back a little in the seat, one arm out the window as I listened to soft music on the portable radio.

I had taken Zone 9, and couldn't help thinking about Sims, and wondering why somebody had killed him. Bradford hadn't been very forthcoming about the investigation. He was supposedly in charge, although a couple of detectives from the state police were actually doing the work. That probably galled him, but he was smart enough to realize he didn't have the experience they did.

I dropped by Erika's, but the lights were out so I didn't stop. I passed the doughnut shop, driving a little farther to a truck stop. It was noisier but nobody bitched at me as I ate.

I was driving on County 8 around two-thirty when I rounded a curve and saw something in the trees glinting as my headlights swept over it. I slowed to a stop, then backed up along the dark road. I turned on the spotlight and swept it through the woods. The foliage was torn up right at the curve of the road, and a blue Nissan was about twenty yards into the bush.

I pulled off the road and turned on the flashers, then took my flashlight and hurried into the woods. The Nissan had mowed down a lot of young saplings and torn up a lot of grass and bushes, but hadn't hit anything major before coming to rest.

There was a guy in the front seat, his head back against the headrest, eyes closed. He looked about forty. He was wearing a pretty wrinkled-looking brown suit. His tie was missing and his shirt open. I reached through the open window and checked his pulse, even though I could see his chest rising and falling. He was okay, as far as I could see, though the fumes coming out of the window gave a pretty clear indication of what had zonked him out.

I shook him and he mumbled something and his eyes fluttered open.

"Wha . . . whaas . . . saatt?" he groaned.

"Out of the car, pal," I said, jerking the door open. His head shook slowly and he blinked up at my flashlight in confusion.

"Come on, out!" I barked, reaching in and grabbing him by the collar. I jerked him toward the door and he fell out onto the grass with a grunt, then stayed there on all fours for a long minute before I pulled him up by the scruff of the neck.

"Le . . . lemme go!" he grunted, shoving at my arm.

I turned my head away in disgust as his breath rolled over me.

"You got a license?" I demanded.

He blinked again, then brought his hand up and rubbed it back and forth across his eyes. He stared at me without any apparent recognition of who or what I was.

"Do you have a driver's license?" I asked loudly and slowly.

"Ye . . . yeah," he said in a sulky tone.

"Let me see it," I said.

"Le . . . lemme alone," he whined in the same sulky tone.

"You're under arrest," I said.

"Whaffeerr?"

"For driving while under the influence. Turn around and put your hands on the car."

He stared at me in confusion.

"I said turn around and put your hands on the car," I ordered.

"Fuck ooooff," he said in annoyance.

I grabbed his arm and turned him around toward the car. He turned back, shoving hard, so I staggered back a few paces.

He turned and tried to climb into his car again and I grabbed him from behind, jerking him back and slamming him against the hood. He struggled again, twisting around and grabbing at my wrists.

I tried to kick him in the nuts but he turned aside and the blow landed on his upper thigh. He cursed and we struggled briefly, hands gripping hands and wrists. I got a foot out and kicked at one of his ankles and he fell to his knees. I let my weight come down on him, knocking him back on his back, then came down heavily atop him, my knee jamming hard into his midsection.

He grunted out air and I got my wrist free, reached back and grabbed my handcuffs, and snapped them around his wrist. He cursed and twisted onto his side, throwing me off. I kept myself on my knees as I tried to pull his other hand around behind him. Then he grabbed at my gun, getting his hand around it and jerking it out of the holster.

I grabbed his wrist in both hands, then jammed my knee down onto it, crushing it against the ground. The gun fell loose as his fingers opened and I grabbed it. He threw a weak punch at me that hit the side of my face, and I slammed the butt of the gun down on the side of his head.

He groaned and collapsed, and I was able to roll him over onto his belly and pull his hands together behind his back. I cuffed the other hand, then sat back on the grass with a gasp of relief, panting for breath and trying to slow the pounding of my heart.

"Son of a bitch," I gasped, jamming my gun back into its holster only after several failed attempts.

I pushed myself to my feet and went back to my cruiser, then reached in and pulled the portable out.

"Patrol Three to Base," I called.

"Patrol Three."

"Can you get an ambulance down to County Eight, about a mile south of Henderson. I got a drunk here who's unconscious with a head wound. I also need a tow truck."

"Ten-four, Patrol Three."

I went back to the Nissan and patted the unconscious drunk down, removing his wallet. His name was Lloyd Robertson. He was a salesman. There was a picture of him posed with a woman and three kids, who I assumed were his family. The guy was a member of the Kiwanis club. Mr. Respectability.

Shit head.

16

It was back to the electronics shop after work. I had little faith in burglar alarms as such. I'd have the security company (surprisingly enough, there was one in Madison) hook one up anyway. What I was after was something else again. I brought one of the bugs from the station, like the one I'd hidden under the rear bumper of Masters's cruiser.

You know something, those electronics geeks love peculiar problems. They sold me an autodial phone, a small radio receiver, as well as a photoreceptor. They took apart the photoreceptor gizmo (one of those things that turn lights on and off as the sun rises and sets), and hooked it into a radio receiver that was set to the same frequency as the bug. When the radio picked up the signal from the bug it would cause the autodial to call the number of my cellular phone.

I thought it looked like an awfully complicated arrangement. They claimed it was simplicity itself. In any event, all I had to do was place them in my home, and whenever the bug came near (I could set the sensitivity of the receiver), I would get a phone call from the machine.

Of course, if I was halfway across the county, that might not help much.

Along with that, of course, I had to get another camera, two cameras, in fact, and more wire. Total cost of everything: another three hundred bucks. That was six hundred dollars he'd cost me so far. I could see now why Goff had thought it best just to let things lie. I was being sort of dumb about it, I guess. Masters had been working as a cop for more than twenty-five years and the county hadn't fallen apart. I don't know . . . maybe I had too much testosterone or something, or maybe I was just being pigheaded, but I was determined to beat that bald son of a bitch.

What with my shopping, it was ten-thirty before I got home. My car still had all its tires, and the door locks worked. I hesitated briefly, then opened the door and listened. I didn't hear any moans or cries of pleasure, so I went in.

There was no sign of whoever Brin's friend had been, but Brin herself was asleep in my bed. Oh, well, a small price to pay not to have all my windows busted and maybe paint or cow shit all over the place.

"Hey, wake up, sleeping beauty," I said, nudging the mattress with my knee.

I bounced the mattress some more and she groaned and rolled over onto her back, opening her eyes, then blinking them rapidly. She looked up at me in confusion for a moment, then looked on either side of her, before looking back at me.

"Hi," she croaked.

"Hello. Long night?"

She grinned tiredly.

"Want me to make some coffee?"

"Would you?" She sat up, slowly and not without difficulty,

and even when she managed it she looked ready to fall back again.

"Oh God, do I have a hangover," she moaned, putting a hand against her head.

"This isn't meant as a criticism, Brin," I said, "but have you ever considered the possibility that you drink too much?"

"Yes, often," she sighed, swinging her legs out of bed. She turned to look at me. "I hope you have a big hot-water tank."

"It hasn't run out on me yet."

"Good," she grunted. She slowly pulled herself out of bed and shambled naked across the room to the door. A moment later the shower went on. I shook my head, reminding myself that she was a big girl and didn't need a mother, then went and made some coffee.

I figured she'd be a while, so I started unpacking the electronic crap and sorting out what I'd need. I did a preliminary survey of the outside, deciding where I wanted to put the cameras and lay the wires, then went back inside and hooked up the receiver and other junk. None of it was much good until I got a bug on Masters's car, but first things first.

Brin spent a long time in the bathroom, then emerged, hangover intact, wearing one of my robes. It was way too big, but better than nothing, and I didn't begrudge it. She dropped heavily onto a stool by the kitchen counter and held her head in both hands. I wordlessly got her some coffee, black, of course.

She took it and held it below her head, inhaling.

I had to laugh. She looked up at me, eyes bloodshot.

"God's punishment," I said.

"I thought that's what your period was."

"God hates women having any fun."

"Yeah? Fuck him."

"Don't let Bradford hear you say that."

"Fuck Bradford too, stuck-up creep," she muttered.

"You don't like the sheriff?"

"Oh, he's okay," she sighed, sipping gingerly at the coffee. "Do you know he had the gall once to try and lecture me about my . . . what did he call it . . . my promiscuity?"

"That must have been fun."

"I told him to mind his own goddamn business. Do you know he thinks 'goddamn' is a curse?"

"He's kind of religious."

"So? That should be my problem?"

"Your boss's problem is always your problem."

"I guess." She took another sip of coffee. "I'm not a slut, you know," she said.

"Who you sleep with is your business."

"But I want you to know. I like you. I don't want you to think I'm cheap."

"I don't think you're cheap."

"Everyone else does."

"That's their problem."

"And mine," she muttered.

"Tell me something," I said.

"Hmmmm?" She gulped some coffee.

"You and, uh, Marty, from Eddie's?"

"What about us? Have we ever done it? Yeah, but not since we were kids. We're just friends now. I'd do it if he wanted, but he'd rather we stay platonic. God knows why. It's not like he doesn't fool around a lot himself. Oh, are you interested in Marty?"

"Oh no," I said, shaking my head.

"He's a great guy, you know. He's smart, really funny, good-humored. He almost never loses his temper and he treats you with respect, doesn't take you for granted."

"I was just wondering," I said.

"Yeah, sure. Want my advice? Go for it. He loves tall women, too, specially blondes."

"I'll think about it."

"Wish I was tall as you," she mused, looking me up and down.

"You know, you're kind of taking a chance in this day and age."

"You mean AIDS? I've seen the statistics, hon. The chances of heterosexual transmission is minimal. Less than three percent of those infected got it that way, and even those usually slept with someone who was in a danger group, like gay, or an intravenous drug user or hemophiliac. Anyway, I use a rubber most times. I've tested negative every time."

"There's still a chance."

"Shit, Caitlin, more people die of cancer every two weeks than have ever died of AIDS. I'd hate to spend my life platonic and then die of cancer or in a car wreck or something. I'll take the fuckin' chance. You only live once."

Brin left, though not before consuming a bowl of corn flakes and commenting, in hilarious fashion, on the sexual proficiency, or lack of it, of a number of deputies.

Then I went to work.

I hid both cameras in trees, plastering leaves all over them. I ran their wires down the sides of the trees and into the ground, then buried them underground (okay, an inch underground, with mostly leaves and cut grass on top), and ran them into my place through the windows. It wasn't going to take a genius to find them, but at night it would take an effort, and I was hoping Masters would have other things to do.

The alarm guy came, and did the doors and windows with magnetic strips and wires. I wanted an audible alarm, to wake the Cunnards, as well as the silent signal to the alarm company. I wanted Masters to have as little time as possible to wreck things and knew, as a cop here, how easy it would be to distract the local car, have it sent to the other side of the zone, then break into a place. With just the silent alarm, he'd have twenty minutes or more to do what he wanted and leave.

When he was just finishing up, the guy Cunnard had called about the paint came and decided he'd have to paint the whole side of the house. I left him to it and went to bed.

It wasn't easy getting to sleep. For one thing, I kept waiting for a brick to smash through my front window. I kept imagining all kinds of scenarios where I'd catch Masters red-handed, ranging from him being humiliated to my shooting the son of a bitch (in self-defense, of course).

For another thing, Brin's little romp in my bed reminded me that it had been some time since anyone but I had made use of it, for sleeping or any other purpose. I wasn't exactly a nymphomaniac like her (okay, unfair, but the girl truly had slept with half the department!), but hell, I really wasn't set up for chastity as a way of life. Maybe I should give Marty a try. My four days off started tomorrow.

My sleep went without incident, and after a careful check around the house that night revealed nothing wrong, I figured Masters (who'd been called in to speak to Bradford that day) had decided to forgo his pleasures long enough to let the heat die down.

I got into the Caprice and headed for work. Ten minutes later I walked into the squad room and over to where Gordie Brandt was going over the evening's reports.

"Hi," I said, sitting down on the table next to him.

"Hi yourself." He pushed the chair back and looked up. "You hear about Masters?"

"Don't tell me he got fired?"

" 'Fraid not. In fact . . ." He pointed across the room where Masters sat at a table, talking with Haggar and Ford.

"Oh, great. You mean Bradford did nothing?"

"No, he's made him work a seven-day shift without pay."

"Straight?"

"No. He'll lose a day's pay off the next seven shifts. The sheriff said if he'd been working when it happened he'd have fired him, but he didn't think he could dismiss him for actions he took on his own time. On a completely different topic, did you know the mayor dropped by this afternoon?"

"Now how would I know that? I was sleeping, remember?"

"So you were. They had a loud discussion in there. Couldn't make out all the details, but you and Masters figured prominently. I don't think the mayor likes you much."

"I wouldn't have to be a genius to know that."

"He doesn't think radical feminists should be on the force, causing trouble for good Christians."

"He doesn't? The mayor wouldn't be a friend of Reverend Tyler, would he?"

"Member of his congregation."

"Uh-huh."

"Also a member of the Loren Pro-Life League."

"Figures."

"It's a small town. Anyway, Masters should be pleading guilty before the court next week. Maybe you'll get some satisfaction there."

"Maybe he won't be able to pay the fine and they'll shove him in a cage where he belongs."

"I think he'll find someone to pay it," he said, smiling.

"His brother-in-law?"

"Or his sister, whichever."

"I'll just have to see he keeps getting in trouble. Eventually Bradford will have to fire him."

"Good luck." He grinned.

He initialed several papers, then shoved them into their proper trays. He got up and stretched, looked at his watch and said good-bye. I turned and found the shift was all there, so I went over to the lectern to gather up the briefing notes.

I looked up from them to find Masters standing in front of me, grinning.

"Get your fat face over in line, Masters," I said calmly.

"I heard Chiari was stayin' at your place, Sergeant." He leered. "I guess she's developin' a taste for pussy now, huh."

"Fuck off, Masters."

"Hell, she's had every guy in town, now she's goin' after the dykes."

"She hasn't had every guy in town, Masters. She'd never stoop so low as to let you touch her. What woman would unless you paid for it?"

"How much you charge, baby?"

"More than you've got in this world, Masters."

"Every whore has a price, don't she?"

"Starting with twenty dollars for insubordination and twenty dollars for obscenity." I smiled sweetly.

"Forty bucks is more than you're worth."

"Masters, get back in line," I snapped, raising my voice. He hesitated just long enough to show his contempt, then turned and sauntered to the wall.

I read out the reports of the day's troubles: a quarrelsome couple that'd had the police there three times since noon, a couple of houses broken into, and a report of drag racers on County 9. Masters held up his hand, a big grin on his face. I ignored him.

"Excuse me, Sergeant," he said in a respectful tone. "But I really had to congratulate you on that excellent piece of police work the other night. You know, when you caught me takin' a little nap."

"I'm glad you have such respect for my police work, Masters," I said calmly.

"Oh yes, ma'am. But I do have one kind of, well, kind of a

warning, like. You see, sneaking up on a policeman, well, ma'am, that can be right dangerous, especially after poor old Sims got his brains blown out the side of his head. I've been a mite jumpy since then, and well, ma'am, I'd sure hate to, well, to shoot you 'cause I thought my life was in danger. I was just, well, warning you, like. If you . . . if you see what I mean, ma'am." He smiled endearingly.

"I guess the answer to that problem is for you to stay awake then, isn't it, Masters?"

"Well, ma'am, you know that's sometimes hard to do. I do my best, of course. Still, I'd really hate for there to be a tragic accident, if . . . if you know what I mean."

"I can understand how you'd be jumpy, Masters," I said. "Why, I remember when I snuck up on Haggar there last week. I was sure afraid something had happened to him. In fact, when I opened the door and he kind of fell out, I damned near blew his fool head off. I had the muzzle of my shotgun about a foot from his face and my finger down on that trigger so tight it's a wonder he's with us today," I said sympathetically. "I get real jumpy crawling around in the bushes myself. That's why I usually take the shotgun with me.

"In any case," I said, looking at the rest of them briefly, "since you didn't get a chance to properly patrol Zone Five the other night, I'll give you another try. You'll get it tonight. And since you have trouble staying awake I'll give you Car Fourteen. Milt Hoover was saying the squeaky brakes damned near drove him crazy this evening. Maybe they'll help keep you from dozing off."

He continued to smile, but his eyes were cold as hell.

17

Working seven days in a row wasn't pleasant, but the advantage to it was that your weekends, wherever they fell during the week, were alternately three or four days long. That was something to relax and look forward to. I was off from 8 A.M. Friday morning to 12 A.M. Tuesday morning. I meant to take advantage of it. The first week had been an exhausting one.

After a week of running around everywhere and trying to get to know the county and the rules at work, all I felt like doing was sitting around the house for a while and taking things easy. I decided to do a little something about my tan, which was fading, too. Working midnights could have you looking like a ghost after a while if you weren't careful.

I got home Friday morning and went out onto the deck. It was bright and sunny, and even at nine in the morning it was getting up there in temperature. With the deck ten feet off the ground here, and no stairs, and with nothing in sight but a long empty field and trees far off in the distance, I considered going nude, but my old Irish upbringing made me chicken out and I wore my bikini as I basked in the sun.

I know you're supposed to be worried about the ozone layer and getting crisped by the sun, but as Brin had said, if one thing didn't get you, another would, and you really did only live once (unless you believed in reincarnation, of course).

I had developed a reasonable tan back in L.A., when I was trying to look good for the doctors, so I used a high tanning lotion as I lay on the deck. I considered what would be involved in getting a pool put in out back, and made a mental note to ask Fred Cunnard the next time I saw him.

I read for a couple of hours, and got a phone call from Brin near noon. The gossip around the station now was saying the guy who killed Sims was probably one of the monsters. Supposedly the state investigators were looking in that direction, checking the backgrounds of all of us. I couldn't blame them. Of all the mean, surly, violent characters wandering around the county at night, the guys in the Monster Squad were probably the worst.

After I hung up I went inside and took a shower, then, not wanting to be dead on my feet later, went to bed for a few hours.

I wasn't sure what to wear to Eddie's. I mean, I wanted to look sexy, but not as if I'd tried. I had a couple of really tight little dresses, but they were out of the question. I didn't want to wear pants, since all Marty'd seen me in were my police uniform and the jeans I'd worn while Goff was showing me around. I wanted to wear something feminine but casual, and sexy but demure.

"Shit," I said, looking into my closet.

After a lot of wardrobe changes I settled on a ruffled knee-length blue skirt and a blue-and-white peasant blouse. For an added touch I wore a pair of cowboy boots I'd bought four years ago and only worn once before. I figured they'd be appropriate at Eddie's.

Brin was working that night, so I went alone, getting there just shy of ten. The place was packed and I barely managed to squeeze through the front door. There didn't seem to be any tables open, and no place at the bar either. Marty was behind the bar working and I began to regret coming so early. He spotted me then and waved me over, shoving two guys out of the way to clear a space for me at the corner of the bar.

"Glad to see you. You look gorgeous," he said, beaming.

"Um, thanks. Thought I'd come see what everyone does here on Friday nights."

"They come here, of course. Unless they're underage, then they drive up and down Center Street all evening. What can I get you?"

"Do you have wine here?"

"What do I look like, a barbarian? Of course I have wine; white or red?"

"White, please."

"White wine, coming up."

He went over to the fridge and pulled out a green bottle of something, then lifted a couple of glasses off the rack, said something to one of the bartenders, and came around the bar to me.

"Come on, I'll show you to your table." He grinned.

"I didn't see any empty tables," I said, worried he'd shove people away from their table for me.

He led me through the crowd to the other side of the bar, where one of the busboys was just setting down a table on the edge of the dance floor. Another busboy carried over a couple of chairs, while the first guy dropped a tablecloth on.

Marty held my chair, his smile only partly mocking.

"Nice to know the owner," I said.

"Hell, everybody knows me," he said, sitting down across from me. He took a corkscrew out of his pocket and opened the wine, then sniffed the cork like a connoisseur and poured for me.

"You drink a lot of wine?" I asked.

"I prefer brandy, most times," he admitted. "And stop being a snob."

"Snob? Me?"

"You look like you were expecting a screw top."

I had been.

"We aren't exactly in the sticks here, Caitlin. Nobody marries their sister here."

"I know. I'm sorry. It just seems very, um, small-town after L.A."

"L.A. is a dump. I lived there for five years and I never miss it."

"Oregon is just a big change from what I'm used to."

"Yeah, you can breathe the air. And you don't have to duck flying bullets all the time. Except around hunting season. I love this place. I know everyone. They all know me. I've got a pile of friends here. There's always something to do if you've got friends, Caitlin. If you don't, L.A. is a lot more boring than Loren County."

"I suppose that's true to a certain extent."

"So tell me about this captain you beat up in L.A."

"How did you know about that?" I demanded. "Nobody here knows about it."

"Sure they do. Pat told me."

"How'd he know?"

"I think the sheriff mentioned it."

"Well, how the hell did he know?"

"Ask him next time you see him."

"I thought that was a secret."

"Hard to keep secrets around here."

"It should be when you're the only person that knows."

"Did you know the sheriff used to be an L.A. cop?"

My jaw dropped and he grinned in amusement.

"Spent twenty years on the Los Angeles Police Department. Became a lieutenant there."

"I'll be damned. How come nobody ever mentioned it?"

"One of those things you don't talk about because everybody knows it. Tell me about you."

"Nothing to tell." I shrugged.

"Why'd you become a cop?"

"I like the job."

"Kind of, er, hard to meet people, isn't it?"

"Mostly when you're a cop you run with other cops."

"Yeah, so I hear. I don't think you have to be quite so clannish here as in L.A."

"You mean, like, I could hang around with, oh, bar owners, for example?"

"For example. Bar owners make great companions."

"Just feed them once a day and let them out in the evening."

"And give us lots of TLC."

"TLC, huh? From what I hear you get more than your share of TLC."

"So how do you like Loren?" he asked, pointedly changing the subject.

"It's nice, kind of quiet and peaceful. I've never really been to a small town before."

"Where you from before L.A.? Don't tell me you were born there."

"Chicago."

"Never been there."

The music changed, a fast song coming on. Marty turned with a start, then grinned at me, standing and grabbing my hand. "Let's dance," he said.

I had little chance to decline and he led me onto the crowded floor, a floor becoming more crowded with each passing second. Apparently this was a favorite song or something. Maybe I'd have to start listening to country radio.

Or maybe not.

We danced through the next three songs before I finally managed to jerk him back to our table, where I fell into my seat and wished for something cooler and more refreshing than wine.

We talked some more, with Marty giving me a catalog of vivid descriptions of the drunken exploits of some of the area's more notorious characters, including my deputies. We danced a lot, and I had a bit more to drink than I probably should have. It had been a long day, though, and despite my nap, I was soon feeling it.

Marty saw me out to my car, reluctant to see me go and, from what I could tell, puzzling out how to seduce me before I could get to the car.

"You know, the problem here is you're driving yourself home." He sighed, as I reached the car and unlocked it. "I can't even drive you home 'cause I'd have to take a taxi or something back."

"Don't worry about it," I assured him.

"Yeah, but you don't have the chance to ask me in for a coffee or something," he said, easing close against me. I grinned and he suddenly bent and kissed me. I was a bit startled but I didn't fight him as he slid his arms around me and pulled me against him. I had a bit of a buzz from the wine, and as he extended the kiss I had the sudden desire to put an end to my temporary chastity.

"My place is right around back," he breathed, pulling back slightly.

I considered it. It was tempting.

"I don't think so," I said slowly. He bent and kissed me

again, putting a lot of effort into it. His tongue slid back and forth against my lips and probed gently against them before sliding a little inside.

I fought it with mine for a few seconds, then pushed him back, breaking my lips free.

"I gotta go," I gasped.

"You don't have to," he said.

"I think I do."

I turned and pulled the door open and he reluctantly stepped back.

"Next time we're gonna have a real date, where I pick you up in my car and get to be invited in afterward for coffee," he promised.

"If you're lucky," I said, smiling at him, then sliding in behind the wheel.

He stepped back as the car started and I waved before putting it in gear and pulling out of the space. I spent the drive home debating whether I'd made the right decision or not. I was tired, after all, but I really would have rather spent the next couple of hours doing something other than sleeping.

Oh, well.

▌18 ▐

I slept late and spent much of Saturday afternoon working on my tan. Saturday night I went out with Brin, to Eddie's, of course. She tried to hold down on her drinking, not wanting me to think bad of her, I guess, but she was as rowdy and boisterous as she'd been the other night, when I'd seen her all over that deputy. The difference was, with no particular date tonight, she was coming on to damned near every guy in the place. A lot of the women were giving her distinctly unhappy looks.

She was dressed in a skintight black sheath dress, which made me ten times as glad I hadn't worn my own. I'd done a little shopping that afternoon and was wearing a soft calf-length suede dress with brown boots. I was glad of the modesty in Brin's company. Whatever she'd done or not done to earn it, she'd gotten a reputation, and I did not want people thinking she and I were, as my mother would say, cut from the same cloth. I know that's cowardly and, in fact, I kind of envied her, acting as she did. I just would never have the confidence, or feel comfortable, flirting up a storm like that.

She was incredibly outgoing, and a helluva lot of fun to be around. Sure, her behavior bordered on the outrageous and drew a lot of looks (some of them disapproving), but I hadn't laughed as much in months. And though her getting hot and heavy with her final selection for a night's soul mate made me feel a little more pressured where Marty was concerned, I couldn't really find it in my heart to blame her. He was pretty cute, after all.

The problem was she'd driven me to the bar, and that made it kind of look as if I'd set it up for Marty to drive me home, despite all my protests to the contrary. I had to invite him in for "coffee," too. I made it clear all the way home, though, that coffee was all he was going to get. Maybe if I'd been back in L.A., things would have been different, but in this small-town atmosphere, where everybody seemed to know everybody else's business, I just didn't want to get a reputation as a "fun date."

So Marty got no farther than my sofa. It took a Herculean effort in self-control to achieve that, and I think both of us knew that the next night, Sunday, which Marty could afford to take off, would probably have us end up in one or another's bed.

On Sunday he picked me up like the perfect gentleman, wearing a tasteful blue suit, drove me into Madison to Ralph's Steak House, wined and dined me, then drove halfway across the county to a really bad movie.

He made up for it later, though modesty forbids my saying how.

I woke around two in the afternoon, slowly, reluctantly. I hadn't drunk enough for a hangover but I was somewhat sore in various places. Marty was gone.

Feeling a little like Brin, I pulled myself out of bed and padded naked to the shower, where I let the hot water massage some of the soreness out of my muscles.

Afterward, it occurred to me that I'd neglected my morning workout with the Solo Flex. On the other hand, Marty and I had worked out with it last night (in ways its makers had never intended, I'm sure), and I don't think I'll ever look at it in quite the same way again.

After coffee on the deck I conducted an inspection of the premises, surprised again, as I had been the last few mornings, that nothing had been disturbed. Either Masters had given up or he had just taken the weekend off.

At least, that's what I thought.

I did my laundry, and the rest of the chores I'd put off all week, then relaxed on the deck again to watch the sun set.

A few hours later I was in the Caprice on the way to the station.

Masters's car was already there. It took only a couple of seconds to slip the bug beneath the rear bumper, barely a pause in my walk across the lot. Feeling a little smug (it had been a great weekend, after all), I made my way through the halls toward the squad room.

Then stopped dead as I passed the bulletin board.

There, on the board, was a full-color, poster-sized picture of me . . . in my bikini. I was on the deck at my place, leaning forward over the railing. The bikini had a string top, and though leaning forward over the rail didn't exactly make me look like Dolly Parton, it sure had given the camera a nice shot of cleavage.

I stood there and stared at it in shock for long seconds, wondering how and when it had been taken. Then I jerked my eyes away, face heating up as I looked quickly up and down the hall. I grabbed the thing and ripped it down, wondering who'd seen it already.

I was so thrown by it that I retreated into the ladies' room to try and think. The poster was a little fuzzy, just a little, and had obviously been taken with a telephoto, a very long-range one. Someone could easily have gotten close to the deck without my seeing him, but that would have given him a shot from ten feet below the rail. The picture looked almost as if the camera had been on the same level.

It had to have been taken from well back, maybe all the way into the trees. That meant a damned expensive piece of equipment.

Face hot, I tore the photo into pieces and shoved them into the garbage, considering the likely reactions of the goons out in the squad room to something like this.

Thank God I hadn't given in to temptation and sunbathed in the buff!

I ran through all the likely things the guys in the squad room were likely to say, presuming they'd seen it, and what my response should be. The worst thing I could do, as I saw it, was make a big deal about it or act embarrassed. I'd have to shrug it off, act completely uncaring.

That was going to be an effort. The thinking behind the poster was clear. Not only was it meant to embarrass me, it was intended to remind me and everyone else that, after all was said and done, all I was was a piece of ass.

I left the bathroom and went down the hall to the squad room again.

There was another poster on the bulletin board, a copy of the first. I ripped it down without breaking stride, crumpled it up and jammed it into a garbage can.

I almost ran into Bobbie Whyte, who put his hands out to fend me off.

"Sorry," I said.

"I see you've found another one," he said, making a wry face. "I tried to get rid of them all."

"All? How many were there?" I demanded.

"The first ones showed up on the bulletin board there, and the one down the north hall, at the start of the evening shift. I got rid of them, then when I came in at the end of the shift, about twenty minutes ago, I found they'd been replaced. I took them off, but I guess somebody's put up another one."

"Another two. This is the second one I've torn down from that board," I snapped.

He made a face and looked back over his shoulder toward the squad room.

"Who did it?" I demanded.

"I don't know but I'd guess one of your guys."

"Where would you get something like this made up in Loren?"

"Not many places. In fact, I don't know any place."

"Where do people get their film developed?"

"Shah's Pharmacy and Madison Drugs. I don't think they do blowups. Maybe they did it at home."

"Equipment to blow up a color shot that big is too expensive for any of the deputies here." I shook my head. "Besides, whoever took that shot did it from a hundred yards off. The telephoto lens alone must have cost a thousand dollars or more."

"Well, I don't know," he said uncomfortably. "I don't know a lot about cameras."

"Hi, Caitlin."

I turned as Brin came in from the parking lot, carrying her shotgun and clipboard. "You seen the pictures yet? You showed her those pictures?" she asked Bobbie.

"I've seen one," I said.

"Good fuckin' thing I didn't come over like I was gonna on Saturday," she said. "They would've got pictures of me in the raw. That's the way I sunbathe."

219

"I wouldn't spread that around or you'll have them crawling around your place next," I said.

"Let them. I do it on the roof. They'd have to fly over."

She didn't know where a person would get a negative blown up to that size, and didn't seem to think it was any big deal anyway. After all, I hadn't been naked, and she seemed to think the picture was pretty flattering anyway.

"Try to arch your back next time," she said, laughing, as she went past into the squad room to file her paperwork.

I glared at her back, then at Bobbie, who shrugged helplessly. "It's no great scandal," he said. "Nothing to be embarrassed about. Like she said, it's just a bathing suit."

"It's not exactly the kind of image I want to present to them," I said.

"Yeah, I know, but what's done is done. Forget about it and they will too."

"Sure."

I went on to the squad room, passing Brin on her way back.

"Brace yourself," she said, giving me a sympathetic punch in the arm as she passed.

They were all there including Masters, who was doing extra shifts replacing Sims, and all eyes turned to me as I walked into the squad room. Most of them were grinning openly. I ignored them, going straight to the lectern and picking up the activity log. It was almost empty, with nothing of significance to report. I glanced over the top of the paper at them, not meeting any eyes, then looked down at the paper again.

"Line up for inspection," I said. I heard them shuffling into position, and finally put the clipboard down.

Haggar and Masters were leering and grinning widely. Pczchornek had his normal scowl on, Mason smiled sympathetically, while Ox looked out the window.

It was then I noticed there were two new posters on the

walls, both of me. One was a copy of the ones I'd seen in the hall. The other one was a full-body pose of me in mid-stride, facing the camera. I turned quickly away from them as Haggar snickered.

"You find something funny, Haggar?" I demanded.

"Nothing, Sarge." He grinned.

"I don't suppose the photographer would like to identify himself," I said calmly.

Nobody came forward.

I shrugged nonchalantly and handed out assignments. I gave Masters Zone 5 again. He was the most likely suspect, and anyway, I couldn't stand the son of a bitch. He didn't appear surprised.

"Mind if I take one of those posters with me, Sarge?" He asked slyly. "Something to keep me awake, keep the blood moving, y'know?"

"Do they belong to you, Masters?"

"Oh no, ma'am. I have no idea where they came from."

"If they're not yours, then you can't have them, now can you."

"Can I have one then?" Haggar asked. "I need something to hang over my bed."

"How about the number of the STD hot line?" I snapped.

"The what?" He blinked.

The STD hot line was a Log Angeles number for people who had or thought they might have a sexually transmitted disease.

"Forget it," I said.

"You sure do take a good picture, Sarge," Pczchornek said. "Course the clothes make the woman."

"Yeah, you ought to dress like that on duty," Haggar said.

"I think you look real pretty," Ox volunteered, to more snickers.

I took Zone 6, entirely because I wanted to see Marty again.

I rushed through the rest of the roll call, then waited until they'd all left to tear down the pictures on the wall. I didn't rip them up as I had the others. Instead I examined them for any sign of what organization might have produced them. I didn't see any markings, so just rolled them up and took them out to the car with me.

I almost chickened out at Eddie's. I was feeling a little awkward. Still, I braced myself and pushed through into the bar.

It was a Monday night, so the place was already starting to wind down. Marty was sitting at a table with several other guys. He noticed me before I was halfway across the floor, said something to one of the others and came forward to meet me.

"Hey, beautiful," he said, hugging me and giving me a kiss. I pushed him back awkwardly.

"Marty," I protested.

"What? Afraid someone'll think we're"—he dropped his voice to a harsh whisper—"doing it?"

"I'm in uniform, is all," I said.

"We can solve that problem right fast. Let me show you to my place," he said, leading me toward the door. I broke free and shook my head, pulling him to an empty table and sitting down. He sighed in regret and sat down as well, pulling his chair closer to me.

"Don't tell me you're having regrets?" he said.

"No, not exactly."

"What? I wasn't any good?"

"You know damned well you . . . were . . . okay," I said.

"Okay? Gee, thanks, but I don't know if my ego can stand such a buildup." He scowled unhappily, giving me a hurt expression.

"Marty," I said, grinning.

"Maybe if I ever go looking for a real job, I can get you to write me a recommendation," he said. " 'He was okay.' "

"Don't forget I have high standards." I shrugged.

"Let's go to my place then and we'll see if I measure up."

"I don't think I can criticize the others for sleeping on duty if I take off for quickies with local bartenders."

"Quickies? Who said anything about a quickie? It's Monday night, for Christ's sake. I got lots of time."

"But I don't. I have work to do."

"Shooters'll be as quiet as here, quieter. Nobody else will miss you. We can take off for a couple of hours without anyone noticing a thing."

"I'll notice. Go take a cold shower."

"Maybe I'll just do some exercises," he said, the corner of his lip quirking upward. I looked away, feeling a slow flush creeping over me. He laughed and I punched his arm, hard enough for it to hurt. He refused to show it, though, grinning and not moving to rub where my fist had struck.

"I hope Brin doesn't take off for these little parties when she's on duty," I said.

"Hey, I'm not gonna rat on a friend to her boss."

"I gotta go. I'll be back later."

He followed me out to the car, trying to get his arm around my waist a couple of times. I shrugged him off. I hesitated at the car, then reached under the seat and pulled out the rolled-up posters, unfurling them as he looked down with a casual grin. His eyes widened as he took in the pictures.

"Do you know where someone would go to get these made up?" I asked.

He took them from me, gazing with interest. I fidgeted, a little embarrassed as he whistled.

"Do you or don't you?" I demanded, reaching for them. He pulled them back.

"Yeah, I know who could make these up, just about the only guy in town. You mean you didn't pose for them? Where'd they come from?"

I explained, trying again to snatch them back. He twisted away, holding them behind his back as he grinned in amusement.

"Guy named Jeff Murdoch runs Madison Printing and Photography on Center Street. He does commercial photography and prints circulars and advertising posters. He does all the political posters during election time too. When business is slow he does weddings, birthdays, portraits, passports, you name it. I bet he could've taken and developed these."

"I'll ask him, now give them back."

"Why? What do you want them for?"

"To show this Murdoch guy, for one."

"He doesn't have that big a business. He'll know if he took pictures of you. Come on, let me keep them."

"Forget it!"

"Why not? They're great pictures."

"I don't want pictures like that circulating around town!"

"I'm not going to circulate them. Besides, you can bet Masters, or whoever had them taken, has lots more."

I tried to reach around him but he held them high above his head and it would have been far too undignified to try and jump up after them. I stared sternly at him and folded my arms across my chest.

"Make up your mind, Marty: either you give those back or you're never gonna get your hands on the real thing again."

"Ahh, come on, Caitlin. I won't show anybody," he said.

"God, keep them then," I sighed, throwing up my hands in disgust.

"I just remembered something that might help you find the photographer," he said. "Murdoch's wife is Mike Ford's sister."

"Oh really."

"Yup. Ford and Murdoch are drinking buddies, not best friends or anything, but they get along pretty good."

I checked on Shooters, then did a quick patrol through the small villages west of the highway. Instead of heading back to Eddie's then, I stepped on the gas and purred through the darkness toward Zone 5.

Masters's one-o'clock report put him near Cedar Road. Whether that was true or not was anybody's guess. I didn't take the chance. Instead I headed to the south side of the zone, where River Road met Fairmount. I figured on driving right through the center of the zone on Fairmount, picking him up on my little radio wherever he was hiding.

To my surprise the thing started beeping before I even reached Fairmount. What was more, the radio showed him south of me, which put him in Zone 8. What was that shit doing in Zone 8?

I had to drive farther west before taking Highway 6 south. I'd lost his signal as I moved west. I was afraid I wasn't going to get it back again, but after heading south at high speed for several minutes the thing started to beep slightly. He was out there, farther south than before, and at extreme range.

I stepped on the gas, hoping to decrease the distance between us. I considered having Toby call him and give him a phony call, but then rejected it. I wanted to know what he was up to. Maybe he was finally going to do something outrageous enough to get him fired.

I waited for the signal to show a turn to the west, toward Madison, and my house, but he just kept going south, passing from Zone 8 to 9. I had closed the range a little, but he was obviously making good time, and unless I wanted to go the lights-and-siren route, it was going to be hard catching him.

I wondered what the hell it was in Zone 9 that brought guys out of their own zones. Then the similarity between Sims and Masters hit me. Both had been assigned to Zone 5, both had driven south to Zone 9. Why? Sims was dead, of course. What, if anything, could Masters tell me about that?

Were the state investigators right? Could one of the other deputies have killed Sims? Masters hadn't been working that night. He could've been the one.

I waited for him to drive onto Beckle and park. Didn't happen, though. He turned east and headed into Ashford instead.

"Shit," I muttered. I considered turning away, but hell, the Ashford cops couldn't have more than one car on the road tonight, if that. The chances of running across it were slim.

I kept following Masters.

We crossed into Ashford, going down poorly lit, poorly paved roads, the odd light shining down on small wooden houses, most in need of a paint job. The receiver showed me closing on Masters, who had probably stopped. I slowed, partly because of the deep potholes, partly to keep from running across him too soon. I wanted to know what he was up to, not catch him parked at a streetlight.

When I was almost on top of him I shut off my headlights and slowed to a crawl, craning my neck to look all around for his car. The receiver showed me right on top of him, and I still couldn't see the car. I pulled over to the side of the road and stopped.

I was on a residential street, though the houses wouldn't have won any awards. They were small, with large yards mostly overgrown with weeds. With the exception of one house, they were all single-story buildings. That one exception was also the only sign of light in the area. All the other houses were dark, and there were no streetlights.

The single two-story job stood out in another way. There were a lot of cars parked around it, and there was obviously some kind of party going on inside. Shapes and shadows drifted back and forth on the curtains of the first-floor windows. The second-floor windows were all alight too, though I didn't see any movement there.

The house was half a block down. I backed the cruiser into

the driveway of a house next to me and got out. I walked slowly up and down that section of street, flashlight in hand, looking for Masters. His car turned out to be parked behind the brightly lit house, empty.

I had two thoughts then. The first was to barge in and find him, probably drinking or something. The second was to steal his car and let him try and explain what had happened to it when he came out.

I reluctantly gave up the first idea. This was another jurisdiction, after all, and not only was I not supposed to be here but I had no warrant to get me inside. I went back to my car and sat in it for a few minutes thinking. I could call . . . whom? I'd have to get two people here, one to drive the other, and the second to drive Masters's car out.

Too much effort.

Too much explaining.

I sat and watched and waited.

A car pulled up in front of the house and parked. A man got out, singularly normal, and walked up to the front door. He didn't knock, but just walked inside. For a few moments I heard music playing before the door closed.

Ten minutes later the door opened again. I focused my binoculars on it, but at first saw little. Then another man appeared and, the door closing behind him, walked down the path, got into a Chevy, and drove off. Five minutes later another car arrived, this time with two men. They both walked up to the house and went in, again without knocking.

If this was a party, there was a peculiar lack of couples.

Another guy came out, got into his car and left, alone.

I'm not the world's greatest detective, but I was starting to realize that what I was watching was one of those whorehouses Goff had told me Ashford sported. I felt a little thrill at that. If I could catch Masters at a whorehouse while he was on duty, that would surely finish him.

On the other hand, there was no way I'd be able to get in there to catch him. And how could I prove anything? I had my camera, but it wasn't anything complicated. It wouldn't take pictures at night at this range, not with the film I had in it. I'd need something that could see in the dark, one of those infrared jobbies. Without a picture I couldn't prove the bum was here. He'd just say I was out to get him, which was true, of course.

I picked up the mike, then hesitated. How could I ask Toby to send a car to Ashford? And whom would I have him send? The nearest car would be Pczchornek in Zone 9. I wasn't very confident he'd back me up about seeing Masters.

The question became academic then as the door opened and Masters strolled out, then sauntered around to the back. A few moments later his car drove around the house, across the lawn, and out onto the street, then past me and down the street.

I'd held my breath but the darkness and the hedge next to my car apparently blocked his sight. I watched him go, cursing under my breath, vowing to get an infrared camera for next time.

I gazed at the house again, then saw something I hadn't noticed before. It was one of the cars parked next to it, in the driveway. It was a silver Jaguar. I frowned, then picked up the binoculars and focused it on the license. It was FISHER. I remembered seeing it in Erika Fisher's driveway when I was looking for her prowler.

I figured at first that her father must be there, and thought unpleasant things about him. Then I remembered what Goff had said about the girl, that she hooked sometimes.

I sat back and watched.

19

M en came and went, usually by themselves. Around three Erika came out and got into the Jag, pulled out onto the road and headed back toward her place. I started the engine and followed.

At fifteen she wouldn't have a driver's license, and even if she did I was willing to bet Daddy didn't let her drive his Jag. He probably didn't let her stay out till three in the morning either, most especially not at whorehouses.

I let her get home, then closed the distance between our cars rapidly, pulling in off the road just as she was getting out of the Jag. She turned, blinking in surprise when my headlights focused on her. She didn't move as I parked, turned off the lights, then got out and walked around the Jag to stand in front of her.

I'd half expected her to be in some kind of leather miniskirt or something, like the hookers wore in L.A., but she was in jeans and T-shirt, looking entirely suburban. She was obviously wary about the timing of my visit, slumping and looking at me from under her eyelids.

"Hi, Erika," I said.

"Hi," she said sullenly.

"Father home?"

"No, he's away again."

"Already? He just got back. Last Wednesday, wasn't it?"

"Yeah, he's just gone overnight."

"Uh-huh." I paused but she didn't volunteer anything else.

"Where you been?" I asked.

"Just driving around."

"Around Ashford?"

She shrugged and looked more sullen.

"How much you make tonight, Erika?"

She shrugged again.

"Why don't we go inside and talk?"

Another shrug. She turned and moved to the door, though, as I followed. She unlocked it and stomped across the floor into the living room, then turned and fell heavily into one of the armchairs, folding her arms across her chest and scowling at me rebelliously.

"How long you been working there?" I asked, sitting on the sofa across from her.

She shrugged again.

I looked around at the luxury surrounding me.

"Nice place," I said. "You obviously aren't hooking for food money." I turned back to her, but she didn't reply.

"I'm not gonna bust you, kid. I'm just curious," I said. "How long?"

Another shrug. "Couple years," she said.

"How come?"

"Something to do. Gives me money for clothes and stuff."

"Your dad doesn't give you money?"

"Not enough."

"Not worried about catching something?"

"If I die, I die," she said flatly.

"Poor little rich girl, is that it?"

She gave me a scornful look, then turned her head to examine the far wall.

"Daddy doesn't love me so I'll go and find some other man who will? Think they'll love you if you fuck them?"

She turned her gaze back to me, eyes cool. "Long as they pay me, I don't give a shit," she said.

"Tough, aren't you?"

"Look, what do you want?" she demanded. "You said you weren't gonna bust me, so why don't you just fuck off somewhere?"

"I got nothing better to do. We discussed that the last time I was here."

"Oh, right, so you're gonna stay here and comfort the poor little rich girl, is that it?" she sneered, voice rising. "Want me to cry on your shoulders and tell you all about my terrible, deprived life? What makes me do such a terrible thing? Well, don't fucking count on it! Or maybe you think you're gonna talk me out of it. Think you can convince me to become a pure little virgin again? Go ahead and try. I could use a good laugh."

"I'm not a social worker, kid," I said. "I'm not Dear Abby either."

"Then why don't you get the fuck out of my house!" she snapped.

"You don't look very pretty with your face all scrunched up and red like that," I commented.

She stared at me blankly, then scowled again. "I really fuckin' care!" she sneered. "Unless you're a customer, of course. Want to fuck me, lady? Cost you a hundred bucks. I'll get all prettied up if you like." Her hands went to her shirt and she slowly lifted it up, taunting me. She pulled it over her bare breasts and slid her tongue along her lower lip in what she probably thought of as a sexy pose.

"What I'd like to do is haul you across my knee," I said.

She let out a whoop of laughter. "That costs extra, lady," she exclaimed. "Especially if you wanna tie me up. Course, you cops have your own handcuffs. I should give you a discount for that."

"You think a cop would screw a whore like you?" I said, sneering right back.

"Oh, fuck! Shit! You are so fuckin' dumb, lady!" She laughed.

"I'm dumb, huh?" I snorted.

"The first guy, my first fuckin' customer, was a cop. Okay?"

"Bullshit."

"He was the fuckin' guy that told me about Boomers! He fuckin' drove me there the first time!" she exclaimed, laughing over my ignorance.

"When you were thirteen? I don't think so," I said dismissively. "No cop would screw around with a little girl."

"Oh, right," she snorted. "Cops around here are such perfect fuckin' people. She rolled her eyes toward the ceiling.

"So how much did he pay you the first time?" I demanded.

"First time? Fifty bucks. I was dumb then. Now I know what things cost."

"Masters always was a cheap fucker."

She shrugged again.

"One thing I'd like to know," I said. "How could you let someone as ugly as him screw you?"

"Just close your eyes and pretend it's Mel Gibson," she said, smirking.

"So Masters drove you there the first time, eh? In his patrol car?"

"I didn't say it was him."

"But it was."

Another fucking shrug. I was really getting tired of them.

"I saw him at Boomers tonight."

"So?" she glared suspiciously.

"Was he with you?"

"No."

"Wanted someone better-looking, huh?" I taunted.

"I'm better-looking than you, honey." She smirked.

"But a lot less expensive."

She snorted and looked away.

"Tell me all about him."

"I got nothing to say," she sniffed, examining her nails.

"Do you know how easy it is to arrest someone for prostitution?" I asked.

She shrugged.

"Do you know it's the policy of the *Herald* to print the names of anyone arrested for any crime right on the front page?"

She looked at me warily.

"I could drag you into the station and book you for prostitution right now. Tomorrow your name, and probably a picture from your high school yearbook, would be on page one as a hooker. Think your friends at school would like that?"

"You said you weren't—"

"I don't like your fucking attitude!" I yelled.

She flinched back and I felt like a bitch, bullying her. But dammit, I needed to get through to her. I wasn't unconcerned about her being a whore, but I'd seen so many teenage whores in my life that I'd given up trying to reform them. In Vice, you went for the pimps. Masters might not be a pimp, but he was still a piece of slime. I wanted information on Masters, information that would at least get him fired and might put the bastard in jail before he found some other little girl and convinced her that whoring was a good career.

I remembered Goff's tales of how interested Masters was in high school girls. Was this a hobby of his or was he into it in some professional way?

"Tell me how you came to meet Masters," I said, keeping my voice hard.

She looked sullen again, but wary, a little scared. She wasn't a tough kid, not like the street whores I'd known. She was probably whoring now partly for money, partly for kicks, partly for some kind of psychological thing, getting back at Daddy for abandoning her, maybe.

"He gave me a ride home one day," she said sulkily.

"From where?"

"School."

"And he suggested right out of the blue that you should become a prostitute?"

She rolled her eyes upward and looked away.

"I don't want any more smart-ass looks, kid. Tell me the truth."

"He dropped by one night, you know, when I was home by myself. He saw the lights on."

"And?"

"And nothing. He dropped by a few more times, you know, when he was in this zone. He was kind of sleazy, but . . . I don't know, I guess I didn't mind."

"What do you mean, sleazy?"

"You know, the way he looked at me, the things he said, like how nice-looking I was, and what a hot body I had, stuff like that. I knew he wanted to fuck me."

"So you let him?"

She flushed a little and shrugged. "After a while. He said I was really hot. I told him how my dad never gave me enough money for stuff and he told me about Boomers.

"He said men would go crazy over me." She gave me an arrogant look. "He said I could make lots of money and have some fun, so I did. So what? Big fuckin' deal. I wasn't a fuckin' virgin anyway. Why not get paid for it?"

"What about this Boomer guy? What's he like?"

She gave me a pitying look. "Boomer isn't a guy. There is no Boomer. It's just a name. The place used to be a Chink whorehouse, and they called fucking 'boom-boom,' y'know, like, 'Let's make boom-boom.' "

"There any Asian girls there now?"

"Sure."

"How many?"

"I don't know, half of 'em."

"They local?"

"Most of 'em don't even speak English."

"I'm starting to get the picture."

And I was, in more ways than one. If Masters was helping whomever it was who ran the whorehouse, procuring young girls for him, maybe he had had a hand in getting that Thai girl. Maybe Sims had been delivering her for him. Had the whorehouse owners killed Sims, or had Masters done it?

"You know any other cops, like a guy named Allan Sims?"

She shook her head.

"You never saw him at Boomers?"

"I don't know. I don't know what the guy looks like," she said sullenly.

"Masters ever bring anyone over here?"

"What do you mean?"

"Come on, honey. I'm sure Masters didn't stop visiting just because you turned pro. I bet he drops by here now and then, and he seems like the kind of guy who'd introduce a find like you to his buddies."

"What's that supposed to mean, a find like me?" she demanded.

"A whore," I said shortly. "You're not Erika Fisher, straight-A student and high school fashion queen, you're just a dirty little whore, and I'm a cop."

"You got no reason to talk to me like that," she said, lip quivering.

"You know about status, Erika? On the scale of life, hookers have just about the lowest status around. Everybody looks down their noses at them. Even the men who screw you think of you as a cheap whore. You think they're impressed by you? Try showing up around their kids someday. See how fast they get rid of you. They don't want someone like you hanging around their sons or daughters."

"You're just jealous, you bitch," she said, eyes watery.

"You've been hanging around adults, all hyped because you can get them all excited. You think that makes you special or something? You think that makes you mature and sophisticated? I bet you do. I bet you think how much more mature you are than your friends. Face it, kid. You're just a cheap blonde for rent."

"You get out of my house, you fuckin' bitch!" she demanded, voice breaking. She rubbed her arm angrily across her face. She jumped to her feet and marched toward the stairs. I jumped up and grabbed her, whirling her around and shoving her against the wall.

"Let me go!" she yelled.

"You've seen it on TV shows, baby," I said, forcing her legs apart, slapping her hands flat against the wall. "Go on, assume the position. I want you to get used to it."

"Leave me alone!" she sobbed.

I didn't. I shoved her hard against the wall and ran my hands roughly over her body. I pulled out several fifties from her pocket and put them in my breast pocket, then pulled her hands behind her back again, not gently, and cuffed them together.

"You know, kid," I panted, shaking my head to clear the hair out of my eyes. "Every hooker in L.A. remembers the first time she got busted."

I gripped her hair, jerking her back from the wall and twisting her around. She cried out in pain.

"They were always scared and embarrassed, and always sure that would be the last time, but then they went back to selling their pussies on the street. I gave up feeling sorry for them a long time ago. So you can quit your sniveling. It's not gaining you any sympathy. Nobody has much sympathy for hookers."

I held her arm tightly as I led her toward the front door.

She struggled to pull away, getting panicky.

"Please! Don't!" she begged.

"Maybe Masters will come and bail you out before your father gets home," I said.

I jerked the door open and pulled the struggling girl into the front yard, then over to my patrol car. I opened the rear door and forced her inside, then slammed it shut behind her.

She spent most of the ride there crying, sobs interspaced with pleas to let her go and promises not to hook ever again. I ignored her, refusing to talk. I was being intentionally coldhearted. The truth was, though I had indeed arrested scores, hundreds, of teenage hookers in L.A., I always felt sorry for them, particularly the new ones.

Besides, I'd kind of liked Erika the first time I met her. She had seemed nice enough, a vulnerable, lonely kid. I was not enjoying playing a bully. But Erika, though she'd been hobbying as a hooker for a couple of years, was still far from hardened. At fifteen, pretty and rich, she still had the idea that everyone would fall at her feet and be nice to her if she just pouted enough. A good shock now might wise her up, make her find another hobby.

I wasn't being completely altruistic, of course. As I said,

I've had lots of experience with teenage hookers. I wasn't about to put a major effort into reforming this one. But there were pictures at the station of the other cops. I wanted her to look at one of Sims, and I wanted her shaken enough to come clean about Masters and his friends.

I got a call from Toby just before I reached Madison, about a domestic dispute. I told him I was busy, coming in with a prisoner, and to give it to Haggar, who was working Zone 7.

I put her in the cage and let her sit there for a few minutes, then went to the file room to get pictures of the rest of the Monster Squad. I went back to her, let her out, then proceeded with a modified form of booking. That included all the usual—fingerprinting, pictures, arrest reports, as well as questions about any sexual diseases she had. I also made her strip in front of me and change into an orange prisoner's jumpsuit. Normally that wasn't done until they got to County. Ironically enough, we'd gotten a few in smaller sizes because of the Thai girl, so I had one that fit her.

I told her she'd be deloused and have to undergo an internal-cavity search at the county jail, then threw her back in the cage for twenty minutes.

I destroyed the reports, fingerprints and pictures, then had a coffee while I waited. When I went back for her and led her down the hall and put her in an interrogation room, she was docile, miserable, and seemed much smaller and younger than before. I undid her cuffs, which I'd kept on the entire time, except while she changed, then sat down across the table from her.

She didn't look at me but stared down at the table, her long bangs hiding much of her face.

I had to fight the urge to go around the table and hug her, tell her everything was going to be all right and I was going to let her go. A lot of cops got compassion fatigue after a while, but I hadn't quite reached that stage myself yet.

I rapped the table to get her attention. She didn't look up.

"Look up at me," I snapped.

She gazed at me dispiritedly, looking at me without meeting my eyes.

I laid out some pictures, some of the Monster Squad, some of dummies. Dummies were just pictures we had on file to include with any picture IDs. I had no idea who the men were, only that they didn't live in this state.

"I want you to tell me if you know any of these men," I said.

"Can I call my dad?" she asked in a small voice.

"No. Look at the pictures. Tell me who you know."

Christ, I felt like shit.

She looked down at them, her eyes moving slowly over the dozen or so pictures I'd placed there. Her hands reached out and hesitantly pointed at Masters's picture, then Sims's, then Ford's.

"I want you to tell me when and where you saw them, and what they were doing."

"At my house," she said. "And at Boomers."

"When?"

"Billy brought them to see me a few weeks after we started . . . having sex; first this one"—she pointed at Sims—"then this one."

"Did they pay you money?"

She shook her head.

"How many times did they come to your house?"

"Just sometimes," she said, sounding half-dazed. "A couple of times a month with Billy."

"When was the last time you saw either of them?"

"Not for a couple of weeks."

"What about him? Ford?" I asked, pointing at his picture.

"I don't know, maybe a month or two."

"You on drugs?"

"No."

239

"They'll test you at County. If you're lying to me I'm gonna be really pissed."

"Just . . . some grass sometimes, that's all. I don't do hard stuff."

"You want a medal?"

She glowered sullenly.

"When you were at Boomers, did you recognize any girls from your school?"

She snorted in disgust and sat back in the chair. "Just one," she said. "That little snot Ginian Tyler. What a fuckin' laugh."

"Ginian . . . the Reverend . . ."

"The dumb cow in the papers. The one that got tossed out the door bare-assed naked by her old man."

"She worked at Boomers?" I asked doubtfully.

"Fuckin' right."

"You're just saying that because you read about her in the papers."

"Bullshit, lady! She was the S and M queen! She acted so fucking snotty and holy at school, then she'd go to Boomers and get tied up and whipped. What a fuckin' joke!"

"Why would she work there?"

"How do I know? Maybe she got her rocks off that way."

"Anyone ever whip you there?"

"Fuck, no. No way I'd go for that shit. Sometimes they'd do, like, bondage, y'know, but that was okay. I didn't mind that too much. But Ginian would go in the Red Room and they'd beat her with belts and canes and shit like that. Sometimes she'd have to be carried out."

"What's the Red Room?"

"It's soundproofed, so you wouldn't hear her screaming, her or the Chinks they made work there, or sometimes the men, the clients, y'know, the ones liked getting whipped by girls."

240

"Did they make Ginian go there?"

"I don't know," she groaned. She put her elbows on the table and covered her eyes with the palms of her hands, rubbing them, then sat back in her chair again. "I don't think so. They never tried to make me. It's mostly Chink girls, cause they haven't got any choice."

"Ginian use drugs?"

"I don't fuckin' know, okay! We didn't hang around together, there or at school. She was a fuckin' snot!"

"Keep your voice down," I snarled.

She looked rebellious and folded her arms across her chest. "I have a problem with this whole story," I said, scowling. "If Ginian worked there, then why would she tell her father she was pregnant? She told me she had to tell him because she didn't have the money for an abortion."

"Yeah, well, that's bullshit. All she'd've had to do was tell James Earl and he would've had her done. Anyway, she had money. She was always flashing it at school. Getting your ass whipped pays big money."

"So why didn't you try it?"

"I told you, I don't go for that shit."

I stared at her. She was definitely losing some of her fear, starting to get snotty again. "Pity," I said. "You'll probably get a lot of it at County. There's a lot of old, fat lesbians there just love beating up pretty little things like you."

She looked sullen and said nothing.

"Sometimes they cut up your face. They're old and ugly and jealous, so they scar you so nobody else will want you. That's after they gang-bang you a few times, of course. You ever been gang-banged by women, Erika?"

I slammed my hand on the table and she jerked her eyes up at me.

"I asked you a question."

"No!" she cried.

"Ever do it with women? Sometimes they're easier on you if you're really good in bed."

"Leave me alone!" she cried.

"It's gonna be some change from that nice place of yours to a cramped little cell with three lesbian women in it."

"You're just . . . trying to scare me," she gulped. "My dad won't let me stay there, anyway."

"You sure of that? Remember what Ginian's father did when he found out she'd been screwing around? What'll your proud daddy do when he finds out his sweet little virgin girl works in a whorehouse screwing anyone with money in his hand? Maybe he'll just let you stay there, let you learn a lesson."

"You're just mean!" she cried, her voice breaking.

"Yeah, kind of. But you ought to see the matrons at County. Guess what they do with their nightsticks."

"You don't scare m-me," she said, her voice breaking.

"Just warning you what to expect."

She looked down at her lap, blond bangs hiding her face.

"That night when you called the police, were you just trying to get Masters over there? Did you think it was his zone that night?"

She looked up, blinking back tears for a moment before dropping her eyes again. "One of the . . . customers followed me home. He wanted to come in."

"Why didn't you let him?"

"He scared me," she said, looking up.

"There's lots of scary people in your business. That's why every whore needs a good pimp to protect her."

She winced and looked down at the table again.

"Course usually it's the pimps that wind up killing you. They're a real nasty bunch."

"I don't have a . . . a . . . pimp," she said, voice quavering.

242

"I'm sure you can find one," I said dismissively.

"I'm not going to . . . I'm going to stop," she whimpered.

"Yeah, right. I've heard that before. Anyway, how else are you gonna feed yourself when your father kicks you out of the house? You'll have to work full-time for Boomers. That's once you get out of jail, of course."

I couldn't get a lot else out of her. All she knew about Sims and Ford was that Masters sometimes brought them by to screw her. She didn't know if they worked for Boomers, though she'd never seen them doing anything there but what all the other men were doing. She had the vague idea that Masters worked for Boomers, but not what he did.

I gathered her clothes in a bag, put the cuffs back on her and led her back to the car, supposedly to take her to the county lockup. She kept her head bowed most of the way home and showed no sign of recognition until I pulled into her driveway and stopped beside the Jag.

I let her out and removed the cuffs, then shoved the bag at her. She looked up at me in confusion.

"I decided to give you another chance," I said.

She looked at the house, then back at me.

"I'll dump the pictures and reports. You can keep the jumpsuit as a reminder." I took out the money I'd removed from her earlier and handed it to her. She looked at it without speaking.

"Maybe you can keep the money with that jumpsuit. They kind of go together anyway."

She looked up at me again.

"You were never gonna arrest me, were you," she said dully.

"Nope. I told you that before."

She didn't say anything for long seconds, though she continued to stare at me. "That was . . . that was really shitty," she said, swallowing rapidly, blinking.

"Yeah. It was."

She took a deep breath, then, trembling slightly, turned and walked toward the door.

"I didn't do it to be mean, Erika," I called after her. "I did it to show you your future. If you think this was rough, kid, wait until you meet the matrons and prisoners at the county lockup. I wasn't kidding about them and what they do to pretty young girls."

Which was why she never would have been sent there, of course. She'd have wound up at Juvenile. I didn't see the need to mention that, of course.

She fumbled in the bag, searching for her keys, then dropped it. She squatted beside it, then pulled her pants out of the bag and jammed her hand into the pocket. She was shaking slightly, and as she rose she dropped the keys. She eased down to her knees, then started to shake. She hugged herself, rocking back and forth as she cried.

I picked up the keys and unlocked the door, then lifted her to her feet and brought her inside. I made coffee while she sat at the table sobbing. By the time it was ready she'd mostly cried herself out, and was just sniffling a little. I slid the coffee in front of her and stroked her head. She jerked away, rubbing her arm across her face.

"Sorry, kid. But I wasn't just saying it. Things would be a lot rougher at the county jail, a lot rougher. I didn't have the heart to beat you up and didn't have the inclination to rape you. Those bitches would rip a pretty little thing like you apart."

"Go away," she whispered.

I squeezed her shoulder, then left. Maybe she'd thank me one day. That's what my parents always used to say when they did something shitty to me. On the other hand, maybe I'd just given her a scary, miserable night. Maybe tomorrow she'd be back at Boomers taking comfort from the men who told her how pretty and sexy she was.

Sometimes being a cop isn't a lot of fun.

244

20

I didn't sleep well or long. The phone woke me up. I was surly and ready to take someone's head off, but when I picked it up, all I got was a dial tone. The ringing didn't stop either.

That was when I realized it was the cellular phone, and the only one who had the number was the autodial machine sitting in the living room. Comprehension was just dawning, and I had just swung my legs around to get out of bed when the sound of breaking glass, followed by a gunshot, made me dive onto the floor.

The alarm bell rang frantically as another shot followed the first, then another, and another and another. Whoever was outside emptied what sounded like a rifle into my window. The fourth or fifth shot collapsed the whole window in a shower of glass as I fumbled behind the bed for the shotgun.

Heart pounding, I raised my head slightly, gazing out the window into the woods facing me, then turned and looked behind at the wall. All the bullets had hit it in a straight line from the window, which placed the gunman directly in front of it. I couldn't see anything in the woods, though.

He fired again, and I thought I saw movement behind a bush. I raised the riot gun and fired the whole clip, spraying ten loads of buckshot around that area.

There was no reply. I tugged the entire drawer out of my nightstand and, hands shaking, fumbled the box of shells open, reloading. I waited a minute, then crawled over to the other side of the room and put my pants on, stuffing my night-shirt in, then pulling on a pair of boots. I debated which door to use on the way out, then decided to use the deck, and drop down to the ground from there.

I shinnied down one of the supporting poles, thinking, as I did, what a great target I'd be for anyone coming around the house.

Nobody did. I moved to the corner and then, using the low hill for protection, ran sideways into the woods.

I wasn't exactly a Camp Fire girl, and creeping noiselessly through the forest was not among my talents. I had to move slowly, very slowly. There's nothing more frightening than moving around trying to find a gunman, and not having any idea where he was. I kept low and tried to keep a large tree at my back at all times.

By the time I'd made my way around to where the gunfire had come from, sirens were getting pretty loud, competing with the ringing alarm bell for decibel count.

Crouching low, I moved among the trees and bushes, sweating, sure of getting shot at any moment. I kept turning around quickly, thinking surely he was behind me, ready to shoot.

A patrol car shrieked down the lane and pulled to a halt in front of my place, kicking up a cloud of dust. The siren cut out and the cop got out, clutching his shotgun, crouching as he hurried to the door.

"Up here!" I called.

He whirled and pointed the gun.

"I think he's gone," I said, "but watch yourself anyway."

Another cruiser, siren wailing, ground to a halt near the first. I kept low as the two men started carefully forward. I still wasn't sure the gunman, likely Masters, was gone.

I was a little worried too that these two day-shift guys wouldn't know me, but a third car raced down the lane, halting suddenly as the driver saw the two deputies advancing toward the woods. Another cop I didn't recognize got out on the driver's side, and the sheriff got out the passenger door.

"O'Neil?" he called.

"Over here, Sheriff."

"You all right?"

"Yeah."

The four of them joined me at just about the same time. I stood up gingerly and looked around.

"The shooting was coming from around here," I said.

"What was it, rifle or handgun?"

"Rifle, sounded like a thirty-thirty."

"Everybody spread out, let's make sure he's gone," Bradford said.

Another car arrived, and the six of us scoured the area, finding half a dozen shells, some footprints, and a lot of torn-up shrubbery where my buckshot had hit.

"Any idea who it was?" Bradford asked.

"I think we both know."

He set his jaw and scowled.

"Come on back to the house. I want to show you something," I said.

He sent three of the deputies away, but Goff and Ed Dunmore, the day-shift sergeant, arrived to replace them. Dunmore dug the spent bullets out of my wall as I showed Bradford and Goff the receiver and relay setup I had.

"And it rang just before the gunfire started?" Goff asked.

"Maybe twenty or thirty seconds before."

"What's the range on this?" Bradford asked.

"No more than a hundred yards."

They looked at each other.

"You realize that this is completely inadmissible," Bradford said. "You had no warrant to bug his car. In fact, doing it was illegal."

"I didn't bug his car with the idea of arresting him for any crime, Sheriff," I said tiredly. "I just wanted a warning if he was going to vandalize my house again."

"Did you bug his patrol car too?" Goff asked.

I nodded and he snorted in amusement. "He couldn't figure out how you found him that night."

"Those bullet holes are too high to have hit you," Bradford said. "He was just having fun."

"There's something else you better know about him," I said. Then I told them about what I'd found last night, and what Erika had told me.

"Shit," Goff said, then looked apologetically at Bradford.

Bradford ignored him, though, looking thoughtfully out the window.

"I'm not sure about the legal technicalities of that," I said. "I don't know if we're allowed to bug our own patrol cars."

"I don't see why not," Goff said.

"The girl's testimony is completely inadmissible, of course," Bradford said. "You could be sued for false arrest there, you know. The fact that you saw her coming out of what you thought was a whorehouse in another jurisdiction hardly gave you the right to enter her house, search her, then put her in cuffs. Nor are you permitted to question her without parental approval or a lawyer present."

"I knew all that. I wasn't planning on arresting her. I just wanted information on Masters and . . . I was hoping to throw

248

a scare into her, maybe make her decide hooking wasn't such a good hobby."

"If her father finds out . . ."

"He won't do anything. He won't want his daughter linked with prostitution in any way, shape, or form."

He nodded slowly.

"It points to Masters, but it doesn't give us a good reason why he'd kill Sims," I said.

Again they looked at each other, then Bradford sat back on the sofa and gave a little smile.

"Sims was working undercover for the state police," he said.

"Sims?!"

"They caught him using his badge to rip off drug dealers in Carson Grove. They decided to use him to get information on the Ashford police, to nose around there. What he was concentrating on was the relationship between the authorities there and the whorehouses."

"He had managed to ingratiate himself with the people there, and did a few odd jobs for them. He knew the place was owned by James Earl Clubb, but he had information there was a second partner, a cop."

"Naturally he thought it was one of the Ashford cops," Goff interjected.

"Naturally," Bradford sighed. "On the night he was murdered, he had been sent to pick up a hooker brought over from Thailand, the girl you found in his trunk. He was supposed to deliver her to someone, we think Clubb's partner."

"He never told them anything about Masters being involved with Clubb?" I asked.

"We hadn't heard anything about that. It's possible he didn't know."

"But if Masters was inviting him in to share Erika's charms . . ."

"At her house. We didn't know that either. Besides, that doesn't mean anything. So Masters visited a whorehouse? So he liked to have sex with this girl? So what? None of that indicates a hard link with Clubb. I'm sure he's not the only cop who's gone to that whorehouse for pleasure instead of business."

"Except it was business for him," I said.

"Maybe."

"Suppose he didn't know about Sims?" Goff said.

"What?"

"He was supposed to meet some guy and pick up a whore. Suppose he meets Sims. Sims puts two and two together, realizes it's Masters who's the silent partner. Masters doesn't want him knowing, so he kills him."

"Why should Masters be afraid of that?" I asked.

"Maybe he knew Sims was working for the staties. Sims had a big mouth. He liked to drink too. He might have told Masters about his working for the state police. After all, he had no idea Masters was the silent partner in that whorehouse."

"But why kill him with the girl in the trunk?" I protested. "That just points right at the whorehouse."

"It might have been a sudden impulse. If he didn't know it would be Sims. If he was just told there'd be a car parked on Beckle and the girl would be in it, then found Sims, what would he do?"

"He'd go over and ask him what he was doing there out of his zone," I said.

"And Sims would ask him the same. It would have to occur to both what had happened," Goff said.

"But how could Sims work for the whorehouse if Masters knew he was working for the staties?"

"And wouldn't Masters have told James Earl about Sims?" Bradford said.

"I got to know Sims a lot more than I would have liked," Goff said. "He wouldn't have told anyone. What he would have done is hint a lot, very smugly. He probably wouldn't have been taken very seriously by anyone."

"But Masters would have been damn suspicious if he found him on Beckle at the meeting place," I said.

"And Sims wasn't much of a quick thinker." Goff smiled sadly. "His normal response to being caught at something while I was his supervisor was to stammer and stutter and come up with a totally unbelievable lie."

"Masters decides to off him right then and there." Bradford nodded.

"We could ask the rest of the Monster Squad if Sims ever talked or hinted about him working for the state police," I said thoughtfully.

"That's not gonna prove anything," Goff said.

"Circumstantial evidence," Bradford said. "We're not going to get any hard evidence on this if it was him. Nobody saw him do it. No way he's stupid enough to still have the gun on him."

"But if it was a surprise he'd have probably used his service revolver," I said.

"He didn't carry one, he used his own three forty-seven Magnum."

"What kind of gun killed Sims?"

"A three forty-seven Magnum."

"If Masters can't produce it, that's another piece of evidence," Goff said.

"The girl links him to Boomers, that's another," I said.

"Don't count on it," Bradford said. "Let's look at this realistically. I don't think there's any way in hell Fisher is going to let his daughter get up in court and testify that she's a whore. So forget her testimony. Forget about this too." He waved around him. "The bug you have on his car is clearly illegal, so we have nothing but suspicions that he's involved here. As for your following him to Boomers, so what? So he went to a whorehouse? Proves nothing. Fact is, we got zilch in the way of hard evidence."

"If the state police can do a check on his bank accounts, find out where he's putting extra money . . ." I started.

"If they find money he can't account for, that's something." Bradford nodded. "But it doesn't prove murder."

"We need to be able to prove he was the silent partner," Goff said. "The guy Sims was supposed to meet."

"The guy who runs that place might not want a murder rap," I said. "He's probably very unhappy about that. He might be able to deal, give up Masters in exchange for immunity."

"I don't like panderers," Bradford glared. "Especially panderers who sell underage girls."

"I don't either, Sheriff, but getting a cop killer is more important than getting a pimp," I said.

"I suppose," he grunted. "Though Sims wasn't much of a cop."

"He was killed in the line of duty," Goff pointed out.

"Only because he was blackmailed into it," Bradford scowled.

"But what I don't get is why James Earl Clubb would send Sims, would even bring him into things, without consulting Masters. I mean, it seems an obvious thing to do. They're both on the same shift on the same force. Why wouldn't he have consulted Masters?"

"We'll ask him when we find him," Bradford said.

Bradford and Goff left to visit the state police investigators and tell them what they'd learned. As for me, after Fred Cunnard had found a plywood board and nailed it across my bedroom window, I went to sleep . . . again.

* * *

My sleep was undisturbed, and I woke eager to find out what had turned up that day. Unfortunately, it is the plight of the shift worker that everyone you want to talk to has already gone home by the time you climb out of bed. I didn't feel confident enough of my relationship with Bradford to call him at home, but I did call Goff, figuring what the hell, so what if he is pissed off?

He wasn't. But he wasn't very enlightening either. They hadn't been able to find any sign of James Earl Clubb, and Erika had refused even to talk to the state police. Masters had produced his .347 and it had been sent to the state crime lab. Their immediate suspicion, based on a close inspection of the gun, was that it was Masters's, but that the barrel had been recently replaced. They were checking local gun shops now to see if Masters had been in one. As for him having extra money, that would take time.

It wasn't, of course, my job to investigate murders, but there isn't a cop alive who doesn't want the ultimate of all investigations. The dumbest flatfoot in L.A., Miami, or Kansas City always wants to be a detective, and every detective wants to work on homicides. They are the top of the charts as far as prestige and excitement are concerned.

Besides, I hated that bald bastard. I'd hated him even before talking to Erika, but after learning he was a filthy pimp I really loathed the bastard.

Masters didn't show up for work that night, having been suspended. Even with no real evidence on the man, Bradford simply couldn't stomach the idea of him driving around in one of our patrol cars again. Goff said Masters was finished, one way or the other. And screw what the mayor thought of it.

I didn't miss him. I was able to talk to a couple of the monsters. Haggar confirmed, in a bored tone, and with much nose rubbing, that Sims had hinted about being an undercover agent of some sorts.

"He was always full of shit, anyway," he said. "Who the fuck cared what he said?"

Pczchornek was less helpful, though he shared the same sentiment. "The guy was an asshole. Why the fuck would I listen to him anyway?"

Ford, who'd been called back to replace Masters, said he'd tell me anything I wanted if I'd give him a blow job.

"Don't you get enough of that from Erika Fisher?" I asked. The sneer on his face dropped off immediately and he took on a wary look.

"I don't know what you're talkin' about," he snapped.

"Funny, Erika told me how Masters would take you and Sims over there for fun and games."

"She's full of shit!"

"I don't think so, Ford. I think you're guilty of statutory rape."

"Bullshit! Prove it!"

"Who do you think they'll believe, Ford—you or sweet little Erika with the big blue eyes and the golden hair?"

"That slut! Nobody'd believe her."

"Why do you call her a slut?"

"She's . . . everybody knows," he said lamely.

"Why don't you just save yourself the trouble and answer my question about Sims?"

"I hardly knew him," he said sullenly.

"He didn't mention anything while you and him were banging the little girl?" I asked.

"I never—"

"Yeah, yeah. Tell me what he said, not where he said it."

"He said something about being some kind of detective, something about being undercover, you know, nudge-nudge, wink-wink, that kind of shit. The guy was a jerk-off. I didn't pay any attention to him." he said.

"Uh-huh."

"That all?" he demanded.

"Yeah. See Erika about the blow job."

"I told you—"

"Yeah, right. You're too much of a prince to screw around with underage girls."

I assigned myself to Zone 9, though there wasn't a lot I could do there. Erika had said her dad was away for just last night, so it wasn't likely I could ask her more questions. I should have asked Goff if Daddy had been home when he'd called on her. Still, I could keep an eye on Boomers, and that area, see if Masters showed, or Clubb.

I'd found a picture of Clubb on file. He had a record for alcohol, drug and weapons offenses. How he'd gotten a license for his strip club was a mystery I'd leave to the state investigators.

Before going into the zone I dropped by Masters's house. The lights were out and I saw no sign of his car, and there was no garage at the dump he lived in. I adjusted the receiver in my car to the frequency the second bug was on but got nothing.

I drove past Erika's house, but everything there was quiet. I kept the bug turned on all night, hoping to pass near wherever Masters had parked. I drove through Ashford a couple of times but didn't pick up a peep.

At eight I saw Bradford. He didn't know where Masters was either, and had no further information. I headed home, but then had another thought.

I hadn't mentioned Ginian Tyler to Bradford, mostly because I wasn't sure if Erika had been bullshitting me, but at least partly because I wasn't sure just how close he and the

Reverend were. I didn't want Ginian getting into more trouble than she already had.

I drove to her aunt's place, a farmhouse a few miles outside town. It was early, but country people, as I'd soon learned, tended to be early risers. Anyway, Ginian had to be at school at nine.

Her aunt seemed surprised to see me, as did Ginian. The atmosphere in the big country kitchen was happy and light, with five kids there besides Ginian. She looked a bit embarrassed as her aunt led me inside, but greeted me politely enough.

Her aunt and uncle were a little dubious about our talking privately, but finally agreed to let the girl come out back with me.

"Is this something about my father's case?" she asked as we walked toward a rough wood fence.

"Well, not really, no. How're you doing here?"

"Okay." She shrugged. "Uncle Jim and Aunt Karen are a lot nicer than my parents."

"How's your back?"

"Huh?"

"Your back, where your father used his belt."

"Oh. Um . . . okay."

"That was an awful thing for him to do."

"Yeah." She nodded, pushing her glasses back on her nose.

"He didn't even pay for it."

"What?"

"Well, he didn't pay you, did he?"

She looked at me in confusion, but the confusion gave way to a sudden wariness that made me certain Erika had been telling the truth. "How much do you usually get for that kind of thing?"

"I don't know what you're talking about," she said coldly.

"Sure you do."

256

"I don't."

"I know all about it, Ginian."

"About what?"

"About Boomers."

"I never heard of it."

"Tell me, were those marks from your father, or had you been working earlier?"

"I don't know what you're talking about," she said, raising her voice angrily.

"I've been talking to Erika Fisher."

"She's a lying little slut!"

"Also been talking to James Earl."

She opened her mouth, then closed it, licked her lips and looked behind her. "He's lying too," she hissed, turning back and scowling at me.

"I'm not here to arrest you, Ginian. And I don't plan on telling people how you earn your spending money, not unless I have to."

"I don't have to listen to this," she snapped, turning toward the house.

I gripped her arm and swung her around again. "Listen to me, you little bitch. I'm investigating a murder. You can either help me or I'll make sure everybody in the county finds out what your part-time job is."

"Go ahead!" she cried, shoving me back. "I don't care! See how the great Reverend Tyler explains that!"

"It won't just hurt him, you know. It'll hurt your aunt and uncle too."

"They won't care," she said with less certainty.

"Won't they? What will they think about having a prostitute living with their kids? They seem like nice people, but . . ." I shook my head worriedly. "When they hear what Erika and James Earl say, who knows what they'll do."

"It's just their word against mine," she said sullenly.

"They have no reason to lie about you. Why don't you just answer my questions. Then there's no reason anyone has to find out."

"What do you want to know?" she demanded, scowling furiously.

"How did you start working there, and when?"

She looked as if she wouldn't answer, then she tossed her head, shoved her hair back and said, "About a year. I ran away from home and went to Ashford 'cause that's where the cheapest places were. But the only place I could find that I could afford was a garbage pit."

"So you went to Boomers?" I asked doubtfully.

"No. Well, not exactly. This guy said they rented rooms to young women there." She laughed derisively. "I went there and that's when I found out it was a whorehouse."

"So why'd you stay?"

"I don't know, okay? Maybe I wanted to rub Daddy's face in it."

"He knew where you worked?"

"Not then."

"You told him?"

She looked away, losing some of her defiance. "No. I didn't have the guts."

"Why did you work in the Red Room?"

She laughed again, shaking her head. "Self-loathing." She shrugged. "I'm into self-destruction. Also I'm rebelling against my father and trying to get back at him by working as a whore. The S and M is a kind of carryover from his belt, you know, from him using the belt on me. I'm emulating . . . if that's the word . . . I forget exactly. I'll have to ask my shrink tomorrow. Anyway, according to her, I like getting whipped, I get off on it, because I need the pain to cancel out all the guilt I feel."

"So . . . you . . . like it when they hit you?" I asked, a little confused.

"I love it," she sneered, eyes hot and challenging.

"How long you been seeing a psychiatrist?"

"My aunt made me go when she found out I'd worked at Boomers."

"How did she find out?"

She turned her head away.

"I guess my father wanted her to know what a whore I am."

"He knew?"

She tsked impatiently and gazed at the house again. "Someone told him. I didn't deny it."

"And what did he do then?"

"Cried, beat the shit out of me, prayed a lot, grounded me. I was hoping he'd send me to live with Aunt Karen but he didn't. Instead he just made me pray for hours on end. Like I give a shit about that."

"So how'd you keep working at Boomers? And how'd you get pregnant? Your father ever touch you like that?"

"Did he fuck me, you mean? No. He wanted to, though. I could tell. The look in his eyes . . ." She nodded vigorously. "He wanted to, all right, especially when he was taking the belt to me."

"So how'd you get pregnant?"

She sighed and shoved her hair back roughly, turning and leaning against the fence. "My father wouldn't let me out of the house at all. He drove me to school, then picked me up afterward. He also made sure my teachers would call him first thing if I missed a single class."

She turned and smiled thinly. "So I fucked a teacher. Wasn't hard. I even got him to use his belt on me."

"You weren't taking the Pill?"

"My fucking old man searched my room and took them," she snapped.

"You couldn't go to Boomers for more, or to get money for an abortion?"

"I wasn't working there anymore, not after my old man found out. He threatened to cause a huge stink if they let me work there anymore. Said he'd lead pray-ins there like he did at the abortion clinic."

"Tell me about Masters."

"Who?"

"Masters, the cop. Big, ugly bald guy."

"Oh, him. I didn't see him much. He was just there sometimes. Sometimes he brought in new girls, mostly Thais or Koreans. He brought in drugs for the whores that used it, too. Him and that scraggly asshole Vernon were big buddies."

"Vernon?"

"The police chief in Ashford. Don't you know anything?"

"Did you see them there a week ago Saturday?"

"I told you, I haven't been there for months."

"And they haven't talked to you?"

"No."

"Masters never stopped by to see you on his own?"

"No," she said, rolling her eyes in irritation.

There was something she was hiding, something she was lying about, but I couldn't decide just what. All this snottiness had a reason.

"What about Ford?"

"Who?"

I described him and she shook her head. "I never saw him."

"And Sims?"

"No."

Something there. I was sure there was.

"How long did you know Sims?"

She hesitated. "He . . . um, was a customer at Boomers sometime."

"Of yours?"

She hesitated again, then nodded slowly as she glanced at the house.

"He beat you?"

"No," she said, shaking her head in irritation again. "I didn't do that all the time, you know."

"How many times did Sims see you outside of Boomers?"

Again there was hesitation, and some fear now. I racked my brains, trying to figure out what she was hiding.

"Just . . . just sometimes," she said reluctantly. "At the meetings."

"What meetings?"

"The Brotherhood meetings. That's where I met him first."

"The . . . the Christian Brotherhood?"

"Yeah."

"How did you come to be there?"

"Daddy brought me," she said, surprised that I wouldn't know.

"Your father is involved with them?"

"He's the leader," she said, laughing at my ignorance.

"I'll be damned."

"We all will be," she sniffed. "According to my old man."

"Did your father know you were screwing Sims?"

Jackpot. She looked down fast but not before I saw how the question had hit home.

"Does your father own a three forty-seven Magnum?" I asked.

"I gotta go." She lurched forward off the fence and strode quickly back toward the farmhouse. I jumped after her, catching her halfway there and swinging her around again.

"Leave me alone!" she cried, trying to shake loose.

"You were out there meeting Sims on Saturday, weren't you?" I demanded. "And Daddy found out."

"No!"

"Saturday was that big anti-abortion meeting. I saw it on

TV. You snuck out while your father was at the meeting! Snuck out to see Sims. Didn't you?"

"No!" she screamed.

"Your father found out and caught you there!" I yelled, shaking her. "He killed Sims, didn't he!"

"No!" she sobbed.

I gripped her arms and shook her violently, making her head whip back and forth. "Listen to me, Ginian," I snarled. "If you protect him you're as guilty as he is. You'll go to jail for the murder of a police officer and you'll be an old woman before you get out!"

Her eyes were teary as she stared at me and her mouth worked without any sounds coming out.

"Pr-protect him?" she sobbed. "Him? I'm not . . . I . . . I can't . . ."

"Do you want to go to jail, you stupid girl?! Tell me what happened!" I gave her another shake.

21

You don't understand," she groaned tearfully.

"Tell me."

"He's . . . he'll kill me if I talk."

"He's your father."

She shook her head vigorously. "He meant it when he said I'm not his daughter. He did. He'll kill me."

"We'll protect you."

"How? The sheriff is his friend. Lots of cops are members of the brotherhood. They'll kill me!"

"Just because the sheriff is religious doesn't mean he'll help your father hurt you, Ginian. I know him. He wouldn't ever do that. And I'd be willing to bet most of the so-called cops in the brotherhood are from Ashford."

"But I caaaaaan't," she sobbed.

"How did your father know you were there?"

She sobbed quietly and I shook her again.

"My . . . my mother," she gulped, sniffling and pulling her arm free to rub her face.

"Your mother?"

"She heard . . . sh-she listened on the extension, to me and Allan, and then she called my dad to tell him," she said miserably.

"He showed up on Beckle. Were you already there?"

She nodded, rubbing tears off her face again.

I was getting real good at bullying teenage girls.

"Why Beckle? Why way over there?"

She swallowed several times, then looked longingly at the house before turning her eyes back on me. "He had to . . . he was going to Boomers," she said softly. "He had this . . . Thai girl he was bringing there. A new girl.

"He wanted . . ." She drew in a deep breath and swallowed again. "He was easy money," she said, looking up at me desperately. "He just . . . he just liked to watch."

"Watch?"

"Girls."

I frowned in confusion for a moment.

"You and the girl? He wanted you and the Thai girl to . . . to do some kind of sex act?"

She nodded unhappily.

I drew in a deep breath myself. Clean-living small-town folk. Right.

"Right there on the street?"

"No, there was lots of bushes to go behind on one side of the street."

"So you and the Thai girl went behind some bushes with him and . . . put on a show . . . while he watched?"

"And my father showed up."

"Jesus."

"Yeah." She barked a laugh. "Yeah, right."

"But Sims was killed in his car."

"My father was really weird," she said quietly. "He didn't yell or scream or even look angry. He was, like, like a robot.

264

He told Allan to leave. Said he wouldn't say anything about it, and told him not to call me again. Allan grabbed the Thai girl and ran back to the car."

"And then?"

"He . . . he took out . . . his gun . . . and he . . . pointed it at me. He . . . put it right against my head," she gulped. "I thought . . . I thought he was going to kill me. Instead he hit me in the head with it. He went out through the bushes and I heard a shot. I wanted to run away but . . . I was . . . I was on the ground . . . and my head was bleeding . . . and I was . . . I . . ."

She was hugging herself tightly, swaying in place. Her eyes were wide and frightened, darting from side to side."

"So when he threw you out the next morning, that wasn't because you were pregnant."

"We were up all night. He beat me with his belt, he prayed over me, he made me pray for hours and hours. He called me names . . ." She shook her head in misery. "At some point I told him I was pregnant. That's why I needed to see Sims in the first place, to get money for an abortion."

"Wouldn't your teacher have given it to you?"

"I guess," she sighed. "But then he probably wouldn't have wanted to see me again. He was scared as it was."

Wow. And I'd thought Erika was fucked up.

The screen door banged and I turned to see her uncle coming toward us, obviously not having liked what he was seeing through the window.

"Oh, fuck," she gasped. "Please don't tell him anything! Please!"

"Your Aunt didn't tell . . ."

She grabbed my arm desperately and rubbed her face hurriedly with her other hand.

"I begged her not to!"

"Just what is going on, Deputy?" her uncle demanded, frowning at us. "Ginian? Are you all right?"

She nodded rapidly, trying to keep her face turned.

"Mr. Jennings, I'd like to take Ginian in to make another statement, clear some things up."

"What things? She's already made a statement."

"Some additional information has come to our attention. I'm not at liberty to reveal it just now but Ginian could be very helpful."

"I don't think I like that. If you can't tell me what it is that she's being accused of, or just what information she has—"

"It's . . . just not something I can say right now."

"It's okay, Uncle Jim," Ginian said.

"I'm afraid I can't agree unless I know more about it," Jennings said.

"It might involve other young girls, Mr. Jennings, it's possible Reverend Tyler was involved in some criminal activities that Ginian could help us with."

"I'm not sure I like that at all." He frowned. "I don't want her being used against her father. I'd still like to think there could be a reconciliation between them someday."

"Ha! Are you kidding?" Ginian demanded. "As soon as I finish school I'm out of here. I'm going to college on a scholarship and I'm never coming back."

"Ginian," he sighed.

"No! Forget it! I'm never speaking to him again."

"Well, then I'll go with you," he said slowly.

"No!" Ginian cried. "I don't . . . I don't want you to come, Uncle Jim."

"What about your aunt?" he asked, sounding hurt.

"I don't want either of you involved. It's bad enough . . . I mean, I just don't want you two to get involved. It's too . . ." She looked away without finishing the sentence. Jennings scowled at me in confusion.

I went toward him, put my hand on his arm, and led him back toward the house.

"You see, sir," I said. "The man who made her pregnant was a teacher at her school."

"You're kidding," he gasped, shocked.

"Yes, and Ginian is very embarrassed about it, and doesn't want you or your wife hearing about the details. Nevertheless, we do want her to give a statement so we can get rid of this man."

"He should be in prison," Jennings growled.

"I agree. In any case, Ginian isn't very comfortable talking about it, and she'd be even less comfortable with you or your wife around. She may be afraid you'll reject her like her father did."

"We would never do that. We're Christians, real Christians, not like that puss-filled windbag!"

"I understand, but Ginian is very, um, insecure right now. It would be better if she went with me alone."

"Well . . . all right, then." He sighed. "I can understand how she'd be embarrassed, though really, it's hardly her fault if some teacher seduced her."

"I agree completely," I assured him.

I left him there and went back for Ginian, then led her around the house and out to the car. He followed, staying a few yards back.

"You let us know if there's anything we can do," he said.

"We will, sir," I assured him, seating Ginian in the front passenger side, then hurrying around to the driver's door. I started the car and backed away as he watched.

"What did you tell him?" Ginian demanded.

"The truth . . . sort of."

"You told him I . . ."

"I told him that a teacher seduced you and you were embarrassed about him or your aunt hearing the details."

She looked at me for a moment, then turned away.

"Hey, from his perspective, that makes you a complete victim. If it was a teacher instead of some kid your age, then you have even less blame than before. That's good, kid."

"Don't call me kid," she sighed. "I'm not a kid."

"If you say so."

I left her in the squad room with a deputy to keep her company and get her coffee, then went to Bradford's office feeling slightly smug.

"He's in a meeting, Sergeant," one of the auxiliaries warned as I put my hand on his doorknob.

"He'll see me," I assured him. I knocked twice, then shoved the door open. Bradford was at his desk. Goff was sitting in front of it, along with two men in suits I didn't know.

"Sheriff, I have to talk to you," I said.

"Sergeant O'Neil," he said, slightly surprised. "Come in. This is Detective Robbins and Detective Parish, from the State Police Office of Criminal Investigations."

I came in and closed the door, then shook hands with the two, who insisted on standing up.

"Is this important?" Bradford asked, his tone saying it had better be.

"I think so, yes. I know who killed Sims."

"I thought we'd already established that," he said in confusion.

"Uh-uh. We were wrong. I have an eyewitness."

"What?" Robbins demanded.

"Maybe you should explain, Sergeant." Bradford sighed.

"First I'd like to apologize."

"For?"

"For not telling you something Erika mentioned the other day."

He frowned but said nothing.

"I wasn't sure at the time if she was just blowing steam,

trying to shift blame, or what. I didn't want to injure another girl's reputation for nothing."

"And?"

"She was telling the truth. Ginian Tyler worked at Boomers until a few months ago, when her father found out."

"Wow," Goff whispered.

"He beat her, and threatened Boomers with daily pray-ins if they let her near the place again. Anyway, it seems that Sims was one of her regulars. She would meet him at the Christian Brotherhood meetings. Did you know her father was the leader?"

He nodded and made a go-on motion.

"Anyway, on the night he died, Sims called her up, or she called him, I didn't get which. He was bringing the Thai girl in and he wanted her and Ginian to put on a show for him. Apparently he liked that a lot, just watching. Ginian called it cheap money.

"Unfortunately, her mother was listening in on the extension and called the Reverend, who showed up while Ginian and the girl were, um, performing."

"Reverend Tyler killed Sims!?" Goff exclaimed.

"Uh-huh." I nodded.

"Wow."

"Where is this girl?" Robbins demanded.

"Sitting outside in the squad room. She's more than a little reluctant to talk. She seems to think her father or his group might kill her."

"Those assholes wouldn't have the balls to kill anyone," Parish scoffed.

"She also doesn't want her aunt and uncle to find out she worked at Boomers. She's afraid if it got out they'd kick her out like the good Reverend did."

"I wouldn't be surprised," Goff said, shaking his head.

"I don't see how we can keep this from becoming public knowledge," Robbins said. "It'll all come out at the trial."

"If you can't give her some kind of assurances along those lines I don't think she'll be willing to testify," I warned.

"Why don't we get her in here and see what she has to say," Bradford said.

"Uh, Sheriff . . ." I started.

"I know. I know, O'Neil," he said, waving me off. "Brian, you'd better leave, and, well, one of you two had better go as well," he said to Robbins and Parish. "The fewer people in here, the more likely she'll be to talk."

By the time Ginian came in, though, she had composed herself, and was adamant in her demands. We spent half an hour trying to figure out a way to keep her anonymous, but there just wasn't one. We sent her out and had Goff keep an eye on her, then discussed the situation.

"What if we confront Tyler?" I suggested. "Maybe he'll confess and save us the need for a trial?"

"Get real," Robbins snorted.

"It's not likely, O'Neil." Bradford sighed. "He'll plead not guilty and give the jury a chance to let him off the hook. He'd be crazy not to."

"But with Ginian's testimony . . ."

"It doesn't matter, O'Neil," he said. "The jury will sure believe he killed Sims, but there's a good chance they'll let him off anyway. Hell, they might even award him a medal."

Robbins nodded. "What did he do, after all? He killed the pervert who was encouraging his underage daughter to perform lewd acts. If the whorehouse connection comes out he'll look even better. He'll have shown patience and tolerance by warning them and keeping the girl at home.

"Who can blame him for cracking when he finds one of the cops that works for Boomers was trying to get her back into prostitution again?

"The only thing he's got against him is tossing her butt out the door naked, but then again, a lot of these people would've done the same, especially after learning, on top of everything else, that the girl was pregnant.

"Trust me. I know juries."

"So you're saying they'll acquit? Even though they know he's guilty."

"It wouldn't be the first time. Or they could just find him guilty of temporary insanity. That's always a nice loophole."

"So what? We're not gonna charge him?"

Bradford and Robbins looked at each other.

"What do you think, Sheriff? They're your people," Robbins said.

"I think they'll come down harder on him for the child abuse we've filed, and even that only if the whorehouse isn't mentioned. I also think his reputation is harmed more by what he did with the girl than it would be for killing Sims. Hell, half the county would cheer him as a hero if all this comes out."

"But how can we not file?" Robbins asked.

"If the girl won't testify, what evidence do we have?"

"We could seize his gun," I said.

"If it was still there, and how do we know we could even get a warrant without the girl's testimony?"

"So he's gonna get away with killing a cop?" I demanded.

"He didn't kill a cop, O'Neil, he killed the pervert corrupting his little girl." Robbins grinned cynically.

"We had a better chance of getting Masters." Bradford sighed dejectedly.

"I don't believe this," I scowled.

"There's no point filing charges on something we can't win," Bradford snapped.

"And what about Masters? I suppose he's coming back now?"

"No damned way that bastard is getting back in here," Bradford said. "Excuse the language," he sighed, sitting back.

"This fucking sucks," I said. "Excuse the fucking language."

Bradford raised his eyes and then to my surprise smiled. "I think, O'Neil, that you're up way past your bedtime. You should get home and get some shut-eye."

"I'll go drive Ginian home," I said.

"No. I'll do it, then I'll stop by and see her father, have a word to the wise."

"You won't tell him Ginian told us?"

"Don't be a fool, O'Neil. Go home and go to bed." I turned and jerked the door open.

"O'Neil."

I turned and glowered at him.

"Do not tell anyone, and I mean *anyone*, about this," he warned.

And that was it. My big breakthrough had accomplished nothing except to let that bald bastard Masters off the hook. I was furious and felt like punching out a window. I settled with pounding my fist on the roof of my patrol car and speeding on the way home. Sims wasn't any loss, really, so I don't know why I should be that upset.

The thing was, even if he wasn't killed because of his uniform, he'd been wearing it when he died, and I damned well didn't like that. I also didn't like people thinking you could kill a cop and get away with it.

The world sucked, and I didn't get much sleep. I kept spinning the details of the case around in my head, trying to find someway, legal or otherwise, to put that scumbag Tyler in jail.

Okay, I know he did me and the county a favor by killing Sims. I could admit that, though not without difficulty. But I still hated him for what he'd done to Ginian. And besides, the guy was the leader of the local Nazis. He sure wasn't any prince.

I woke up in no better mood after a couple of hours' sleep than I'd been in before going to bed. Even the monsters at work seemed to sense it, and the roll call went off without incident for once.

I took Zone 9 again, don't ask me why. I was heavy on the gas pedal for a while, but the cool night air started to calm me down after an hour or so. What the hell. Tyler wasn't the first scumbag I knew was guilty who was going to get away. I'd find some other way to make his life miserable.

Without consciously making the turn, I found myself on Erika's street. To my surprise the lights were on both upstairs and down.

I turned into the drive and stopped behind the Jag. The trunk was open wide, and as I got out of the Caprice I could see girls' clothing inside, much of it still on hangers.

I went to the front door but before I could knock it opened and Erika, arms laden with clothes, a yellow panda and a small box, almost ran into me. Her eyes widened as she jumped back.

"Hi, kid," I said.

"What are you doing here?" she blurted.

"Came to see how you were doing. You going somewhere?"

"I . . . uh, sort of."

"Where's your dad?"

"Daddy's right here," said a voice behind me. Before I could move, something hit me on the back of the head and I fell forward onto the polished wooden floor as Erika screamed and jumped backward.

I couldn't see or think straight for long moments as I felt myself dragged forward by one arm. I reached down, pawing at my holster, but felt my gun pulled out before I could get my fingers on it. I was turned over, and though the pain in my head was still fierce and hot, I looked up to see Masters crouched above me, smiling triumphantly.

"Glad you could join us, Sarge," he drawled.

"Billy," Erika said in a tremulous voice.

"Shut the fuck up," he snapped. "Get your shit into the car now or we're leaving without it."

She shuffled past and to the door as Masters grinned down at me.

"Too bad you didn't come by a little earlier, when we had more time," he sneered. He held my wrists together above me with one hand, then groped my breasts as I struggled to roll away. He cursed and backhanded me across the face several times. I was dazed by the pain, and was hardly aware of what he was doing for several seconds.

"Coulda had some fun, you an' me," he said, his face coming down close. You woulda loved that, wouldn't you, dyke?"

He gripped my hair, pulling it hard, forcing my head back as his lips came down on mine. His tongue pushed into my mouth and I bit it. He cursed, jerking back and slammed his fist into my face.

"Fucking cunt!" he snarled, holding his mouth.

I spit at him, mostly blood. He jammed his hand down on my throat, squeezing. I clawed at his hands and he bellowed in pain and rage, jerking them free, then swinging his fist down again as I tried to twist over. It slammed into the side of my head and he cursed in pain, even as I shook my head in numbed confusion.

I was half over on my side, at least my upper torso. He gripped my hair again, trying to slide his arm around my throat. I slammed my elbow back, aiming at his throat, but catching him in the cheek. He fell off and I scrambled up, but then had the legs kicked out from under me and fell heavily again.

He jumped atop me, his weight crushing me into the floor, then he jerked my arms behind me and I felt the cold steel of handcuffs forced tight around my wrists.

"You know what I'm gonna do, cunt?" he panted. "I'm taking you with us. We'll stop along the way and play a little before I dump you."

"How far you think you're gonna get in that Jag?" I gasped, gulping air.

"Far enough, baby. Things are way too hot for me here. Me and the girl are headed south. Bradford can wander around the trees lookin' for me till he's a little gray-haired old man. Where's your key?"

"Lost it," I said.

He slapped me again, then groped me some more, or at least I thought he was at first, until he ripped open my breast pocket and took out the key.

"Have to punish you for lying later, babycakes." He grinned.

He gripped my hair and pulled me to my feet by it. I cried out, the pain intense as I scrambled upward to relieve it. He forced me toward the door just as Erika came in again. Her eyes were wide as she stared at me.

"What are you doing?" she gaped.

"Shut up and get in the fucking car," he ordered.

"But—"

"Get in the car!" he roared.

She turned and scrambled out the door again.

"Obedient little pussy, ain't she?" He laughed. "She'll bring big bucks in L.A."

"Pimp," I spat.

"You weren't so old and ugly, I'd put you on the street too, baby," he said, shoving me out the door. I staggered and almost fell but caught myself before he could grab my hair. He grabbed my arm then and pulled me over to the back of the

Jaguar. Erika was sitting in the front passenger seat and looking out at us anxiously.

"You drive the Jag for now," he said to her. "I wanta drive the cruiser away from here."

He shoved me into the trunk. I had a holdout gun in an ankle holster, and had a few seconds hope of retaining it, but he gripped my foot as he shoved me in and felt along it, jerking the gun out.

"Thought I was dumb enough to forget this?" He snickered.

He shoved my legs inside and stood there for a moment, looking down.

"This is the way we drive all the whores around," he taunted.

"You're a credit to your uniform, shit head!" I snarled.

"You'll see what kind of credit I am later, bitch." He smiled, his eyes leering as he looked me up and down.

"Don't have anything else on ya, do ya?"

I didn't say anything and he grinned. "We'll do a strip search—no, a cavity search—when we stop," he taunted. I winced as the trunk slammed down, leaving me in darkness.

There was some muffled talk between him and Erika, then the Jag's engine started up and it lurched forward. It bumped slightly as it went over the curb, then settled down to a smooth ride.

I was lying on a pile of clothing, so bumps didn't matter anyway. What did matter was the switchblade in my pocket. I'd gotten in the habit of carrying one when I was a hooker. It was practically part of the uniform.

It wouldn't do me much good with my hands cuffed behind me, of course. But I was sure I could solve that. I was reasonably thin and wiry, and as the Jag moved down the road I struggled to force my wrists under my behind. It was a lot harder than I remembered it, and took some time and effort, but I finally managed to slide them over my butt and drag my legs through.

With my wrists cuffed in front of me now, I was able to get a hand, not without effort, into my pocket and draw out the switchblade. It clicked open easily. But then what? I'd only been thinking as far as getting it out, getting some kind of weapon to hold between me and Masters. I had no idea what to do now.

Surprise would be difficult. As soon as he opened the trunk and saw my arms were in front of me, he'd be wary. I would only have one chance, and it wasn't for the squeamish. Shooting someone was easy, you just pulled a trigger. Stabbing someone was a lot tougher.

I struggled to roll onto my knees. The roof was just high enough for me to kneel with my head down. That was no damned good, though. It would take too long to get up. I tried again, after much effort getting into a squat, my head way down between my legs.

The car bounced and I was thrown onto my side again. I tried to get back into position but it bounced again and again as Erika took the Jag down a rough road, very rough. I figured we were going down one of the logging roads.

My heart pounded faster and the adrenaline surged in my veins. I was not . . . I WAS NOT going to get played with, raped, by that stinking pig, then be found by hunters a few months from now with a bullet in my head. I held the knife in one hand while I grimly clutched the edge of the trunk with the other and got myself into position again.

Just as the car stopped I was able to position myself on my feet again, my butt on the floor and head between my legs, pressing against the lid. I was coated with sweat, but hardly noticed, all my concentration on the lid, waiting for it to open. As soon as it did I was going to come flying out like a jack-in-the-box.

I shifted position a thousand times in a few seconds, then

had the heart-stopping thought that he might have Erika open it. I heard her voice then, protesting, the words inaudible.

I thought back to all those police reports I'd read on women kidnapped and murdered, and some of the vile, sickening things that'd been done to them before their deaths. If I couldn't kill him and couldn't get away I was going to jam the knife into my own chest, better to die clean.

I shifted my weight constantly, ready to rush upward immediately. I heard the keys in the lock and prayed harder than I ever had before.

The trunk rose and I put all my strength into shooting upward. My knees, as I rose, slammed into the curving overhang below the door and I screamed in pain as I fell forward against a surprised Masters. The pain was so intense I almost dropped the knife. I still don't know how I held on to it.

He fell back, with me tumbling across the edge of the trunk after him. Desperately I swung the knife in a long, violent arc and heard a howl of pain as I fell forward onto the ground. I tried to get to my feet but my knees wouldn't support me and I collapsed as Masters slammed his foot into my stomach.

I rolled backward half under the car as he kicked the knife away, snarling in rage. I saw a thick dark line cutting diagonally across his belly. He tore open his shirt and gazed at the deep slash, wincing and gasping in pain. Erika screamed as she came around and saw it, her eyes and mouth wide.

"You . . . you fuckin' whore," Master gasped. "You stinking bitch! I'm gonna kill you so slow, so fuckin' . . . slow," he groaned.

He kicked at me and I rolled farther under the car. He snarled in fury and stood there for long seconds as I scurried around and tried to crawl out the side. Then he raced around and caught me by the hair, dragging me out as I clawed at his face.

He howled again, shoving me back as he held his face. His

eyes bulged and his skin, even where my nails hadn't slashed it, was bright red in the moonlight. I tried to get to my feet again, but the pain in my knees was still too great. Masters started forward, murder in his eyes.

"Stop!"

Neither of us paid the girl any attention. I tried to get back under the car but Masters grabbed my leg and dragged me back several yards.

Then there was a loud crack of noise, and dust spurted up a few inches from my head. I yelped and rolled over a couple of feet, turning to stare at Erika, who had my gun in her hands. She looked as if she were ready to have a heart attack as she looked at me, then she turned and pointed the gun at Masters, who was glaring at her furiously.

"What the fuck are you doing?!" he screamed, a world of anger and frustration in his voice as he stomped toward her.

"Stop!" she cried. "I'll shoot you!"

"You dumb little cunt! You couldn't hit a fucking barn!" he snarled.

"I will! Don't!" she cried, backing away as he moved toward her.

"Gimme the gun!" he demanded.

He grabbed it with both hands, trying to jerk it away, and in a panic, or by mistake, Erika fired.

I actually saw, or think I saw, the bullet blow out his back. I'm still not sure. He was flung backward, the gun flying away as he landed in a heap in the dirt a half dozen yards from my feet. He lay there, not moving. Erika didn't move either. She stared down at him in appalled shock.

Long seconds passed, then she sobbed and clamped her hands together over her mouth, turning to stare at me. I let out a long breath of air and fell back onto my own back.

"Oh my God! Oh my God! Oh my God!" Erika whimpered.

"Thank him for me too," I said in a hoarse voice.

22

The shock of almost being arrested hadn't done a lot for Erika, but killing a man seemingly had. She didn't turn into the princess Daddy had wanted, but at least I never heard of her hooking again. Her father was probably as shocked as she was by what had happened, and resolved to spend a lot more time around her.

He didn't follow through on it after the first few months, but two years later unbent enough to send her to an arts program at UCLA rather than Harvard Law School.

My knees were so badly bruised I couldn't walk for several days. I'd put all my power into slamming them up into the steel, after all. What a bonehead.

This time I didn't have to stay in the hospital, though, and nobody called my parents.

Bradford was a little annoyed at me, said I was causing him too much paperwork. Goff was annoyed at having to supervise the Monster Squad again, or what was left of it, but only a little. Ox was enraged that Masters had almost killed me, and made me promise to bring him the next time I was going anywhere dangerous. After all, we were cousins . . . sort of.

Boomers was closed down, not by the state police, but by the INS and FBI, who charged James Earl Clubb with a bewildering variety of federal crimes, everything from slavery to hiring illegals.

Some of the guys dropped by my place the day after, excluding Goff and Bradford. Brin told me about a guy she'd found who was the ultimate sex machine, Ox used my Solo Flex, Bobbie Whyte complained that he never did anything exciting, and Pczchornek, to my intense surprise, dropped by to ask uncomfortably how I was feeling . . . and when I might be up to arm-wrestle again.

The biggest surprise of all, though, was when Brooks showed up. Oh, he hadn't come all the way there to comfort me. He hadn't even known about my run-in with Masters until he'd arrived and talked to Bradford. He stayed for a week, spending most of his time fishing with Bradford. He managed to drop by every other day, insisting each time that I put on my uniform, including my cowboy hat, for him. I never did.

I was stuck at home for ten days while my knees healed. Coming so soon after my enforced sick leave from the LAPD, that could have been excruciatingly boring. It wasn't. Marty came over to look after me and make sure I stayed off my feet. He also seemed to think I'd heal better and faster without any clothes on. An interesting medical theory that we didn't quite put to the test.

By the time I returned to work, Ford had quit and disappeared, and the monsters I was left with didn't seem quite so monstrous anymore. None was particularly friendly, except Ox, but I was able to get rid of the alarms and got no more nasty presents.

Working as a deputy sheriff wasn't exactly thrilling, not most of the time, anyway, but after my first month had passed I didn't feel any regrets at leaving the LAPD or the city itself. Loren kind of grew on me. So did the job.

I never did wear the stupid cowboy hat, though.